KILL GAME

Check out this thrilling new series:

FEARLESS® FBI

#1 Kill Game

#2 Live Bait (coming soon)

FEARLESS FBI

KILL GAME

Francine Pascal

SIMON PULSE
New York   London   Toronto   Sydney

First Simon Pulse edition June 2005

Copyright © 2005 by Francine Pascal

SIMON PULSE
An imprint of Simon & Schuster Children's Publishing Division
1230 Avenue of the Americas, New York, NY 10020

 Produced by Alloy Entertainment
151 West 26th Street
New York, NY 10001

SIMON PULSE and colophon are registered trademarks of Simon & Schuster, Inc.

FEARLESS is a registered trademark of Francine Pascal

Printed in the United States of America
10 9 8 7 6 5 4 3 2

Library of Congress Control Number: 2004117303
ISBN: 0-689-87821-4

KILL GAME

Gaia

Every now and then, when I'm sure that I've absolutely exhausted every other option for self-analysis, I allow myself to look back on my teens. And then I cringe. From all those memories. The word *lost* just wouldn't do those years justice. *Confused* wouldn't really cut it either. More extreme terms are required to describe me back then. *Clinically depressed?* Not exactly. *Tragically misinformed* is more like it.

Of course, my "teens" only ended last year, but still, some of it seems so far away now—just a murky gray cloud in my head. Names and faces from the Village School in New York . . . Tammie Deegan and Megan Stein and the rest of the FOHs. I've already forgotten the details of their faces. With each year at Stanford they turned more and more into poorly drawn cartoons in my head; clichéd characters played by bad actresses in another mediocre movie about bitchy cliques and high school growing pains.

But other memories feel so fresh it's like the last four years of college never even happened. The look on the face of my best friend turned boyfriend turned best friend again, Ed Fargo, when I turned around and left him for good in that dark alley on Forty-seventh Street. And of course . . . Jake. I don't want to think about Jake.

The point is, there were so many things I thought I knew about myself back then—when I was seventeen. But I've finally begun to realize . . .

Maybe I didn't exactly know everything I thought I knew? As in . . .

1. I thought I would never live to see twenty. I was wrong.
2. I thought that if I did live to see twenty, I'd be telling my story Holden Caulfield style, sitting in a white loony bin robe, strung out on Zoloft and lithium, talking to a kind but unresponsive therapist. Also wrong. And most importantly . . .
3. I thought that the dismal state of my life would never change.

This, as it turns out, was wrong, too. If there's one thing I've learned now, after three years at Stanford University, it's that things do change.

It just happens *very* slowly.

I finally ended up with a life that works for me. Right in time to graduate.

It wasn't easy. Not after what had happened to Jake. I mean, I'd watched him, my seventeen-year-old boyfriend, get shot in the chest. I watched him die on the floor right in front of me. And I knew he'd died for one reason and one reason only. He'd gotten close to me. He'd fallen into my tragic little vortex and become another one of its victims. That's why I've been careful not to make any real friends at Stanford.

Well, I guess there was that Kevin Bender guy. He was a senior transfer who definitely challenged me for the title of "Biggest Loner on Campus," but he was sort of a quasi friend. We probably would have been fine if we hadn't had that weird night at the library. I'd been a little too nice to him and I think he got the wrong idea. After that, I really had to pour on the distance.

So there really are no Stanford friends. That's one of the reasons I'm able to graduate so early. It's also one of the reasons I've never let my dad visit me up here, even though he's coming up now for graduation. I just didn't think he'd want to see this new careful life of mine. Not that it's a bad life. It's not. Like I said, it works. I have acquaintances, of course. People I say hello to on the quad every day. There were study group partners, and lab partners, and professors who've given me nothing but straight A's. But I've never really gotten to know any of them, and they've never really gotten to know me. And that's how I wanted it.

It's taken me three long years of self-imposed psychological boot camp, but I think I've finally managed to achieve some sort of Zen-like balance at Stanford. Well, not exactly Zen-like. More like stoicism.

It doesn't quite qualify as "happiness." But I have come to accept it as a close enough facsimile. Especially when you compare it to the endless psychodrama that my life used to be.

No, this will be good. This graduation thing will be fine. I mean . . . I think this will all be very good.

TEARS OF JOY

Gaia couldn't stop fidgeting in her black graduation gown. The nylon fabric felt uncomfortable in the early-summer weather. The California sun was hot and bright, and the air was clear and dry. Gaia was used to all that—in three years she'd come to accept the endless parade of picture-postcard days. After years spent in the humid, foggy summers and whipcrack-cold, snow-drenched winters of New York City, the uniformly perfect weather was actually a nice change.

The rooftop of the Roth Library in Palo Alto was a wide, tiled expanse lifted six stories off the ground on one side of the Stanford University campus. Gaia and her father stood near its center, surrounded by dozens and dozens of Stanford graduates and their parents and friends. A catering table had been set up along one side, serving champagne and wine and hors d'oeuvres on expensive-looking white plates. Stanford knew how to throw a graduation party—and this year the university community were enjoying the added benefit of this brand-new library rooftop plaza, probably, Gaia thought, named after some wealthy donor somewhere who had enjoyed a postcard-perfect graduation day like this one and had never gotten over it.

So why aren't I enjoying this?

4

Gaia wasn't sure. Part of the problem was her father. He wouldn't stop *looking* at her, for one thing, and when he did, his eyes kept filling up with tears. Sure, they were tears of joy, but she still couldn't deal. She had hardly ever seen her father cry, with the exception of the darkest day of her life, and that was the last thing she wanted to think about on this auspicious occasion. She did everything in her power to avoid his glistening neon blue gaze, but there was no way to dodge his words. He wouldn't stop talking about her mother.

"I just wish she were here to see this." His voice cracked slightly on the last syllable. "Summa cum laude from Stanford—in three years, Gaia. She would have been in seventh heaven today."

"Yeah," Gaia said. He probably hadn't meant to mention her mother and heaven in the same sentence right now, but the unpleasant effect was palpable.

Say something else, she told herself. She kept avoiding her father's gaze by staring at the other students. They all looked so ridiculously happy. They had grins like infants: completely guileless and wide, revealing their perfect, featureless joy. Other moms and dads with cameras circled around, taking photograph after photograph and filling the rooftop with their tuneless chorus of, "Cheese!" over and over. And many of them, like Gaia's own father, were crying.

Talk to Dad. He needs this—he needs this day more than you do.

It had been true since he arrived—since that uncomfortable moment they'd spotted each other at the airport the day before, when Gaia saw her father's beaming face and thought,

I'm really in for it. Since that moment her father had been in nonstop pride-o-rama mode, a font of endless congratulatory remarks. Looking around at the other graduates in their identical black gowns, Gaia wondered how they were all doing it— how they were putting up with it.

But that's easy, Gaia thought. *They've got friends.*

It was really as simple as that.

It was supposed to be one of the greatest days of her life. She was graduating from Stanford University with the highest honors. She had worked her ass off to finish school in three years. She was supposed to look like they did. She was supposed to *feel* like they did. But she didn't. Something was missing. And it wasn't just her mother.

She raised her hand to her mouth and let out a faint cough to mask her discomfort. A hollow sort of ache crept up in her chest. Though the truth was, she'd been plagued by that sensation all day—even when she'd walked up onto that stage and accepted her diploma. She'd heard all the people applauding as she shook hands with the dean, but their applause had felt so devoid of meaning. It had felt like such an empty victory— because the people here didn't really know her at all.

"Gaia, smile, for God's sake." Her father laughed, squeezing her shoulders. "This is the best day our family has had in a long time. Aren't you walking on air? I haven't even seen you in a year."

"I know," she said, feeling a wave of guilt pass over her.

"Oh, it's all right," he assured her. "I understand. I do. But I'm here now, so . . ." He grabbed hold of her hand and took a step toward the crowd, clearly expecting Gaia to guide him through a host of gleeful introductions to her dearest friends and respected professors at Stanford, but Gaia didn't move. Instead she threw her arms around her father and hugged him tightly.

"I really did miss you, Dad," she said, resting her chin firmly on his shoulder. "I really did."

"I missed *you*," her father said, hugging her back. "God, we haven't even talked about your plans. When can we get you moved back to the city? There are so many people I want you to meet—I've talked to some friends at the Agency about you already, and they're dying to—"

"Dad." Gaia's body suddenly went very stiff. Her dad could obviously feel it in the awkward silence. He slowly dropped his arms from her shoulders and took a step back, which was very much what Gaia wanted him to do.

"What?" he asked quietly. "What's wrong?"

Gaia crossed her arms and lowered her head, staring down at the red sunlit tiles of the roof. She needed to remain quiet for a moment so she could control her frustration.

"We've already had this talk," she said, speaking directly to the ground. "I thought I'd made myself clear."

Her father let out a long breath. The bright yellow light was bringing out all the new speckles of gray that had cropped up in his dark hair. "Look . . . sweetheart . . . I *know* we've had this talk. And I understand your reservations. *Of course,* I understand. But Gaia . . . the worst is behind us now. Your uncle Oliver is not a threat to us anymore. This family is free and clear now. We can start again in New York, and you can talk to—"

"I'm *not* going back to New York. I told you that." Her

7

volume had taken an unfortunate leap. A few classmates turned in her direction, and she strained to lower her voice. "I am never going back," she added in a self-conscious whisper. "And I won't be having any 'talks' with any intelligence agents. We've been through this. That part of my life is over, Dad. It's over and done with."

"Gaia, they're just talks. I'm not saying you need to *join* the CIA or anything like that. I just think my friends at the Agency have a lot of knowledge to impart. They might have some ideas for you. Some job ideas, some ways you might be able to put all your incredible gifts to work—for the city, for the country, who knows. The sky is the limit for you—"

"No," Gaia interrupted calmly. "No, you're not listening. Why won't you ever hear me on this?" She glanced back at the crowd and then pulled her father farther from the party, over to the waist-high ledge of the roof, where they could have more privacy. "Look, you have to listen to me, okay? Please. Because I can't keep making this speech. I *don't* want that life. That was your life, not mine. I don't want my 'incredible gifts.' I don't want to use them, I don't even want to think about them anymore, do you understand? They're not *gifts,* Dad, they're curses."

"How can you say that?" He leaned closer and kept his voice low. "Gaia, you have more skills than half the experts in this country, and I should know. I trained you for half your life. You're stronger than they are, faster than they are, and you *fear nothing.* How can you not want to *use* that? To help people—to make a difference? How can you look at that as anything other than a blessing? It's like you're turning your back on everything that makes you special. Everything that makes you unique."

"Exactly," Gaia stressed. "I don't want to be special. I don't want to be unique. I want to be a normal person with a normal life. Look at me. Look at this gown. I look just like them." She pointed out to the crowd of joyful graduates. "And I just want to be happy like them."

"But you're *not* happy, Gaia. I've been watching you all day and I've barely seen you crack a smile. Is that how you want to go through life? Denying who you are?"

Gaia couldn't respond at first. She hated hearing those words come out of his mouth. He made it sound so much worse than it was.

"You know what?" she said finally. "This is happy for me, okay?" She pointed to her face. "This is as happy as I get. And I'll take it. Believe me, after everything I've been through . . . I'll take it."

She turned away from her father and headed straight for the hors d'oeuvres table. She was going to drink some wine and eat some cheese and have loads of delightful chitchat with the rest of her classmates, whether they knew her name or not. She was going to enjoy this day whether she liked it or not.

My father calls it a blessing and I call it a curse. Though I admit, I've gone back and forth on this one more than a couple of times. To be honest, I've grown a little tired of trying to sort out the philosophical repercussions of the whole thing. I mean, yes, I am a genetic oddity. Yes, I was born without some chunk of DNA, and that freakish mutation has left me incapable of experiencing fear. But how many more times am I supposed to map out all the pros and cons before I can figure out once and for all whether I love myself or I hate myself?

I actually found an old list of pros and cons I'd written out when I was in high school. It was scrawled in the back of an old notebook that I'd brought with me to Stanford because I'd thought it was blank. It definitely rings of the old me:

BEING FEARLESS: LATEST PROS AND CONS LIST
Instead of MacGregor's Pop Quiz

Finished the quiz in two minutes and I'm freaking bored.

PROS

1. *Undaunted by knives, vicious dogs, criminals twice my size, nuclear weapons.*
2. *No trouble with heights, spiders, the dark, airplanes, circus clowns, the unknown, the end of the world.*
3. *Free to kick enormous amounts of ass.*
4. *That's all I can think of. . . .*

CONS

1. *Can't really enjoy roller coasters or haunted houses (trouble finding thrills in general).*

2. *Everybody who knows about me wants a piece of me (literal or figurative), thus people around me get hurt or die.*
3. *That annoying blackout period I have to go through after a fight—one day I could end up on a railroad track and get flattened.*
4. *Have no idea what it feels like to be brave.*

CONCLUSION: *I wish I were normal (that's the 5,835th time I have reached this conclusion).*

I guess maybe everything doesn't necessarily change. I wrote that list when I was seventeen, but I'd still very much have to agree with the conclusion today. Like I told my father: these supposed gifts of mine . . . I don't want them. I don't want to have über-eyesight, bionic hearing, superhuman speed, or muscles of steel. I don't want to be fearless. But I don't want to be afraid, either. I want to be that thing I still don't quite understand. That thing in between that everybody else is. Just a college graduate who doesn't scare too easily. It shouldn't be all that hard to pull off. Just as long as I stay out of trouble. I've managed that for three years. I don't see why I shouldn't be able to manage it for three more.

"Was that your dad?"

Gaia was staring blankly at the table of hors d'oeuvres when that unmistakable deep voice whispered in her ear. She recognized the voice immediately.

"Hey, Kevin," Gaia said, turning around. Kevin Bender was right there, his black graduation gown emphasizing his pale, mottled face and thin blond hair. As usual, he stood a bit too close—but on the few occasions she'd spent time with him, she'd gotten used to it. "Yup, that's my father," she confirmed, munching on a baby carrot. "In the flesh."

"Okay." Kevin smiled shyly, his plain face twisting pleasantly into the unfamiliar expression. Kevin *never* smiled—or rather, he never *fake* smiled. It was something Gaia liked about him. "I'm guessing it went a little something like this." He broke into his imitation of the stereotypical father: "What are your *plans,* Gaia? What are you going to *dooo* with your life?"

"Something like that," Gaia said, swallowing the carrot. "Let's not talk about it."

"Okay," Kevin said agreeably. "What should we talk about?"

"I don't know," she said. "Something normal. What do normal people talk about at graduation? I mean, *besides* their 'plans for the future'?"

"I have no idea. Ask one of *them.*" Kevin pointed with disdain to another gang of shiny happy people huddling up for another photo op.

"I think I'll pass," Gaia muttered.

Kevin nodded soberly. "We've got so little time to talk about anything *real*," he agreed. "It'd be a shame to waste what little time we've got left on trivial stuff."

"Um—" Gaia wasn't sure what Kevin meant, but on the few occasions she'd spent time with him or talked on the phone with him, she'd gotten used to that, too. "I guess you're right."

At another part of the rooftop Gaia's father had engaged one of her professors in a spirited discussion—or at least, half spirited. Tom Moore was talking animatedly, and the professor was nodding patiently. *They must hate this day,* she thought. *All the teachers—they have to listen to everyone gush.* As she watched, her father glanced over, smiling yet again, and she was glad to have Kevin by her side.

See, Dad? I have friends—or at least one friend. See how normal I am?

"Look at all these people, about to begin their empty lives," Kevin remarked, gazing around at the graduates. "They'll all look back on this with sappy fond memories of all the friends they made—so many they've already started to forget the names. But we know better, right? We only have memories of each other—of the brief time we had before the end."

"What?" Gaia looked at him and saw the way he was looking back. She didn't want to admit the obvious—that Kevin had a little bit of a crush on her—so she didn't object. "I guess that's true. I sure didn't connect with anyone *else* here, Kevin."

"*Connect,*" Kevin said. "Exactly the word I was going to

13

use. We *connected*. Listen, Gaia, there's something I wanted to talk to you about before this ends."

"Hey, grads!"

Gaia saw Kevin flinch as the high-pitched, bubbly voice intruded on their conversation. A well-built, muscular young woman with a long black ponytail stood there, holding a tray of wineglasses. She was dressed in the same outfit as all the other catering personnel. Kevin still looked alarmed, as if the woman's voice had given him a very bad fright.

"Glass of wine?" the waitress asked, beaming.

"No, thanks," Gaia said.

"Okay!" the woman replied in her bubbly voice. "Well, I'm here if you need me!"

"Right," Gaia said, sharing a perplexed glance with Kevin. "Good to know."

"As I was saying," Kevin went on in his painfully shy way, "I'd like to talk about something."

"Fine," Gaia said, glancing around at the oppressive sea of graduates and caterers. "Let's get out of the line of fire here."

"Follow me," Kevin said obligingly, taking her hand and leading her toward the low parapet that bounded the roof. Gaia was so startled by the gesture that she let herself be pulled along that way.

They made their way across the roof and settled into the sunny corner, looking out over the vast Stanford campus, with its winding white walkways, tall green palm trees, and terracotta roofs. Kevin seemed to have fallen deep into his own thoughts as he gripped the ledge and gazed out at the clear blue sky. The long silence grew too uncomfortable, and Gaia finally felt the need to break it.

"So what did you want to talk about?"

"Well, I just figured, you know . . ." Kevin smiled self-consciously and lowered his head as the wind tossed his baby-fine hair. "Since it's all going to end now . . . that I should let you know . . ." Kevin's voice tapered off into silence again.

"Let me know what?"

"Um . . . Just to let you know that . . . I always liked talking to you, Gaia. I mean, I liked . . . being with you."

She laughed awkwardly but then saw that it was the wrong response. Kevin's expression had grown very earnest and serious. Gaia suddenly realized that this wasn't going to be the kind of delightful graduation chitchat she'd been after. Her chest grew tight with discomfort. "Well, I liked talking to you, too," she said.

"Yeah," Kevin went on, looking down over the ledge. "And I wish—you know, now that it's all going to end . . . I'm just saying . . . I wish that I'd gotten to know you better while we were here. I wish we could have gotten closer. You know what I mean? Much closer." Kevin looked up and locked his eyes with hers. And now with the sun shining directly on his face, she could see just how pale Kevin had become—how dark and deep the circles under his eyes had gotten.

"Yeah," Gaia finally admitted. "I'm sorry we couldn't have been closer." It was a vapid, Hallmark card thing to say, but she couldn't think of anything better. "Closer is not my forte, Kevin. I'm sorry."

"Yeah, well, you certainly don't have to worry about it now,"

Kevin said. "I totally understand how you feel. Believe me."

"You do?"

"Sure, I do," he replied, peering at her through his increasingly wary eyes. "I mean, why try to make connections with people that you know will never last, right? Why make the effort? Wasn't that our philosophy here?"

Gaia shook her head. "No. No, it wasn't that. It was way more complicated than that, Kevin."

"Oh, come *on,*" Kevin snapped. "It's not so complicated. You and I are the same, Gaia, I know we are. We were never going to make any friends at this place. We never gave a crap about these people and they never gave a crap about us. And why would they? All they give a crap about is themselves. I mean, look at them. Look at all these sad, pathetic automatons, posing for pictures and holding up these stupid diplomas like they *mean* something. You know they're telling themselves some crap about how they're going to leave this place and go out and save the world, but the only people they really want to save are themselves. They just want to make enough cash to send their kids to this school so their kids can make a ton of cash and send their kids to this school and on and on and on like a freaking machine—"

"Kevin, what the hell is wrong with you?" Gaia grabbed Kevin's shoulder. She had never seen this look on his face before, and she'd never heard him talk this way. The things he was saying were depressing enough, but combined with this new look in his eyes, it was downright disturbing. "Are you okay?"

"Nothing's wrong with me; it's *them.* They're just completely in the dark. They're all just drinking their wine and whooping it up like there's some big bright future ahead of them, but you and me, Gaia, we know the truth, right? We know the truth. There *is* no big bright future. They just don't know it yet. They have no idea that today is their last day."

Gaia stepped in front of Kevin and took hold of both his arms. "Kevin, you need to chill. You're freaking me out, okay? Cut it out."

He turned back to Gaia and gave her a piercing stare that she couldn't even begin to read. "I want to show you something," he said quietly. "If I show you something, will you promise not to scream?"

"Kevin—"

He pulled his hand inside his sleeve and brought something out from under his gown, presenting it proudly to Gaia. It looked like one of the joysticks from a flight simulator game—black with a small red button at the top. A metal wire ran from the bottom of the joystick down under his sleeve. Kevin wrapped his fingers tightly around the shaft.

"What is that?" she demanded. "Kevin, what is it?"

"It's the way out," he said. "And it's a rude awakening for all these ignorant, soulless people." He ripped the Velcro of his gown open with his free hand, revealing the taped-up package at the center of his chest. It was strapped to his body by the metal wire from the joystick. The top of the package looked like a digital clock readout, and the number 20 was flickering at its center.

A bomb. Oh my God—he's got a homemade bomb.

Gaia forced herself not to move. She wanted to look

around the roof and gauge how far away the other partygoers were, but she kept her eyes fixed on Kevin's.

"Good-bye, Gaia," he said, backing slowly away from her. "I really do wish we could have been closer, like you said. But it's all over now." His thumb hovered over the red button.

"Jesus, Kevin, what are you doing?" Gaia hollered. "What the hell are you—?"

Suddenly Gaia heard a crashing noise—somebody had dropped a tray, it sounded like. A surprised gasp went through the crowd.

"*Freeze!*" a high-pitched voice shouted. "FBI! Drop it! Drop it *now*, Bender!"

FBI—? Gaia thought she must have heard wrong. *What the hell?*

She whipped around to see the bubbly catering woman standing at the center of the roof. She had dropped her tray of glasses to the ground and was thrusting a huge automatic handgun forward with a two-handed grip, aiming squarely at Kevin.

An agent—the waitress is a freaking FBI agent.

Gaia felt like she was dreaming; the logic of what was happening to her had veered so quickly that she'd barely had time to understand it, let alone react.

An inexplicable sensation had suddenly invaded her senses. It was something like nausea, only ten times worse. The sickness spread out through her lungs and her stomach—penetrating her core with this unbearable pressure. She clenched her fists and tried to shake it off, but even the simple act of shaking seemed momentarily impossible. It was like a sudden glitch

18

in all her motor functions, and she had no explanation for it.

A rash of confusion and screams broke out in the crowd—some of the partygoers flattened to the ground at the sight of the gun. Some of them just stood there in shock. Gaia had no idea where her father was—she strained to see, but she couldn't find him.

"Move away from him, ma'am!" the ponytailed FBI agent yelled.

They knew, Gaia realized suddenly. *That woman's here because the FBI knew Kevin was going to do this—*

"Oh, that won't really make a difference," Kevin shouted. He was holding the trigger out in front of him, and with his other hand he'd grabbed Gaia's wrist. "Once I hit this button, the whole roof goes to kingdom come. Me and my darling here will be first on the list at heaven's gate."

The agent thrust her gun into the air and fired off two warning shots that echoed over the campus rooftops. Each shot was like another bolt of pain through Gaia's center. She slammed her eyes shut for a moment just to cope with the nauseating aftershocks in her chest. And that's when she finally realized where this god-awful feeling was coming from . . .

It was the gun. Gaia hadn't seen or heard a gun since that horrific night—the night that Jake was shot. She'd sworn off all the violence as of that evening, and she'd made it through all these years at school without even a glimpse of a loaded weapon. Now the sight of that gun was bringing it all back. Images of Jake's murder were flooding her head and torturing her with this unbearable feeling. It wasn't fear, of course. The shots didn't frighten her. It was just the purest kind of repulsion. A supreme and stagnating discomfort. And Gaia needed to get the hell over it. Fast.

"Drop the trigger, Bender," the FBI agent repeated. She had to shout to be heard over the screams of the crowd. "Drop it or die."

"But I *want* to die," Kevin argued. "Anyway, if you shoot me, I'll still push the trigger."

The screams of the crowd had gotten louder. Over the parapet Gaia could see passersby on the quad gathering into a crowd, gazing up at the roof. There was no way to get them to scatter.

"Put it *down,* Bender," the FBI agent ordered. "Don't make me shoot. You do not want to do this." She began to move slowly toward them as Kevin backed himself up against the ledge, pulling Gaia with him.

"No, you're wrong about that," Kevin said. "See?"

Almost casually, he squeezed his thumb down on the red button.

Everyone on the rooftop screamed. It was deafening. The rooftop had devolved into pure chaos: black robes were flying in every possible direction and no direction at all, like a flock of panicked crows who had forgotten how to fly.

Gaia had to shake it off right now—the flashbacks, the paralysis, all of it. There was no more time to indulge her damaged psyche. She took a deep breath and she swallowed it all down—all the memories and all the promises she'd made to herself. And finally her thoughts became very focused and very clear—clearer than they had been in a long time. Because she knew what she had to do. There was simply no way to get all those people off the roof in twenty seconds. She had to get *Kevin* off the roof. That was the only way to save everyone else. And she was the one person on that roof who could do it.

"Congratulations, everyone!" Kevin hollered. The digital clock on the center of his chest had begun to count down from twenty. "Twenty seconds to impact! So say your good-byes to each other and then say good-bye to your bright and sunny futures."

Without wasting another second, she pulled her wrist from Kevin's grip, ducked her head, and dove at his midsection just as the clock on his chest struck fourteen seconds. She heard the loud *whuff* sound of their impact, the muffled clatter as they smacked against the parapet, pinwheeling upside down, slipping and plunging straight toward the ground.

Walking on air, Gaia thought randomly. The wind slammed up against her face, pounding her eardrums and whipping her hair high over her head. All the peripheral sounds seemed to fade away—the crowd's helpless cries, her father's useless pleas to try and stop her. All she could hear now was the steady beating of her heart as it pumped pure adrenaline through every one of her limbs.

Kevin clasped his arms desperately around her waist and shut his eyes as they plummeted. But Gaia's eyes were wide open. There was no fear, only focus. She knew her targets. She'd known them before she'd even left the ground. She prayed for dear life as she thrust out her hand and grabbed onto the first Stanford flag on the side of the building. The flag ripped away from its pole just as she managed to grapple the flag below it, tearing it clean off its pole as their fall grew slower. She focused in on her last target, folding her body tightly around Kevin's as they finally soared into the building's billowy white awning.

They slammed into the awning with an ear-shattering thud, forcing the entire canvas to fold in on itself as it dipped and dipped, tearing tack by tack from its frame until it had enveloped them in a thick white parachutelike ball on the ground.

The ground. She had gotten them down to solid ground. Still breathing and with all their limbs intact. But her job wasn't done yet. Not by a long shot. She hurled the awning off them and fixed her eyes on Kevin's chest as he lay there in a state of shock. The clock was down to six seconds. *Five, four . . .*

She smacked her hands down on his chest and ripped the front of his T-shirt right off, grabbing the bomb and all the wires with it. *Three, two . . .* She sprang up from the ground, took two running steps, and hurled the bomb with every ounce of her strength, rocketing it high into the air.

"Get down!" Gaia screamed.

There was a brief moment of absolute silence—and then a ball of fire, exploding in the air like some kind of ungodly fireworks finale. The deep, deafening sound seemed to echo through the entire campus as the ground shook below her.

And suddenly there was total quiet. Nothing but peaceful silence as the black cinders fell harmlessly from the sky.

Gaia knelt on the green grass, realizing that the explosion had momentarily deafened her. She felt a strong hand come down on her shoulder and another reach for her arm. The hands helped lift her back to her feet. When she finally looked up, she realized there were in fact three men helping her to rise. She saw the wide smiles on their faces and the confounded amazement in their eyes. And then she noticed the insignias on their dark blue windbreakers:

FBI

Three unmarked cars had pulled up beside her—Gaia was still in her silent world, and she wouldn't have known except for the dust clouds and exhaust against the bright sky. Kevin Bender stumbled and fell as he was thrown into one of the cars. An agent still had his hand on her shoulder; he squeezed it, and Gaia realized he was trying to tell her something. . . .

"I'm sorry?" Gaia yelled. She could hear herself, muffled— but her hearing was returning.

"I said," the agent yelled distantly in her ear—she could barely hear him, like a shout from miles away—*"it sounds like there are a lot of grateful people up there."*

"What?"

The agent pointed. Gaia followed his gesture upward.

And finally her hearing came back. The dull roar intensified until she recognized it.

Clapping. They're all clapping. . . .

It was true. All the way up on the roof of the Roth Library the entire senior class, and all of their parents and friends, were leaning over the ledge and showering Gaia with applause. And in the middle of the rooftop crowd, silhouetted against the flawless blue sky, was her father.

Gaia wanted to wave—but she couldn't move. She was so stunned by what had happened, and how *fast* it had occurred, that she could barely think straight. But one thing was certain.

That nagging sense of emptiness that she'd felt throughout her graduation day, that sense that something was missing . . . it was gone.

For at least this one moment, Gaia felt whole again.

FEDERAL BUREAU OF INVESTIGATION
TRAINEE ENTRANCE INTERVIEW FORM

Note: **This document is an official record of a trainee entrance interview.** In accordance with FBI regulation #27EE-1 this form must be provided at the time of the interview and subsequently submitted to J. Edgar Hoover Building, Washington, DC, by the interviewing personnel supervisor, accompanied by any and all requested documentation, including medical forms or releases, referral letters, photographs, and other material.

THE APPLICANT NAMED BELOW **MUST** BE FINGERPRINTED AND PHOTOGRAPHED **IMMEDIATELY** FOLLOWING INTERVIEW PROCEDURES.

Please PRINT or TYPE information into the form below and provide signature.

NAME OF INTERVIEWEE: Moore, Gaia   **HEIGHT:** 5'10"
WEIGHT: 125 lbs   **EYES:** blue   **HAIR:** blond
NATIONALITY: United States   **BIRTHPLACE:** New York City
EDUCATION: The Village School, New York, NY
BS, Stanford University (2005), honors in chemistry
NEXT OF KIN: Thomas Moore, New York (father)

I, the undersigned, hereby submit to evaluation for participation in the Federal Bureau of Investigation's Special Forces Training Program. I solemnly swear (or affirm) that the information provided above is accurate and truthful.

Sign here:

Well, here goes, Gaia thought.

Alone in the air-conditioned waiting room, Gaia let herself slump in her chair—and then quickly straightened up. The room probably had hidden cameras.

Taking a deep breath, Gaia uncapped her pen and wrote her name. The steel tip of the ballpoint nib scratched loudly on the form, pressing against the metal clipboard they'd given her. For the fifteenth or twentieth time she glanced over the information she'd written, checking to see if she'd made a mistake. Her handwriting looked fine, she thought—not too childish, not too messy or too neat.

That's ridiculous. Nobody's paying attention to my handwriting.

Except that probably wasn't true.

Looking around at the bare, beige surroundings, shivering in the freezing air, Gaia reminded herself where she was. As soon as she'd arrived on the top floor of this gleaming downtown Palo Alto office building and walked through the spotless glass doors that read Federal Bureau of Investigation (and below that, Regional Field Office #421), she was in a super-controlled, constantly observed world. The people who worked her were the world's master detectives and investigators—if she thought they wouldn't pay attention to her handwriting, her clothes, her way of speaking—maybe even find a way to gauge her heart rate or blood pressure—she was kidding herself.

It had been seven or eight minutes since the receptionist had handed her the entry form and shown her into this spotless waiting room. The smooth metal door had a complicated electronic lock, and it hummed and thumped as the door shut, locking her into the windowless room.

Good thing I'm not claustrophobic, Gaia thought. But that was silly—if you were claustrophobic, they wouldn't want you as an FBI agent.

Gaia had arrived ten minutes early, dressed in her best (okay, her only) suit, carrying the medical forms and reference letters she'd been told to bring, The suit itched her neck and was tight across the chest—it had been a gift from her father, who apparently expected her to immediately enter "the job market" once she'd gotten her diploma.

Well, here I am in the "job market," Dad, she thought. *Probably not the one you expected, though.*

In the five weeks since graduation Gaia had spent every day preparing for today. Maybe it was all that buildup that was making her so nervous.

Can I look at my watch again? Would that make me look too impatient?

Gaia told herself she was being silly. Nobody cared if she looked at her watch—if they were even paying any attention, which was only a theory. She couldn't see any obvious places for hidden cameras. Besides, she'd only done it twice in eight minutes.

Gaia looked at her watch. Nine minutes.

Are they going to make me wait exactly ten minutes? Start the interview precisely at—

With a loud, electronic click and hum, the door swung open.

"Gaia Moore?"

A young woman stood in the doorway. She might be thirty-five, Gaia guessed. She was strikingly attractive, but she had managed to nearly conceal that fact behind a buttoned-up black suit and an austere Peter Pan shearing of her dark red hair. She wasn't smiling, exactly—but she wasn't frowning either. Gaia rose quickly to her feet, clutching all her paperwork.

"Yes?"

"Special Agent Jennifer Bishop," the woman said, extending her hand. She did smile then, warmly, and Gaia felt much more comfortable. The smile seemed completely genuine; it was nothing like the dozens and dozens of obvious false smiles Gaia had encountered in her young life. They shook hands—Gaia nearly dropped the metal clipboard but caught it at the last moment. "How do you do? Is all your paperwork ready?"

"Yes, ma'am," Gaia said, holding out the forms.

Ma'am? That was a new one. Gaia wasn't sure if she'd ever called anyone "ma'am" in her life. But it hadn't happened on purpose—she had just blurted it out without thinking. Bishop seemed to take it in stride, as if she was used to being treated respectfully.

"Well, shall we begin?" Bishop took the paperwork and gestured Gaia toward the door. "Welcome to our fifth California base station," she went on, leading Gaia down a wide, gray-carpeted corridor toward a glassed-in guard's station with a metal gate in front of it. A tall, muscular man sat there in a marine's uniform. Gaia seriously wondered whether she could take him in a fight; if she did, it would take a long time. "Let's just get this over with," Bishop said.

"Raise your arms," the marine said, rising to his feet. He

waved a white metal wand around Gaia's body, accompanied by a squealing noise. Then he nodded. "Go ahead, ma'am," he told her, pressing a button that buzzed and opened the metal gate.

Okay, I'm a "ma'am," too, Gaia realized. That was another first.

"Our pursuit of your friend Kevin Bender was conducted out of this field office," Bishop went on as they passed through the metal gate and circled around another corner. "Not that that was one of our proudest moments. If I'd been in charge of that one, believe me, nobody would have been asleep at the switch."

"You weren't involved in that, Agent Bishop?"

"Oh God, no," Bishop said. Gaia caught the distaste in her voice.

Should I not have asked that? Did I insult her somehow?

Gaia understood why the FBI wouldn't be too proud of what had happened on that rooftop. Although it had been five weeks since that insane graduation day, to Gaia, it might have been yesterday. All the time Gaia had spent working out, running, and preparing for this interview as best she could, she'd been haunted by that fragile, lost look in Kevin's eyes just before he released the bomb trigger.

"I don't know *how* they missed it," Bishop went on in a hushed, conspiratorial voice, ducking her head as she confided in Gaia. It was an appealing gesture—it put Gaia much more at ease. "I looked over the report and couldn't believe the mistakes. They'd been watching him for *months*—they had the explosives traced; they had his phone numbers and profile; they knew he was going to do something soon. To me, it was *obvious* he'd make his move on graduation—I took one look at his profile and figured that out. But only *one* agent on the roof? Please. It's just lucky you were there."

Lucky I was there. Gaia felt a surge of pride and was surprised at how strong the feeling was. But then, just as quickly as it had arrived, the feeling washed away.

They had his phone numbers, she thought, remembering the conversations she'd had with Kevin during the school year. *Does that mean they were watching* me, *too?*

Bishop walked quickly, her high heels clicking on the carpet. They were walking past numbered offices. Gaia looked around avidly, trying to get a glance at what was going on behind the half-opened doors, but she couldn't see anything interesting. "Maybe I'm being too hard on my colleagues," Bishop went on. "I specialize in psychological profiling—I've got very high standards. I don't do fieldwork anymore—I create and supervise the recruiting and training programs in Virginia. This time of year I circulate around our field offices, talking to applicants."

She's a profiler, Gaia marveled. *The real thing.*

Gaia was starting to like Agent Bishop—her brisk, no-nonsense manner, her easy, obvious intelligence and the sweetness and friendliness beneath.

Special Agent Bishop used her electronic card to open a metal door. Its identification plate read Conference 12. The now-familiar buzz started and the door clicked open. Inside was a wide, windowless room with a large oak table. Gaia entered the room—and all her hopes about the interview fell away.

The room wasn't empty. A man stood at the table. His presence was forbidding, to say the least. There was a thick file on the table in front of him, with a large FBI emblem printed on its face.

"Gaia, this is Special Agent Brian Malloy," Bishop said. "Agent Malloy is the director of the FBI's training facility at Quantico."

Gaia noticed the man's tightly cropped, slicked-back hair first. It was jet black, slightly graying at the temples. She couldn't quite discern his age—his skin was so taut around his strong jaw but deeply creased around his dark eyes. But what she noticed the most was that he didn't smile. Not in the corners of his mouth, not even in his eyes. He looked like he was reporting for military duty, and Gaia was instantly convinced that he had to be an ex-marine or ex-navy.

"Ms. Moore," Malloy said sternly. "Our problematic new applicant. Let's get started—and maybe you can explain why I shouldn't cross your name off right away."

FBI RECRUITING TRANSCRIPT
AUDIO FILE #245C7
RECRUIT NAME: Gaia Moore
ADMINISTRATING AGENTS: Brian Malloy,
Jennifer Bishop (assisting)
RECRUIT PRIORITY: *Classified*
(as per Malloy, op. code 45 red)

BISHOP: This is Special Agent Jennifer Bishop, ID code G44.

MALLOY: Brian Malloy, A71; special agent.

BISHOP: Questioning potential recruit Gaia Moore, as per Special Agent Bishop. Please note that Ms. Moore has been informed that this interview is being recorded for our records as per regulation #27EE-1 and Ms. Moore has complied.

MALLOY: Confirmed.

BISHOP: Gaia, I'd like to thank you again for joining us today. And the bureau thanks you as well.

MOORE: Thanks for taking the time to see me.

BISHOP: So, Gaia, what brings you here? Why are you interested in the FBI?

MOORE: Well, I guess you could say it started five weeks ago. The incident we were just talking about—the, um, Kevin Bender incident.

MALLOY: Please note for the record that the applicant is discussing case docket #1661, Palo Alto, code name Sapphire.

BISHOP: Go on, Gaia.

MOORE: Well—something happened right after it was over.

The funny thing was, we were talking about not knowing what to do next. Kevin and I were. We'd had conversations like that before; I'm sure the whole class was having that talk. Then suddenly he had a bomb, and I had to do something fast, and the next thing I knew it was over, people were actually clapping, and I felt this amazing feeling. Suddenly it was like I'd found something I really wanted to do.

MALLOY: Situational euphoria. It's a common field occurrence—we do everything we can to discourage it.

MOORE: What?

BISHOP: He just means that there's an expected adrenaline rush after the kind of stunt you performed. It's easy to fall into the trap of overinterpreting those feelings.

MOORE: Wait a minute. Let me finish. It wasn't just that moment. If you'd let me finish, I would have explained that I've been thinking about this ever since—I've spent five weeks researching the FBI, and with each passing day I've become more convinced that it's the right career choice for me. That can't all be adrenaline, can it? There isn't that much adrenaline in ten people.

MALLOY: Let's not start off on the wrong foot here, Ms. Moore.

MOORE: Sorry.

BISHOP: As you know, Gaia, Operation Sapphire didn't go the way this office planned. However, thanks to your actions, the day was saved, as were the lives of many people. It's for that reason that we've decided to bend the rules and consider you.

MOORE: Bend the rules?

MALLOY: Yes—that kind of reckless, impulsive action, especially when performed by a civilian, is a red flag: it shows us that there are dangerous anti-authoritarian tendencies in a person as well as an element of anarchistic heroism that ordinarily would disqualify someone for consideration by the bureau.

BISHOP: Brian, let's not overstate the case. There's also the matter of Gaia's remarkable abilities, which would seem to prepare her for the grueling routine of our trainees, if she can get past the extreme antisocial tendencies that have governed her college experience and the illegal and immoral vigilante actions that have plagued her life in New York.

MOORE: What? How did— What are you—

MALLOY: You're an intelligent young woman, Moore, so I'm sure it comes as no surprise that we have produced a highly detailed and elaborate file on you since you were the only person Kevin Bender maintained contact with at Stanford. As you can see, I've got the file here, and it's quite thick. It shows elaborate signs of arrested social development, combined with obsessive academic and athletic achievement.

MOORE: Arrested—Sir, I'm sorry, but I don't understand. You're saying that you've got a file on me making me look bad because I was Kevin's friend?

MALLOY: Forget Bender. You're missing the point. He's the reason we took a good look at you, and you can't blame us if we're disturbed by what we see. Frankly, I was very surprised that you decided to apply to be an agent; quite honestly, I don't see how you fit the profile at all.

BISHOP: Brian, just a minute. Gaia, please understand—since you are here, we fully intend to give you fair and unbiased treatment as an applicant. Please don't think we're picking on you—it's our job to ask these questions.

MOORE: That's okay. It doesn't bother me.

MALLOY: Ms. Moore, my day is long. I'm not interested in what does or doesn't bother you; I'm interested in why an obvious head case such as yourself would want to pursue law enforcement. Now, will you look at this photograph, please?

What the hell?

Gaia watched as Special Agent Malloy pulled a black-and-white photograph from the thick file in front of him and held it up. She was trying very hard to calm down, to get out of the combative frame of mind that this man's questions had put her into. She forced herself to stare at the picture.

The photograph must be at least five years old. It was an image of Washington Square Park, near where Gaia had lived for so long in New York City. Gaia was at the center of the image, swathed in an old gray sweatshirt and a pair of faded army pants. Her arms were extended outward as she sent a thick-necked skinhead soaring over the park's stone chess tables. His head was just about to collide with the trunk of a huge, leafy tree.

"Does this ring a bell?" Malloy asked. "According to reports, you did serious damage to that boy. And if these pictures are any indication, it looks to me like you enjoyed it."

Gaia stared at the look on her paler, more youthful face in the photo. It was a look she had never really seen before since there had never been any mirrors in the park. She stared at her own eyes—focused with cool razor-sharp attention on her victim. But just barely showing in the corner of her mouth, there was something else. A snarl or a sneer . . . or maybe even a smile? It was actually a bit disturbing to look at.

Gaia had been such an emotional mess in those days. She remembered all too well how she used to take such pleasure in taking down the scumbags in the park. That particular brand of vigilante justice had been her only real solace, her only release. But she wasn't proud of it. Staring at that almost imperceptible smile in the corner of her mouth, Gaia felt a surprising amount of shame creep into her heart. Yes, they'd all deserved what they'd gotten—the muggers and rapists of Washington Square Park fell somewhere below insects and rodents in the order of species—but still, perhaps she had taken a little *too* much pleasure in punishing them.

"Where did you get these?" Gaia asked. "Who took these pictures?"

"They're from our Manhattan field office," Malloy replied easily. "About ten minutes after Kevin Bender called you the first time, the computer recognized your caller ID and routed this information to us. Violent behavior of this nature tends to be noticed by the bureau, Ms. Moore. Especially when the behavior is repeated time and again."

"What would you say about this picture now, Gaia?" Bishop asked gently.

"Well, that was a long time ago—five years and two months, I think," Gaia said, sitting up straighter in her seat. "And if I recall correctly, that—that lowlife was about to mug a young girl at knifepoint."

Malloy paused for a moment—probably impressed with Gaia's near-digital memory. "Yes, that's true," he said finally. "And that is precisely my point. If you saw a potential crime in progress, why didn't you call the police rather than attempt to 'handle' the situation yourself?"

"It was two A.M. in Washington Square Park, sir. Where was I supposed to find a cop? I mean, if I'd known there was an FBI agent hiding in the bushes and taking my picture, I would have called *him*."

Gaia caught a glimpse of Bishop smiling. Malloy didn't share her mirth.

"This does show remarkable combat skills," Bishop said appreciatively. "She disarmed a man twice her size, neutralized him, and saved a girl's life that night."

"Remarkable or not, this was *vigilante* behavior, Agent Bishop—part of a long-standing pattern of violence and antisocial behavior." Malloy frowned, looking like some kind of fierce submarine captain. "How often have you performed such an act—for example, a violent act like the one in this picture—that you *felt* was justified when in fact it was a matter for law enforcement?"

"I've never performed any 'violent act' that wasn't justified."

This isn't going well, Gaia thought worriedly. The optimistic good mood she'd been in when she first met Agent Bishop was entirely gone. *I'm losing control of this conversation—if I ever even had it.*

"Gaia, we're wondering where this pattern begins," Bishop told her. The young woman's voice, as usual, was smoother and kinder than Agent Malloy's harsh barking of questions, and it calmed her down. "We understand that your father was involved with the Central Intelligence Agency and that you lost your mother in a family tragedy right here in the Golden State when you were twelve years old."

Gaia suddenly flashed back to that kitchen. That house in the mountains where the family vacationed. She could practically hear the gunshot and her father's as the blood washed over the white tiles. After eight years she couldn't stop the images from flooding back into her mind—or the lump from edging into her throat, threatening to bring her to tears.

"My uncle accidentally shot her," Gaia said evenly. "He was trying to kill my father—his twin brother—and put an end to their long-standing sibling rivalry once and for all. It was a long time ago. After that I was in foster care for many years."

"Interesting coincidence," Malloy said harshly, "given what happened three years ago in New York—another accident brought about by sibling rivalry."

The hatchet-faced special agent was pulling out another photograph, and right then Gaia felt a chill from the exaggerated, arctic drone of the room's powerful air conditioner. Because she knew what the photograph was going to show.

DYSFUNCTIONAL GRIEF

No, Gaia thought, her eyes turning down toward the metal table. *No, come on. Don't show me that. That's not fair.*

"Look at the picture, please," Malloy ordered.

Gaia kept her eyes riveted on the table. She wouldn't look at the picture. "I know what it is," she said.

"Gaia, you have to look," Agent Bishop said softly.

It was exactly what she expected to see, and it hit her like a battering ram.

It's him.

Jake.

Gaia had done everything she could not to think about him. Which hadn't gone very well. Of course she thought about him all the time. But seeing an actual photograph of his dead body . . . lying there bleeding on the floor . . . it made her truly hate Agent Malloy for that one moment. How could he do this to her? How could he force this picture down her throat?

It was a crime scene photograph, of course—taken by the CIA agents that very night when they'd stormed that uptown apartment. Gaia hadn't even remembered them taking crime scene photos then, but why would she? She'd been completely oblivious to anything other than Jake's vacant eyes as he breathed his last few breaths.

Jake . . .

Gaia still remembered every second—how two jealous, angry brothers had ended up in a horrible face-off and how the bullets had flown like spray from a fountain, punching through Jake's body just a few seconds before the CIA arrived.

Ms. Moore? Are you all right? one of the nameless, faceless agents had said. *It's over—it's all over.* But she knew she would never be all right again.

Stay with me, Jake, she had ordered desperately, clutching his hand and staring at his fading eyes. *Listen to me. Keep your eyes open. You stay with me.*

But he was gone.

Now Gaia couldn't take her eyes off the photograph. She scanned the length of the three-year-old picture again and again, from Jake's closed, lifeless eyes down to the blood-drenched T-shirt on his chest. And then, as her eyes drifted to the left side of the frame, she realized what she had missed at first glance. It was lying right there, just a few feet from Jake's body, staring back at her, reflecting the glint of the flashbulb.

The gun. The murder weapon itself—sitting there on the floor right where Gaia had knocked it from the killer's hands. That one little piece of goddamn steel had done it all. One effortless squeeze of the trigger and Jake's life had been ripped away. She could hear the shots again, echoing through her head like no time had passed.

Suddenly that awful feeling was invading again. The same feeling she'd gotten on the roof when that FBI agent had drawn her weapon. Gaia's eyes focused in on that gun and she fell prey to another surprise attack of unbearable nausea. Her chest couldn't expand to breathe, and her eyes slammed momentarily shut. Her hands clenched into fists, and before she knew it, she had crumpled the side of the photo in her hand and let it fall back down on the table.

Jesus, Gaia, keep it together, she told herself. *Shake it off, for Christ's sake. They're watching every single move you make.*

She heard Bishop's voice across the table, sounding slightly muffled as all the blood rushed to her aching head.

"Gaia, do you need some water . . . ?"

"What?" Gaia snapped. She bit down on her tongue, trying desperately to release the crippling tension in every one of her muscles. "No, I'm fine," she lied, still not quite able to hear herself.

Agent Bishop ignored Gaia's response and poured out a quick glass of water, handing it over to Gaia.

41

"Thank you," she uttered, trying to unclench her teeth, "but I really am just fine."

In truth, she was suddenly parched as all hell.

Just drink it and freaking relax, she howled at herself. *You are blowing this interview.*

She picked up the glass and forced it to her lips. But her hand was still too tense. The glass slipped from her grip and toppled over. The moment lasted no more than two seconds, but it felt like an eternity to Gaia. She could only sit there and watch as the water spilled out across the table, soaking the photo of Jake, turning his skin into wet blotches of black and gray. It continued its course, sprawling out into tiny rivulets and rolling toward Malloy, forcing him to snap up his thick manila folder from the table.

Gaia quickly snatched the glass back up and placed it squarely on the table, but the moment had already happened, and there was nothing she could do to take it back.

The room fell deafeningly quiet as Malloy stared back at Gaia, holding his file up by his shoulders as the water trickled down over the edge of the table in front of him. Gaia stared at him through the painful silence.

"I'm sorry," Gaia said as nonchalantly as she could. "Do we have a towel? I can—"

"It's fine, Ms. Moore," Malloy said coldly. "We'll get someone in here to clean it up." He placed the folder on the chair next to him, looked down at his watch, and then turned to Bishop. "All right," he said. "I think we're done here. Ms. Moore, thank you for coming in today. We'll review the information and you'll receive a letter within—"

"Wait a minute," Gaia interrupted. "We're done? How can we be done?" Her eyes drifted over to Bishop with confusion, but Bishop wouldn't look at her.

"Yes," Malloy replied, packing his file into a briefcase. "We're done. I've seen everything I need to see."

"What have you seen?" Gaia shot back. She knew it was inappropriate, but she didn't care. She had to say something here. She had to speak up and quick because she knew what was happening. It was obvious. Malloy had already made up his mind about her. He might has well have handed her the rejection letter right then and there. "What have you seen?" she repeated, trying her best not to sound as frazzled as she was. "You've seen me spill a little water by accident? *That's* why we're done?"

Malloy set his briefcase on the floor and then leaned across the table, pressing his palms down in the puddle as he looked Gaia dead in the eyes. "Let's not fool ourselves, Ms. Moore," he said calmly. "If you expect me to believe that moment just now consisted of nothing more than a slippery glass, then you not only insult me, you insult this entire organization."

"What?" Gaia squawked defensively. "I don't know what you're talking ab—"

"And if you truly have no idea what I'm talking about," he interrupted, "then you require even more psychiatric attention than I thought."

"*Excuse* me?"

"It's nothing personal, Ms. Moore, believe me. But it wouldn't take a trained professional to understand what just happened to you."

43

"Nothing happened to me," Gaia insisted. "I spilled some water."

"You *lost* control," Malloy declared. "I showed you that photo and it produced an involuntary reaction."

Gaia suddenly fell silent. She didn't know what to say.

"What is it you think we do here, Ms. Moore?" Malloy pressed. "We build psychological profiles. We listen, we watch, we perceive, and then we draw conclusions. I could tell a hundred different things about you when I handed you that photo. You, apparently, can tell nothing. I can tell that it's been three years and you still have not recovered from Jake Montone's death—you have yet to move past it. That kind of dysfunctional grief is unacceptable for our kind of work, Ms. Moore. Do you understand that? We need to move on from grief in three *days*. Sometimes three minutes in a life-threatening situation."

"But I *have* moved on—"

"Please don't delude yourself." Malloy was no longer listening to a thing she said. He spoke each point with clipped efficiency—each word slashing away at Gaia's ego. "I can also point out to you the exact moment that you lost control because that is what we do here. I can tell you that your eyes drifted from the right side of the photo to the left. From Montone's body over to the murder weapon. And that is when it happened."

"When *what* happened?" Gaia huffed.

"The gun," Malloy said, standing up straight. "You saw that gun and you were no longer with us, Ms. Moore. You were back there. Watching your boyfriend get shot—hearing him get shot. You showed all the symptoms of a post–traumatic stress reaction. Your eyes glazed over, the memories took hold, your breathing became labored, and you experienced a momentary lapse in motor function. It's a textbook case."

"That's ridiculous," Gaia insisted.

"Is it?" Malloy replied. "Agent Bishop, you're an expert profiler—do you think I'm being ridiculous?"

Gaia turned to Bishop, who still wouldn't look her in the eye. Bishop looked at Malloy for a moment and then, sounding almost defeated, she finally turned to face Gaia.

"No," she said quietly. "No, it's not ridiculous. I'm sorry, Gaia, but I don't think you're ready. Maybe after a few years of good therapy. After you've worked out some of these issues."

Gaia turned away from them both and focused her eyes on the table. The blood was coursing through her veins so fast now with frustration, confusion, disappointment, desire. . . .

Post–traumatic stress? Wasn't that like a phobia? Wasn't that a fear-based reaction? If so, then it was categorically impossible for her to experience. It's not that Gaia was afraid of guns; she just despised the sight of them with every ounce of her being. And yes, maybe she was so sickened by them now that it was a bit beyond her control. But that couldn't be a good enough reason to reject her. She couldn't accept that.

"You can sign out at the front desk," Malloy said. "They'll see you out to the lobby."

They began to head for the door, and quite suddenly, almost in spite of herself, words began to pour from Gaia's mouth. Words from some part of her heart that she had worked like hell to stomp out over the last three years. The part that contained all her truest feelings and desires. The part that simply couldn't compromise anymore.

"Just *wait* a second," she demanded, looking up at Bishop and Malloy. "Please, just . . . wait."

They honored her request and stood at the doorway in silence.

"Look . . . I need this, okay? I need to do this. . . ."

Malloy glanced at Bishop and then turned back to Gaia. "There are plenty of other applicants who need this, Ms. Moore. I'm sure you need many things—"

"No, you didn't let me finish," Gaia snapped. "I need this. And you need me."

Malloy's eyes widened slightly. "Oh, is that right?" he asked dubiously.

"Yes, that's right," Gaia said, staring at him without blinking. "This organization *needs* me. You think you know me. You think you know what I'm capable of, but you don't even know half of it. And I keep trying to deny it—I've spent years trying to ignore who I am, but I *don't* want to ignore it anymore. I can't. I've wasted so much time trying to dodge my true calling. But *this is it.* I swear the Fates designed me with a purpose, and that purpose is the FBI. This is what I was born to do. And we have to respect that. I have to respect it, and so do you."

"Gaia," Bishop said, "respect has nothing to do with it. We respect your skills; we just don't think you're psychologically prepared for—"

"But how will I ever *be* psychologically prepared?" Gaia stood up from her chair. "Yes, I have some issues. But I need to defeat them here and now. With your help, with your training. And if you don't give me the opportunity, if you don't make the right choice, then we all lose. I kiss my destiny goodbye and you lose something much worse than that. You lose the best goddamn agent the FBI has ever seen. Pardon my French."

The room fell very silent. The drone of the air-conditioning was the only audible noise. Gaia suddenly felt deeply uncomfortable. She felt like she had just made a very big mistake.

Malloy flashed Bishop a harsh glance and then turned back to Gaia.

"I want you to listen to me, Ms. Moore," he said. "I want you to understand something. The Quantico training course is the most difficult and challenging program of its kind in the world. The twenty-four elite trainees embark upon an intense ten-week program that presents them with a near-constant battery of challenging and difficult testing and training situations designed to tax an individual's intellectual and physical persistence, fortitude, and stamina to extremes. Do you understand?"

"Yes," Gaia said. What the hell was his point? Was he just trying to rub it in?

"We can only offer the opportunity to a very small, carefully selected group," he went on. "We have no patience whatsoever for weakness or failure."

"I know that," Gaia shot back. "I get it. You've made your decision already; you really don't need to explain it any further."

"I should hope not," Malloy said. "Fine. Then we'll see you on base in two weeks."

Gaia's frown suddenly fell from her face, leaving only a rather clueless confusion.

"I'm sorry?" she uttered. "I thought you'd already decided to—"

"I just changed my mind, Ms. Moore," Malloy said. "Would you like me to change it again?"

Agent Bishop cracked a subtle smile.

"No, sir," Gaia said as a smile began to creep up on her face. "No, I wouldn't. Thank you, sir."

"Don't thank me yet, Moore," he said. "You've just made me a whole lot of promises. Let's see if you can keep them. In the meantime, I suppose congratulations are in order." He stepped forward and shook Gaia's hand. "Welcome to Quantico, Ms. Moore. Welcome to the FBI."

someone was pulling a trigger and a bullet was being unleashed

OVERLY MUSCLED YOUNG MAN

Left. Right. Right. Left. Balance—breathe—

Gaia's feet were whispering along the dirt track, scuffing on the sharp tops of the rocks. She wanted to look *down*—every instinct told her to glance at her feet and check her progress, but that was the wrong move. If she took her eyes off the space directly in front of herself, she'd smack her face right into one of the treacherously placed horizontal wooden beams or spiderwebs of taut ropes across her path.

In the two weeks that followed her meeting with Agents Malloy and Bishop, Gaia had worked hard to prepare herself for this moment.

The first day.

The first chance she had to prove that she was more than just a head case.

The obstacle course was incredibly hard. The terrain changed very fast, and the course turned and twisted so it was impossible to see what was coming next. One moment Gaia was running along level ground through trees—and she could see the other trainees around her. Then the ground would drop away unexpectedly, and she would have to choose one of the widely spaced rope bridges and pull herself across a deep crevasse. The next moment she would whip around a corner and have to run through narrow, sandy channels of rock, trying to keep her balance without being able to see much of anything beyond the passing rock walls and the sky overhead. Then the rock channels would end and she'd be leaping through thick walls of foliage, like she was now, avoiding the obstacles that threatened to slam her to the ground.

Gaia had no idea how long this was supposed to take. She'd never seen this sadistic an obstacle course before. It had all started in a heartbeat. One minute she'd been standing there in line with the other trainees, and the next minute that bullet-headed drill sergeant Conroy was barking out orders and firing off a starter pistol. He hadn't been one to waste words. "Run the course," he'd shouted. "Don't stop, don't fall. Best time wins."

Gaia had barely gotten a good look at the two dozen or so other FBI trainees as they'd assembled on the parade grounds on this hot, baking morning—a mere two hours after they'd all arrived at Quantico. There had barely been time to change and run out here. Gaia had only managed to notice a couple of her fellow trainees: Peter Pan Girl and Farm Boy.

They'd all looked pretty tough, lined up in their fatigue pants and their FBI T-shirts. She'd noticed Peter Pan girl then because her haircut reminded Gaia of Agent Bishop. She'd also noticed Farm Boy—a sinewy, overly muscled young man with a reddened tan and a blond crew cut that stuck up from his head like a manicured lawn of sun-bleached hair. Farm Boy had a swagger and a wide, easy grin Gaia instantly hated, and she twisted her head away quickly before he could catch her looking at him.

Now, running over the uneven ground, Gaia could barely see the two trainees flanking her. She had crossed the first rope bridge right ahead of the girl with the dark, pixie-cut hair— and Peter Pan Girl was keeping up. And blond crew cut Farm Boy was gaining on her. Gaia could hear his breathing right behind her. The rest of the trainees were far behind.

This was the kind of simple, clear activity that Gaia loved. Nothing to worry about but her speed—nothing to fret over but her agility. A clear blue sky and clean country air. Moving at speed, with the wind blowing her hair and coursing across her body as she ran, with that familiar burn and ache in her muscles, Gaia felt close to nirvana. *I like this place already,* she thought, wincing at the growing pain in her limbs as she moved, *and it's only the first hour of the first workout.*

"Two minutes ten," Sergeant Conroy's voice boomed over the loudspeaker.

Gaia felt her legs aching as she sped up even more. She checked her watch. That meant thirty seconds since she'd reached the end of the opening sprint and entered the obstacle course. She rounded a corner in a channel of ten-foot rocks and saw a huge rope wall about ten seconds before slamming into it. She heard her breath catch as she slowed her pace just a fraction so that she'd hit the rope with her right foot raised to catch on the second rung of the rope wall. *Going to hurt,* she thought pointlessly as her upper body snapped into the taut ropes like a tennis ball hitting a racket. She was right—the ropes lashed her like sandpaper-covered wires. *Don't feel it. Climb.*

Gasping for breath, her arm muscles burning with fatigue

as she pulled herself to the top of the giant, sagging rope wall, Gaia could see around herself again. She could see the bright, vast blue dome of the Virginia sky and the last leg of the obstacle course in front of her. She wasted half a second on a glance backward.

Nobody's even close, Gaia thought excitedly. The nearest trainee she could spot was still quite far behind. *I'm the fastest,* she realized, experiencing another rush of the joyful adrenaline she'd encountered all along this vaulting, twisting pathway.

But the last leg would be brutally hard, she could see. The webbed grid of ropes continued horizontally, forming a bridge. It was clear what she had to do: hang suspended beneath the ropes, pulling herself hand over hand while risking a twenty-foot drop into a not-very-soft-looking muddy field. Then it got even more fun: at the other end she would have to climb down a structure made of rough-hewn wooden logs . . . and then sprint up a rocky incline to a wide, grassy hilltop where a neon orange rope had been strung waist high. The finish line.

Nobody ahead of me either, Gaia confirmed as she swung under the ropes and started moving. She could see nothing but converging strands of rope and the muddy fields and the sky. *I'm going to w—*

Suddenly the ropes flexed wildly, making her bounce in place and almost lose her balance. Someone had just swung down beneath the bridge right behind her.

"Comin' through," sang out a cheerful male voice.

Gaia struggled to keep her grip as the bridge bounced up and down. To her dismay, Farm Boy pulled into view, his tanned face streaming sweat, his upper arms flexing like powerful tree trunks as he easily pulled ahead. He even smiled at her pleasantly as he passed, as if they were strolling along an avenue—and continued on his way to victory.

Without thinking, Gaia pulled herself upward and started clambering along the *top* of the rope bridge.

"That ain't going to help," Farm Boy yelled cheerfully. "You're wastin' too much energy on the lateral vector."

Show-off, Gaia thought furiously. *I already can't stand this guy, and it's only been ten seconds.*

As it turned out, Farm Boy was right—it was nearly impossible to do. It was clearly not the way you were supposed to run this particular course. But, Gaia realized, as she tilted perilously to one side and then the other, somehow managing to keep her grip, it could be done.

"You're wasting too much energy on . . . talking," Gaia managed to wheeze. It wasn't a very good comeback, but she was determined to show him that she wasn't too exhausted to talk. Behind her, she realized, other trainees were catching up, moving onto the ropes, making them shake even more.

"Nice . . . try," Farm Boy gasped as he pulled himself ahead even faster. Somehow he had enough breath to taunt her while the muscles in his arms corded and bunched, pulling him forward. "Second . . . place."

"Two minutes fifty," Sergeant Conroy yelled, his voice distorted by the bullhorn. Gaia could see him now on the other side of the finish line, watching the trainees' progress.

"If they have an 'annoying' competition . . . you'll win easily . . . but not this . . ." Gaia puffed.

The ropes were swinging up and down like plucked guitar

53

strings as Gaia climbed neck and neck with Farm Boy. She could barely see his face staring up at her as she clambered past his fists, moving on all fours like a spider navigating a web. "Nooo—" a female voice called from behind them—the ropes pitched madly upward as someone lost her grip and fell to the muddy ground below. Farm Boy was losing his grip, too—Gaia could see his knuckles whitening with the effort.

Gaia finally made it to the end of the rope bridge. She let go, dropping to the grass with a heavy thump just as Farm Boy dropped behind her. Somehow he landed on his feet—Gaia could only see a blur as her own sweat streamed into her eyes—and now they were running up the grass hill toward the orange rope. It was three paces ahead, shimmering in her vision.

Gaia dug down deep, and with the last of her strength she dove forward, toppling onto the hard ground and pulling the rope with her. Sergeant Conroy's whistle blasted in her ears as she rolled onto her back, her entire body in pain, the sun dazzling her eyes.

A dark silhouette blotted out the sky as she lay there, panting.

"Here—stand up," Sergeant Conroy's rough voice barked out. Gaia could see his face upside down—and his hand reaching down toward her.

"Three twenty-three," Conroy said, his weather-beaten face barely registering a ghost of a smile as he looked at his chrome stopwatch. "That's a record."

Beside her, Farm Boy was doubled over, his hands on his knees, looking like he might throw up. He raised his eyes, gazing at her, and Gaia could read his expression as easily as if it were a roadside billboard. He didn't like to lose.

"Good—good job," Farm Boy wheezed. His chiseled face was soaked in sweat, as was his T-shirt. Gaia could see the veins popping on his neck muscles. Behind him, Peter Pan Girl was leading the rest of the recruits up the hill, brushing mud from her shoulders, recovering from her fall.

"Thanks," Gaia said. A strand of hair had dropped over her face and she pushed it out of the way. "You too." She tried to keep the triumphant smirk off her face—and she succeeded. Mostly.

"Cut the chatter," Sergeant Conroy snapped at them. "Start running."

Start *running . . . ?* Gaia was sure she'd heard wrong. He might as well have asked her to start flying. But the drill sergeant was pointing past the top of the hill, indicating the beginning of a dirt track that led off across the Virginia grass and out of sight.

"Yes, sir," Farm Boy said, having recovered his breath. "How far, sir?"

"Five miles," Conroy said, in a tone that suggested he could barely tolerate the question. He raised his voice to include the other recruits, who were streaming over the finish line behind them one by one. "Five-mile run, people," Conroy yelled. "Follow the track. Uneven ground. Finish at the firing range."

Farm Boy didn't need to be told twice. He was already sprinting ahead, his shoes kicking up clouds of dust from the dirt track. Gaia firmly ignored the screaming pain in her legs and ran to catch up. Peter Pan Girl and two other trainees were right on their heels.

"Your luck's . . . about to change," Farm Boy whispered as they ran side by side. Incredibly he was pacing her. He'd recovered his breath as quickly as she had.

Gaia didn't answer. She couldn't come up with anything clever fast enough. She just pulled ahead.

FEDERAL BUREAU OF INVESTIGATION
FIELD REPORT—QUANTICO SPECIAL FORCES TRAINING PROGRAM
DAY: 1
REPORT: Physical exam
SUPERVISOR: Sgt. Wesley Conroy, Physical Training Director, ID code M12

SUMMARY

All twenty-three Special Forces trainees reported for duty on time, in their required attire. Under my supervision the trainees began the endurance/stamina/problem-solving exercise ("obstacle course") at 0900 EST. This was immediately followed by a single lap on the grounds' dirt running track ("track #1"), constituting 5.24 miles of uneven terrain.

Following the run (which lasted 45 minutes), the trainees reported for examination at shooting range 6, where they each performed in a standard GX-1 handgun training exercise. This occurred nearly without incident (see below).

At 1100 hours EST the trainees were released from duty for lunch. The remainder of the afternoon is designated an off-duty period of "free play" to be followed by the introductory trainee dinner and briefing in preparation for the commencement of "practical applications" tomorrow morning under the supervision of Special Agent Jennifer Bishop, ID code G44.

NOTES

All trainees performed adequately to exceptionally. The winner of the ES/PS obstacle course was trainee Gaia Moore (F), who set a time record of 3:23. She was followed in an extremely close second place by William Taylor (M) at 3:24, in what appeared to be a closely fought personal competition. Other trainees did equally well, although Moore and Taylor's time was not matched; only one trainee (Perkins, M.) failed to complete the obstacle run and is being recommended for dismissal (see attached file).

Competition between Moore and Taylor continued into the five-mile run with interesting results (see below). However, events in the firing range drill were problematic for Ms. Moore. It is my recommendation that a psychological profile report be made on Ms. Moore as her behavior during the commencement of the FR drill may warrant further examination and appraisal.

Full report to come—Conroy, M12

The sound hit her first. *That* sound.

She thought she was ready for it. But she wasn't. And because of that, she almost lost the race to that irritating Farm Boy with his blond crew cut and self-satisfied smirk.

It was that unmistakable noise, that concussive, flat, dead *boom* that meant someone was pulling a trigger and a bullet was being unleashed, about to smash through flesh and bone and blood and change things forever. There was just no mistaking that *boom.*

Boom. Boom. Bullets were flying. Ahead of her guns were going off; there was no doubt. And despite the heat and the pounding exertion of the run, Gaia felt cold.

Because somehow she'd managed not to think about this eventuality since it first came up in her interview with Malloy. Until right now, as she and Farm Boy led the pack of trainees through a hot dust cloud toward the Quantico firing range, their shoes pounding the dirt track as they paced each other.

The firing range was a wide, shallow field divided into parallel tracks, almost like an outdoor bowling alley. At the end of each track was a motorized steel mechanism holding the customary paper targets with their segmented silhouettes of menacing figures. The gunfire was coming from a single figure at the nearest track: a young woman with fiery red hair, dressed in a pair of blue overalls with a bright yellow FBI insignia on the back. She wore enormous black ear guards as she fired a series of perfect bull's-eyes, and the sound got louder and louder as Gaia approached.

"You realize . . ." Farm Boy began, panting with exertion, "we're not supposed to be racing. . . ."

"Who's racing?" Gaia said. She didn't look over at him; she just gazed ahead at the rapidly approaching firing range. ". . . Just . . . faster than you, that's all. . . ."

"Slow down," he panted.

"You first."

But Gaia *was* slowing down and not only that; she realized she was shaking. *Boom, boom* went the gun. *Stop,* she wanted to shout. *Stop shooting.*

That was when Gaia lost her balance.

Her feet had caught on a flat rock in the dusty track, and before she toppled to the ground, Farm Boy had caught her, but then he lost his balance, too, and they both tumbled to the ground. Farm Boy was on top of her for just a moment, his weight pressing her down before he rolled easily to one side and sprang to his feet.

"You all right?" Farm Boy asked in his too-perfect southern accent.

"Fine," Gaia muttered, ignoring his outstretched hand and climbing to her feet. Her face was burning with embarrassment.

The other trainees were approaching behind them, and Gaia wasn't sure whether they were squinting at her or not. Had they seen her fall? Gaia didn't want to think about it.

Gaia

I don't mind making mistakes. I've made a lot of them, and I'm sure I'll make many more.

I don't even mind falling down like some kind of clumsy jerk just when I'm winning a footrace. It's not that. It's losing control. A few weeks ago I successfully argued the point against Agent Malloy. But he was right. He had a good point. I didn't want to admit to him what it was like seeing that picture of myself fighting in the park back in the old days. But he had my number completely.

Out of control. And what's worse, *emotionally* out of control. Enjoying the fight and letting that emotion rule my actions. Prowling Central Park for petty criminals just to make myself feel better. Pretending I don't know what drives a junkie or a desperately hungry homeless kid or a borderline mental patient to attack innocents in the park. Turning myself into judge and jury just to rid myself of that awful, powerless feeling.

I swore I'd never go back. I told myself I could live a disciplined life. If it meant being alone, so be it. There are worse things. When you're alone, you're safe. Without anyone close to you, you're that much more invulnerable.

I've learned that lesson the hard way.

And now here I am at the ultimate temple of discipline and control—the paradigm of playing by the rules, of leaving the law in the hands of those who should administer it. Of *enforcing* the law. And what happens?

First, I get drawn into a stupid competition with a kid from the Farm Belt just because he's spent too much time building up that upper body he's so proud of. Just because I want to smack him, I have this urge to knock out those perfect teeth of his, and it has nothing to do with him. I'm just angry because I couldn't deal with the sound of gunfire and he *saw* me lose control.

The rest of that hour is difficult to remember. I was determined to get my feet back on solid ground. I stood there breathing regularly and waiting in line with the other trainees and when my turn came, I stepped up to the range and took the gun.

It felt awful.

I hated that dull metal weight in my hand. I hated the slick, oily sound of the safety catch being released, of the clip locking home, of the slide notching backward.

But the funny thing was, something else seemed to awaken inside me. Old physical memories of target practice with my father back in the Berkshires. And suddenly I remembered what it felt like to shoot.

Before I knew it, I was in the right stance, with my arm flexed, and without flinching I began squeezing off shots. And when the gun smoke cleared, I realized that I was hearing the sound of the other trainees applauding, and when I peered at the target, I realized that I'd emptied the entire clip into the bull's-eye.

Was it just to put Farm Boy (whatever his name is) into second place? Maybe. (And he didn't like that one bit—I could tell from the sour look on his face, even though he tried to cover it over with that grin of his.) The acrid smell of gun smoke made my eyes water, and for a moment I was back in that kitchen. That kitchen, where my mother died.

The other trainees were staring at me as we all lined up for Agent Donat's speech. She talked about weaponry and about what we'd learn in the weeks to come—ballistics, hidden holsters, all the tricks of the trade—but I have to admit, I was barely listening. I was confused.

Tomorrow you'll begin practical applications, Donat told us, her red hair shining in the sun. *Sleep well tonight—you're going to need it. And congratulations on your first day at Quantico.*

And when she dismissed us and all the trainees walked back toward the dorms together, I actually had a moment when I felt like part of something. Not an outsider, but an *insider*—a team member.

I hate guns—but I shoot really well. Is that why I'm here? Am I facing every contradiction in my life, really facing them all for the first time? Not whining and running like a teenager, but actually *dealing?*

Maybe I am.

Gaia hadn't known what to expect from FBI dorms. She had images in her head of military barracks—gleaming white cinder block walls, army trunks, tightly made bunks you could bounce a quarter on. So she had been mildly surprised the night before to find more or less conventional dorm rooms. They weren't that different from the single rooms she'd occupied all three years at Stanford.

Except that this wasn't a single room. It wasn't just the two beds that filled Gaia with trepidation as she dropped her luggage and accepted the keys from the assistant. It was the evidence of life—the traces left by her roommate. The other occupant (*Sanders, Catherine* according to Gaia's computer printout) had already arrived. The other bed was made (bright orange bedsheets and a quilt) and there was a poster up (a Claude Monet poster, reminding Gaia of the Metropolitan in New York with a sudden pang) and one of the desks now bore an iMac and a stack of books with titles like *Learning JavaScript* and *Intermediate UNIX*.

After her flight and all the paperwork and fingerprinting associated with her arrival at Quantico, Gaia had been too tired to deal with the mysterious Catherine Sanders, art lover, computer hacker, fancier of the color orange . . . whoever she was. Gaia wasn't sure she'd *ever* be ready. Why couldn't she have a single room? Her experiences in shared rooms—the "residency halls" and other temporary housing in New York, filled with students whose parents were "absent" for whatever reasons—had never been good.

All she wanted was to sleep and get ready for her first training day.

But Catherine Sanders never showed up that night.

Now, approaching her dorm room door, with the smell of gunpowder on her hands and every muscle aching from the morning's exertions, Gaia glanced down at the brushed steel doorknob, reaching for her keys—and saw that the door was open.

"Hello?" Gaia pushed the door inward, entering the room. The lights were out and the shades were drawn—it was difficult to see.

When her eyes adjusted, Gaia saw a figure stretched out on the other bed. At the sound of Gaia's entry the girl stirred, raising herself on her elbows to look at Gaia. She had dark hair in a pixieish Peter Pan haircut. Gaia recognized her.

"Hey," Catherine said. She sounded surprised. "I didn't know *you* were my roomie."

As she moved closer, Gaia saw that the girl hadn't changed her clothes—there were traces of dried mud on her FBI T-shirt. Catherine reached to shake hands. "Catherine Sanders—how are you? Don't call me Cathy."

Fair enough, Gaia thought.

"Gaia Moore."

"Gaia Moore from New York City, right? I never would have guessed. I had you pegged as a West Coast girl all the way."

"Um—" Gaia wasn't sure what to make of that. *I'm doing real well in the conversation department so far,* she thought. "Stanford. I went to school in California. But I'm from Manhattan originally."

"No kidding." Catherine winced in exaggerated pain as she moved to sit all the way up and turn on a lamp. The light illuminated her pretty face, her dark brown eyes, and her black hair. "I visited New York once. I can't imagine *living* there."

"Most of the time, neither can I," Gaia said. And to her surprise, Catherine laughed. An actual, bona fide laugh—not a sarcastic fake laugh.

"I'm from Philadelphia," Catherine went on, stifling a yawn. "Mmm. Sorry. I got in late, so I ended up crashing in my dad's hotel room. He took me out for a late dinner . . . and sure enough, I was tired this morning and fell off the ropes. Not like you." Gaia realized that Catherine was looking at her admiringly. "That was pretty awesome."

"Thanks," Gaia said awkwardly. "Did your dad take off?" she asked politely.

"I think so; by now, yeah. Hey, are you hungry?" Catherine asked. "It's lunchtime."

"Sure—I could eat," Gaia said. She had sat down on her own bed and caught another whiff of the gunpowder residue on her hands. "I think I want to take a shower first."

"Yeah, good call," Catherine agreed. "I thought I'd wait since there was such a line. Let me know if it's thinned out, okay?"

"Sure," Gaia said.

See? It's easy, she told herself. *Talk. Listen. Don't be fake. Don't hide behind word games; don't cop an attitude. You don't have to.*

As Gaia moved out of the room with her towel and her toiletries bag, she realized she was smiling. She had nothing to worry about—Catherine had picked up one of her geek books and was scanning along inscrutable lines of machine code. And then, just as she hurried away from her dorm door, she ran smack into Farm Boy—soaking wet, wearing nothing but a towel.

"Well, hi there," Farm Boy said, grinning his patented grin. It came out as, "Hah there," to Gaia's city girl ears. "I'd call you clumsy, but I know better."

"Um—sorry." It seemed to be Gaia's day for awkward opening lines. She couldn't think of anything to say—and the fact that Farm Boy's trim, muscular body was right in front of her, barely concealed by a towel, certainly had nothing to do with it.

"Will Taylor," Farm Boy said, holding out his right hand (while catching his towel with the other hand before it could slip off). Gaia was momentarily at a complete loss as to where to place her eyes. "From South Carolina. Pleased to meet you."

"Gaia Moore," Gaia managed, shaking his hand. "Um . . . what are you doing here? This is a female floor."

Will nodded soberly. "It is . . . it surely is." He pointed. "But for some reason known exclusively to the FBI, it's the only floor with a pop machine."

Gaia squinted at him like he was speaking a foreign language. "A pop . . . oh, a *soda* machine," she said. "Well—use it and go back to wherever you came from."

"Yes, ma'am," Will said agreeably. "But before I do, I have to tell you how much I admire your athletic prowess, Ms. Moore."

Was he kidding? She couldn't tell. Gaia was staring back at his blue eyes, mainly because she was absolutely determined that he not see her skating her eyes down his body, even inadvertently. "Well, you came up a close second," she said.

"I can't understand it," Will agreed, shaking his head sadly. "That's one occurrence I'd relish, Ms. Moore, if I were you . . . since I can fairly well guarantee it will never happen again. I'm a track champion, which I only mention in the interest of warning you about things to come if we should ever meet again on the field of battle."

"Right," Gaia scoffed, trying to move past him and toward the floor's common bathroom. "The 'field of battle.' You're making me think this is *Gone With the Wind* or something. And call me Gaia."

"Gaia—Goddess of the earth, right?" Will said thoughtfully, stepping back in front of her.

"That's—" The remark was so unexpected that Gaia was genuinely flustered. "How did you—"

"I've been to college," Farm Boy told her. "We've got book learning south of the Mason-Dixon line, Ms. Moore."

"Very funny," Gaia muttered. *Another brilliant witticism,* she told herself. There seemed to be no end to her verbal cleverness today. "Will you please just let me by?"

"Who's stopping you?" Will backed to the wall, making an exaggerated show of waving her by.

"Thanks," Gaia muttered, edging past Will and moving as quickly as she could toward the bathroom door.

Insufferable, she told herself as the door swung shut behind her and the familiar smells of soap and shampoo and perfume and damp tiles assaulted her nostrils.

And he LOST, she reminded herself. *Imagine what he'd be like if he'd beaten me. Why am I even thinking about this?*

68

The bathroom was clean; the white tiles were spotless, like everything else here. For a moment it almost felt like the last of Gaia's natural confusion and anger were washing off along with that morning's dirt and grime. She had won the competition. And nobody was giving her a hard time about it. Everyone was nice. It was like she was jumping at shadows that weren't there, expecting, inevitably, that when people saw the things that she could do, trouble of one kind or another would result.

But so far, it hadn't.

Strange.

Catherine

When kids say, "That's weird," or, "You're weird," it's an insult. I never got that, my whole life. Weird is good. I'm "weird"— and I love it.

As far as I'm concerned, the FBI is no big deal—it's just the coolest, most elite collection of weirdos in the world. These people are crazy; they know how to do everything, and they love being good at everything. I can totally relate to that. I can already tell that Gaia is that way too—but for some reason, she seems uncomfortable about it. Like she minds being "weird."

But there's no downside to being "weird." Okay, I admit it would have been nice to have one or two more friends when I was a kid. Like, having *any* would have been a plus. But I didn't even have a fighting chance.

Back then, in Philadelphia, I wore thick glasses (still do) and read a lot of books (still do) and messed around with computers all day and all night (yep . . . still do). As a girl, I didn't care if people looked at me and thought, *Weird.*

In high school the "plot thickened," as they say. I discovered boys—but not the way most girls do. I discovered them because they were the ones hanging around all the computers. My big passion, from then to this day, was code.

Machine code, mostly—computer languages, scripting languages, all the arcane and beautiful operations that happened on tiny silicon chips in machines and devices all around me every day. Everyone's cell phone, wristwatch, personal computer; their cars, their portable music players—to my eyes it was a supercool sea of microchips, each brimming with little bits of secret code, all interacting and communicating and humming at the speed of light, all at once. I felt like one of those "naturalist" dudes with a butterfly net and a microscope—except that the bugs I liked were made of numbers. So if you could figure out how numbers worked, you could figure out how *everything* works. *That's* power, as I see it.

So that was how I met boys—geeks, mostly; weirdos like me, but it got me used to the concept of having males around. Most of the time, in geek clubs or whatever, I'd be the only girl, and later, in high school, once I had a figure and all, it meant they would treat me like Zena, Warrior Princess, or someone had come into the room. But that was fine.

When I met Brian, it was like he never realized a girl could "outgeek" him. After we met on campus and even on our first date (using up his precious Dave Matthews tickets), I would catch him giving me this look, like, *How can you be a girl I like and at the same time know more than me about programming?* I could tell it made him even more into me. That wasn't too bad at all.

Maybe Gaia's life has been different. Maybe she hasn't been lucky that way. Maybe she's still worried about the big distinction between "weird" people and "everyone else."

If that's true, hopefully she'll get over it soon. And this sure is the right place for it.

I'm curious to see what happens to her here. Just like I'm curious to see what happens to *me.*

NO FOOD SOURCE

The FBI—specifically, a woman named Bishop—had recruited Catherine one bright afternoon in Boston, where she'd traveled with a college programming club (all boys except her) to the CompLife Expo. They'd spent three days in the enormous convention center gawking at the supercomputers and attending the conferences while getting ready to show off their big project in the final day's competition. It had taken days for her club to figure out how to make a splash in Boston.

"We can make a 'fuzz tracker,'" Catherine had told her club one night as they devoured a mushroom pizza and three plastic bottles of Jolt cola in her boyfriend Brian's dorm room.

"A fuzz buster?" Cliff, who had really bad acne but was otherwise the most charming boy Catherine knew, hadn't heard right. "So what? You mean, pick up cop radar on the highw—"

"A fuzz *tracker.*" Catherine's mouth was full of pizza and she swallowed impatiently. "Picks up police computer activity."

"How?" Sam said. He was over by the stereo, putting another Beck album on. "How would you get access to it, for starters?"

Catherine had shrugged. "That's easy. It's already around

us, on the Internet, on radio and CB channels, on phone lines. You just have to organize it."

"Are you crazy? Nobody could do that," Brian protested loudly. "You'd need a supercomputer."

"*We* can do it. With an ordinary office PC," Catherine said between chugs of Jolt. "If you listen for two minutes, I'll tell you how."

In the end, Catherine had done most of the work. It was like solving a puzzle—the legality of what they were doing never even entered their minds. That Friday in Boston, while she and her bearded colleagues showed off their handiwork—effortlessly displaying police records, arrest reports, even paychecks and billing stubs on the little monitor they'd lugged from college, Catherine had no idea that Jennifer Bishop was intently watching her from the side of the convention hall.

Catherine smiled, remembering that day. She had been so flattered by the attractive young FBI recruiter's attentions (although she'd found Bishop's boss, the grim-faced Agent Malloy, more than a little intimidating). She had even gotten a short haircut without necessarily admitting to herself that she was copying Bishop's style—or that Bishop had become something of a role model. Today, relaxing on her favorite orange bedsheets in her sunny new dorm room on her first day of FBI training, Catherine allowed herself a moment of unabashed pride. *I made it,* she told herself. *I'm here.*

Gaia had been in the shower a few minutes when there was a knock at the door.

"Come in," Catherine called out, closing the *PC World* magazine she'd been leafing through.

The door swung open. A young Asian man was standing there, smiling pleasantly, his hand on the doorknob. He had shiny black hair and pale skin, and he was impeccably dressed in an untucked blue dress shirt, khaki pants, and well-shined black shoes.

"Hey," the young man said. "I'm sorry—am I bothering you?"

"No." Catherine tossed the magazine aside.

"The dining hall's closed," the young man told her, hooking a thumb to point behind himself. "I just walked all the way over there and the door's all boarded up. There's, like, no food source at all."

"There's a candy machine," Catherine said. She could hear through the wall that the shower had stopped—Gaia would be returning in just a moment. "If you're dying."

"No, I just wanted to see who was around and, like, spare you guys the walk," the young man went on. Catherine had decided he was Chinese American; she had figured him for Korean at first, but the modeling of his face looked more Chinese. "I don't know about you, but my entire body's dying after that routine this morning. There's no reason we should *all* trudge over the fields to that locked mess hall. I'm sorry—Kim Lau." Kim stepped into the room and extended his hand.

"Catherine Sanders." They shook hands. "Welcome to the girls' floor."

"Hi," Gaia said, coming into the room behind Kim. She was wrapped in a towel, and her long wet hair was swept back from her face. Kim seemed utterly unaffected by the view. "What's going on?"

"Hey, I know you—you're Supergirl," Kim said, smiling amiably at Gaia. Even with the loose-fitting, perfectly tailored dress clothes, Catherine could tell that Kim was in very good shape—the muscles on his forearms and the wide cast of his shoulders gave it away. "Gaia Moore, right? This morning's decathlon winner."

"Kim was just saying that the dining hall's closed," Catherine explained. "Which sucks because I'm *really* hungry. Aren't you?"

"'Decathlon' would be ten," Gaia said, pulling open a drawer. "It was only two events."

"Well, it felt like ten. Listen, should we go to one of those restaurants in town?" Kim asked. "Didn't they give us a list or something in the orientation package?"

Catherine's stomach was growling—she realized that she was hungry enough to endure whatever passed for cuisine in tiny, rural Quantico. "Sure," she said. "How about it, Gaia? Even a *biathlon* can make you hungry."

Gaia shot Catherine a look. "Whatever you say," she said. "Let me get dressed and I'll meet you downstairs."

PREPARED FOR COMBAT

Gaia was thinking about luck.

Not "fate" or anything so grandiose. Just "luck," as in the bad or good variety. At the moment she was crammed into the backseat of her new roommate Catherine Sanders's Nissan Altima, which wasn't a particularly large or roomy car.

Catherine was driving, and Kim Lau, the friendly trainee from the men's floor, was in the shotgun seat. Outside, through the window that Gaia was pressed up against, the Virginia landscape was rolling past: fields and small rural outbuildings and farmland, gas stations and billboards, all catching the slanted sunlight of afternoon. Someone named Brad Thompson, another trainee, was sitting next to the other window, and between Gaia and Brad, with his blond hair brushing against the Altima's roof, was Mr. Southern Gentleman Farm Boy, Will Taylor.

Gaia had tried as hard as she could to avoid this seating arrangement, but there had been no way—Kim had just climbed into the front seat, and then Will had gotten in, and before she knew it, she was pressed up against him, pulling the door shut, and counting the minutes for this little excursion to be over.

"Well, this is very nice countryside," Will said agreeably.

"Uh-huh," Gaia said, her eyes fixed out the window. She could see that Catherine was following signs for Quantico. They were moving through a more economically depressed area. She had seen at least one trailer park, and they'd just passed a row of small houses, some with peeling shingles, some with laundry lines stretched across their backyards, some with barbecue grills on their porches, some with rusting cars that had "For Sale" signs, their chrome gleaming in the evening light.

How did I get here? Gaia thought idly. It wasn't an unpleasant question, necessarily. It just kept hitting her what a new, unfamiliar place she was in. So far from Manhattan, from California—from everywhere she'd called home before.

"I imagine this is a big change," Will said.

"What?" Gaia turned to look at him. The illusion that he'd been reading her mind was startling—but then, she firmly told herself, it was luck. Just blind luck: the same kind of luck that had arranged for the five of them to arrive outside at the same time and end up all piled in the same car, with Farm Boy pressed up next to her.

"Well, you're a city girl, aren't you?" Will went on pleasantly. She could smell his aftershave—too much of it, as she would have guessed. "And a Yankee, obviously. In fact, I'd guess you're from New York City."

"Brilliant," Gaia muttered, turning her attention back outside the car window. "You're going to make a great investigator."

"All right, you two," Catherine said, peering at the road signs as they slowed at an intersection. "Kim, what's the name of this place?"

"Montano's steak house," Kim read from the page in his hand. "When we get to town, look for something called MacDougal Street."

"It's one of four restaurants," said Bradley, the trainee none of them knew. "Which sounds like we're dealing with one swinging town."

Catherine laughed, but Gaia, watching the landscape roll by, brushing her drying hair back from her face, was thinking that it was fine. She could use a break from subway systems and freeways, Starbucks and crowded sidewalks, office-building lobbies, the constant sound of passing planes.

As she watched, the car passed something beautiful— Gaia was pretty sure she was the only one who had caught it. In the middle of a large, mowed field, on the outskirts of town, was a World War II memorial. She was sure that was what it was—even though they were moving pretty fast. But she could make out a bronze statue of an infantry soldier, crouched in his bronze uniform, rifle extended, prepared for combat. His helmet was silhouetted against the sky as they drove past. The beautiful part—the element that caught Gaia's attention—was the flowers. Somebody had put a bouquet of white roses into the barrel of the soldier's gun.

It was interesting. Seeing the gun dressed up with the white roses struck Gaia differently than seeing a bare gun. No nausea. No loss of control. There was something touching about it.

"Montano's steak house," Catherine yelled out, pointing at a garish yellow-and-red illuminated sign. "Oh, it's not looking good at all—"

"Yikes," Kim agreed. Gaia peered past his shoulder at the shingled building with its dirt parking lot and neon Steaks and Chops sign and decided it didn't matter.

As Catherine parked and Gaia opened her car door (as quickly as she could to get away from Will's leg pressing against her), she was startled by the buzz of insects and the incredibly fragrant country air. It was so tranquil, so disarmingly relaxing, that she found herself nearly intoxicated by the simple, plain aroma.

"Air smells nice, don't it?" Will said amiably, climbing out of the car behind her.

Stop reading my mind—I don't like it one bit.

"I'll have the sirloin," Gaia told the waitress. She was a short, middle-aged woman with thick glasses and a plaid vest. Her plastic name tag had a Montano's logo, and it identified her as "Margie." She had introduced herself, too, so there was really no way anyone could avoid catching her name. Then she had brought them all water in yellow-tinted glasses and a plastic basket of bread sticks and cellophane-wrapped crackers.

"Yes, ma'am; sirloin steak," Margie agreed, scribbling on her notepad. Gaia could see that her hair was dyed. "How would you like that done?"

"Rare," Gaia said.

"Baked potato? Fries? Garden salad? House chowder?"

"Salad and potato," Gaia said. She made herself smile at Margie. You never did that in New York—she'd developed the habit in Palo Alto.

The steak house was actually fairly large once you got inside. Gaia, Kim, Catherine, Will, and the other trainee—*Bradley,* Gaia remembered—were at a table near the front, with a red-and-white-checkered cheesecloth cover and heavily laminated wooden chairs. About half the tables were full, with families, single diners who were obviously townies, and a couple of other trainees. Quiet, bland Muzak played in the background. Margie seemed to be the only staff, except for two teenage busboys in red vests with barely visible mustaches Gaia had seen when she and her group came in. It was going to take a long time to get their food—it was obvious.

Catherine, apparently realizing this, was munching on bread sticks. "You've got a big appetite," she told Gaia.

"I do indeed," Gaia said. "Where are you from, Kim?"

"Boulder, Colorado," Kim said. "My mom teaches at the university. We moved there when I was a kid—I was born in Chicago."

"And what's your story?" Catherine went on, brushing crumbs from her lips. "What are you interested in?"

"Playing jazz piano," Kim told them. "But sociology, mostly. More recently, criminal psychology. All the 'ologies' having to do with the mind. I kind of have a knack for it."

"That's what you focused on in college?" Will asked politely.

"Besides boys, yeah."

Will, predictably, needed a clarification. "You're homosexual?"

"Yeah, but you can just say 'gay,'" Kim told him, smiling. "Unless you like sounding like a hick."

"Touché," Will said, smiling back. Gaia was forced to admit to herself that there wasn't an ounce of bigotry in Will's question. He was just blunt. "Wait, you're the one I heard about, right?" He was pointing at Kim. "Some of the guys were talking on my floor. You're the prodigy—the one who got those advanced shrink degrees before you turned twenty?"

Kim looked embarrassed. "Well—yeah," he said shyly.

"You play piano?" Catherine asked Kim. She was still munching bread sticks.

"Yeah," Kim said. "For years, actually. My parents forced

me to take classical lessons—the cliché of the Asian musical genius. No, thank you. I rebelled by switching to jazz."

Something was bothering Gaia—some kind of nameless feeling about the room they were in. She couldn't place it, exactly, but something seemed wrong. Glancing past her companions, Gaia looked at the faces of the other diners, trying to see if their expressions were somehow part of what was bothering her. But they all looked normal. She could see one little girl in a pretty yellow dress, eating her mint ice cream dessert with perfect table manners. Her legs didn't reach the floor. She was a picture of perfection—yet to Gaia's eyes, there was something wrong with her.

"My boyfriend plays clarinet," Catherine was telling Kim, speaking with her mouth full. "Like, jazz clarinet. I go hear him at this place whenever he does it."

"Jazz clarinet—cool," Kim said, impressed.

"We're all freaks," Catherine said easily. "Why play boring music?"

"Asian musical genius." Will was marveling at Kim—smiling too much, Gaia thought; probably to show off those teeth he was so proud of. "Why does nobody talk about the cliché of the white southern genius?"

"Because there ain't no such thing?" Gaia said sweetly. "That could be it."

"You're not very modest." Catherine was laughing at Will, who widened his eyes, all wounded.

"What do you mean?" Will pointed at Kim. "Dr. Lau here calls himself a 'genius' and nobody bats an eye. That's not fair—you're all pickin' on me."

We're all freaks, Gaia repeated to herself. She was watching Kim's hands on the table, his fingers drumming on the paper place mat that showed the recipes for cocktails.

Gaia remembered that very clearly in the minutes and hours to come because it was at that moment, that exact second she was contemplating her unusual dining companions and watching Kim's fingers drum on the table, that she heard *that sound,* crashing through the air like thunder, almost seeming to make the air split apart with its deafening boom and crash.

I'm dreaming, she thought crazily. *I'm having a flashback or something.*

But in that frozen instant it was clear to Gaia that everyone in the room had jumped. Her ears were ringing—there was nothing imaginary about it.

A gunshot.

"Nobody move!" a hoarse male voice screamed. "Nobody move or this bitch is dead!"

A woman screamed. Looking over, Gaia saw that it was Margie, the waitress. She had screamed in the act of falling to the floor.

At a table near the kitchen—a larger, round table, flanked by six wooden chairs—a young man in a black business suit and a ski mask was holding a revolver in the air and clutching a young girl to his waist. As if in a dream, Gaia realized that it was the perfect little girl she'd seen earlier—the one in the yellow dress. She had dropped her ice cream spoon to clatter on the floor, scattering green drops of mint ice cream everywhere.

The girl was screaming in terror. The man had her clamped

against himself. The gun was bellowing smoke—it had been just a few seconds since he'd fired it upward. Gaia could see the hole in the plastic foam ceiling that the bullet had made. The rest of the table's diners were screaming, too, and cowering away from the man with the gun.

Where did he come from? Gaia thought. She noticed that her fellow trainees hadn't screamed or panicked—like her, they were all looking coolly over, assessing the situation. All except for Will.

At first Gaia thought Will had vanished. Then she saw him—on the floor. Will had dropped to the floor and was crawling toward the exit and out of the room.

What the hell?

After all his posturing and bragging, Mr. Farm Boy had no backbone at all. Gaia couldn't say she was surprised. Even the "bravest" person could fold in the face of real danger.

But not me, Gaia thought. She was already calculating the distances as the man with the ski mask lowered his arm and pressed the gun against the screaming girl's ear.

"Nobody move or this bitch is dead!" the gunman repeated. "Now, nice and slow—everyone put their watches, wallets, and jewelry on the tables in front of them."

Gaia fixed her eyes on the man's head, testing the strength of her chair with her right hand. But she had missed her chance to throw the chair. With his arm in the air, the gunman had been a perfect target, but now it was impossible. There was too much of a risk that he would accidentally pull the trigger. She had to get the gun off the girl—and there was only one way to do it.

"I'm not going to tell you again," the gunman screamed more urgently. The girl in the yellow dress wailed.

Gaia didn't give herself time to think. Absolutely no time had passed; everyone else was still frozen in their chairs, startled, looking like statues with their mouths open. Gaia catapulted herself forward, charging straight at the gun, just missing Kim's shoulder as she landed in a fighting stance on the carpet between the restaurant's tables. Predictably, the gunman took the gun off the girl and pointed it at Gaia, giving her the expected second and a half to drop and roll and dodge the bullet he fired into the floor where she'd been crouched and then giving her another half second (while the recoil knocked his shooting hand backward) to leap back up and aim a kick at his head.

"Gaia!"

Catherine's voice, behind her.

Without thinking, Gaia ducked her head to one side.

Blam! This gunshot was so loud, Gaia thought for a moment that she might have permanent hearing damage. The bullet had come from right behind her—it must have whipped right past her ear from behind, although she hadn't felt the wind (as had happened to her one or two times in the past). She could see a fresh bullet hole in the wood paneling in front of her.

Second gunman, she thought furiously. *There's a second gunman, and I missed him. Stupid, stupid—*

Gaia ducked her upper body forward and jabbed her right leg straight back without looking and felt the heavy *smack* as her shoe connected with flesh.

It was all happening fast—and Gaia was glad that her muscles, still aching from the morning's exertions, weren't failing her—but that *sound* continued to freak her out, that horrible grave-yard sound of the firing gun that went right through her every time she heard it, sending her back to that place and time in New York she never wanted to think about again.

She was on top of the asshole in seconds, pinning him to the carpeted floor. Behind her the other gunman—the one she had never even seen—was slowly rising off the floor. Gaia had to stretch and kick him again, trying for his gun hand and managing to catch his wrist so that the gun thumped to the floor.

Why is no one helping? Gaia thought in frustration. *Two gunmen . . .*

But she knew the answer to that. It had been years since she'd done this, but she was used to that frustration. *They're scared,* she reminded herself. *They can't move yet because they're scared. Give Catherine credit for warning me about the would-be head shot.*

The crowd was still yelling. Right then the first gunman managed somehow to pull his right wrist out of Gaia's grip, where she had his arm pinned to the floor—and Gaia heard the unmistakable clicking sound of an automatic's hammer being pulled back. She felt a cold steel pressure on her left cheek—and knew it was the barrel of his gun.

"Good-bye, bitch," the gunman said.

Great, Gaia thought distantly. *I've finally found something I want to do, and now I'm going to die.*

It was ironic.

Gaia ducked her head in defeat—and then suddenly

slammed it forward and upward, deflecting the automatic just as it went off. Another bullet sailed past her head—again with no wind—and then Gaia had regained her leverage and knocked the gun away. Karate chopping the man's shoulder, Gaia pulled herself upward onto her knees and then grabbed him by the shirtfront. "You son of a *bitch*," she shouted, staring at the black-masked face. "Putting a gun to that *little girl's* head . . ." Gaia had to keep herself from beating the man senseless. But just then a bell rang.

The bell was very loud—it penetrated all the other sounds in the restaurant. Suddenly all the patrons stopped screaming. It was like a switch being flipped—one moment the room was full of panicking diners; the next it was as calm and quiet as a corporate ballroom. With a loud series of clicks a row of harsh, bright ceiling lights came on. The Muzak stopped playing.

What the hell?

"All right, show's over," a familiar female voice yelled out from the kitchen door. Gaia knew the voice instantly: Special Agent Jennifer Bishop.

"You can get off me, miss," the man under Gaia said calmly. "The exercise is concluded."

Exercise—?

Looking up, Gaia saw that Bishop and Agent Malloy were striding into the room from the restaurant's kitchen. Bewildered, she rose to her feet—the second "gunman" actually helped her stand up.

"Nice kick," the man behind her said, pulling off his ski mask. He was nursing his wrist. "I'll be feeling *this* for a couple of days."

All the restaurant patrons suddenly became extremely calm and collected, regaining their feet and brushing themselves off. All of them were looking at Gaia.

And Gaia had a familiar feeling—again something she hadn't felt in years, but it was so vivid that it was like it had never gone away in all the time she'd spent studiously avoiding combat.

They know, she thought helplessly. *They saw me do that, and now they know—they know I don't get scared.*

But Gaia corrected herself, looking at their faces. All she saw was dispassionate admiration, not shock. They didn't have that look of seeing something bizarre or even impossible.

They're FBI personnel, Gaia reminded herself. *Nothing fazes them. I'm just a woman who's trained to fight, that's all. They see it every day. It doesn't make me fearless.*

My secret's safe.

"Well done, Atkinson," Agent Malloy was saying to the first gunman. He wore the same perfectly pressed charcoal gray suit as always, Gaia noticed. "And you too, Miss Trent."

"Thank you, sir," the little girl in the yellow dress said. It was hard to believe she'd been screaming a few seconds before. She looked as poised and precocious as a child actress—which, Gaia realized, was probably what she was.

That was what I noticed, Gaia realized. *When I thought she looked strange before.*

"Hey—you all right?" Catherine said. She had come over and was squeezing Gaia's shoulder sympathetically.

"What? Yeah," Gaia said, pointing at the wall. "Thanks for saving my fake life."

They both looked over, seeing the smoking hole from the gunshot that had "missed" Gaia's head. Had the actor fired blanks? *Probably,* Gaia thought, noticing an artificiality to the "bullet hole." She was amazed at how thorough the simulation had been.

"You're pretty levelheaded," Catherine commented. "You didn't *know* it was fake, did you? When the bullet just missed you."

"What? *No,*" Gaia insisted. "Are you kidding? I nearly had a heart attack when the gun went off."

I'm doing it, she thought. *Faking fear.*

"Trainees, may I have your attention, please?" Agent Bishop said. It wasn't necessary—Kim, Catherine, Gaia, and the others were staring keenly at her. It was obvious that none of them knew what to make of what had just happened.

"Congratulations on the successful completion of your first exercise," Bishop went on. "Now you know why the dining hall was closed and locked today. A scene nearly identical to this has taken place in each restaurant in town in the last twenty minutes. The purpose of the exercise was twofold: to test your acumen in a time-sensitive crime-fighting situation . . . and to introduce you to a basic fact of your lives as FBI trainees. *You must keep your wits about you at all times—* because you will never be able to predict when we will be observing and testing you. On the Quantico base or here in town—it makes no difference at all. No situation is off-limits. We need to know how each of you will react to hostile, dangerous situations. Can you think on your feet or not?"

All the "restaurant patrons" were patiently listening. *They're all actors,* Gaia realized. *This whole scene is a fraud—every-thing that's happened since we walked in here was part of a test.*

"At any moment," Bishop said, striding back and forth, directing her attention to the trainees in the room, "anywhere on our campus or here in town, day or night, no matter what else is happening, you can be plunged into a training exercise. Don't try to figure out the rules of these games because *the rules are constantly changing.* The only way to succeed is to maintain at all times the disciplined behavior of an FBI agent."

"You all did well," Agent Malloy said in his rough voice. "By which I mean nobody panicked or lost their cool. But there's one trainee who did a superlative job. It isn't often that someone 'wins' the first exercise. But in this case we have a clear winner."

Kim and Catherine were gazing at Gaia, and Gaia was getting ready to speak—she was trying to figure out the most appropriate way of responding as Malloy singled her out. Should she say, "It was nothing, really," or just, "Thank you, sir," or, "I was just reacting naturally—"

"Will Taylor," Agent Bishop announced, "deserves your admiration and respect for a truly remarkable bit of deductive thinking."

What?

Gaia was completely confused. She followed Agent Bishop's smiling gaze . . . and saw Will walking into the room, pushing the two mustachioed busboys ahead of him. The busboys were smiling. They each had their hands tied behind their backs. Looking down, Gaia saw that Will had bound their wrists with torn tablecloths.

"Him?" Catherine blurted. "I'm sorry, but we're confused,

ma'am."

"Do you want to explain, Taylor?" Malloy said.

"Yes, sir." Will seemed to be trying not to look *too* smug—but his answer made clear that there was nothing he wanted more than to explain his own brilliance. Despite her annoyance Gaia wanted to hear, too. She was still baffled.

"There are five empty tables," Will said quietly. He didn't have to speak loudly—he had the whole room's attention. Everyone looked around. Will was right: five abandoned restaurant tables, covered in dirty dishes and discarded napkins. "The whole time nobody cleared those tables—see the leftover plates, half-full glasses, spilled food? But in the twenty minutes we were here, nobody touched those tables at all."

That's true, Gaia realized ruefully. *And I completely missed it.*

"But there were two busboys," Will went on. He was removing the "busboys'" makeshift handcuffs as he spoke. "And I couldn't figure out where they had gone. Why weren't they doing their jobs? What were they doing instead? So when the masked man here pulled out his gun, I realized it had to be a diversion. Why rob the restaurant patrons when the real money is in the safe? It only made sense that the real action was happening somewhere else. And sure enough"—Will clapped the two "busboys" on their shoulders—"I found these two in the office, cracking the restaurant's safe. Full of cash, by the way. So that was the score."

And one gullible FBI trainee, Gaia thought helplessly. *Stupid, stupid . . .*

"Tomorrow morning," Agent Bishop concluded, glancing around at each of the trainees in the room, "your practical training program will begin. The smart trainees among you will realize right now that you can learn a great deal from what happened here today. You're training for the Federal Bureau of Investigation, and in my opinion there's no higher calling, nor is there one more difficult." She pointed. "Remember what Mr. Taylor taught you in this restaurant."

The room was applauding; Gaia realized they were actually applauding Farm Boy and his brilliant maneuver. It was just too much. Everyone was clapping except Malloy—who was looking at her.

Unfortunately, it was very easy to read the man's expression. His rough, leathery face was drawn; his eyes glittered in the restaurant's harsh overhead lights.

This is what I was afraid of, Malloy seemed to be saying. *This is why I didn't want you—why I argued with Bishop. Because you haven't got it. You aren't FBI material, are you? You're a fighter—that's all you are. Just a girl with a good kick who'd put innocent bystanders at risk with her impetuous behavior.*

Gaia stared back at Malloy. She didn't know what to think. But she felt ashamed. *It was the sound of the gun,* she wanted to tell him. *You have to understand—it was the gunfire. It was the danger to the girl.* But he *did* understand, Gaia realized in despair. He knew all about Jake. He'd shown her the pictures. That was the whole point. He understood her completely.

Gaia broke her gaze away from his, turning her eyes down to the drab carpeted floor.

FEDERAL BUREAU OF INVESTIGATION
FIELD BEHAVIOR DIRECTIVES

Attention, trainees: The directives outlined below constitute **mandatory** rules of behavior for FBI agents in the field. When interacting with civilians or local and state police, interrogating witnesses, collecting evidence, detaining or arresting suspects, or engaging in self-defense, pursuit, or combat operations, agents must adhere to the letter and spirit of these directives. Doing so ensures that the Federal Bureau of Investigation can maintain its unparalleled standard of professionalism, fairness, and effectiveness. Failure to abide by these directives can compromise investigations, endanger agents and civilians, and irreversibly impede and limit the bureau's effectiveness in investigating crimes, protecting the innocent, and bringing criminals to justice.

1. **IDENTIFICATION:** Agents must identify themselves by name and refer either to the "Federal Bureau of Investigation" or the initials "FBI" before interrogating, questioning, arresting, or detaining anyone.

2. **SEARCH AND SEIZURE:** Agents may not enter upon private property unless explicitly invited. In circumstances where this is not applicable (for example, locked doors or presumably empty rooms or buildings), agents may not force entry until they have repeatedly solicited invitation by any and all means possible, including knocking on doors, inspecting windows, and loudly announcing their presence. **Agents may not forcibly**

enter, search within, or seize items from within private property without first obtaining a court-issued warrant.

3. **USE OF FORCE:** Even in situations where civilian safety is at issue, agents may not instigate fighting or combat without warning and only if every other avenue of peacekeeping has been exhausted. Persons considered a danger to themselves and others may only be forcibly restrained after they have been issued more than one verbal warning, accompanied by the agent's clear identification of him or herself and the bureau.

4. **CRIME SCENE INVESTIGATION:** Agents arriving at or entering upon a potential crime scene must strictly obey the following rules: There must be **no trespassing** or **physical contact** with the scene in question until permission is granted by a licensed FBI criminologist, and any agent so arriving or entering upon such a location **must** call for assistance and criminology support **immediately** (or as soon as is reasonably possible after such particulars of the crime scene as a present or fleeing suspect have been sufficiently dealt with).

For more information, please consult your FBI training manual and other documentation available through the Quantico Base Command Offices.

extremes of physical and mental endurance

THE LIVING NIGHTMARE

Here we go, Kim Lau thought, gazing up at the flawless blue sky. He stood on the concrete court, his black hair blowing around his face in the morning breeze. His hands were clasped behind his back, just like the other twenty-one trainees who were standing around him. They all faced the southern edge of the FBI campus's outdoor courtyard, where Special Agent Jennifer Bishop stood on a raised platform, holding a microphone. A table in front of Bishop held a row of twenty-two holstered firearms and twenty-two FBI identification badges.

"Good morning, ladies and gentlemen," Bishop began. Her amplified voice projected loudly from a pair of enormous black speakers. "And welcome to the practical applications training course."

A murmur of excitement ran through the crowd. Kim felt it, too. He had heard about the legendary FBI-PA course—it was often referred to respectfully in classes he'd taken—and now he was about to learn firsthand what it was all about.

"Behind me," Bishop went on, her voice echoing over the courtyard, "is the battlefield where you will form teams and combat each other for the honor of victory." As she spoke, she gestured behind her back, where they all could see a one-lane asphalt service road and beyond that the buildings and trees and houses of a small village.

Hogan's Alley, Kim thought, staring across the road. *There it is.*

"We're standing at the perimeter of Quantico's state-of-the art 1.2-acre training arena, which we call 'Hogan's Alley,'" Bishop went on. "Hogan's Alley is an artificial town—a complete, controlled environment right here in the middle of our Quantico campus. As you're about to discover, the area behind me contains an exact simulation of a real town. It has stores, homes, parking lots, movie theaters, even a small park."

Kim already knew a good deal about this famous "artificial town"—he had read a book about the FBI before coming here as well as studying their Web site. He listened as Bishop got to the interesting part.

"The town behind me is filled with people. They're all 'simulations,' too—actors and FBI personnel trained to play roles. They're very good at their jobs, ladies and gentlemen—in less than fifteen minutes, when you enter Hogan's Alley, you'll be unable to tell that you aren't in a genuine, living and breathing American town. It looks pretty, doesn't it?"

Kim had to agree. Gazing across the road with the other trainees, he could see the crisp rooftops and gables of the town, standing proudly against the cloudless sky like a picture postcard.

"Don't be fooled," Bishop told them. The speakers magnified her voice. "Beneath that sunlit surface a nightmare is beginning. Something very dark and sinister has entered this place—a murderous presence that has already begun taking lives." She pointed behind herself, looking out at the trainees. "Somewhere, lurking out of sight in the buildings behind me, a serial killer is on the loose. As we speak, the killer's maniacal work has already begun, although the 'townspeople' don't know it yet. All the clues necessary to solve the crime are in the town behind me. And it will be your job to track the killer and apprehend him. That, ladies and gentlemen, is the object of the game."

Wow, Kim thought excitedly. He actually felt a chill go down his back even in the warm sunlight. *This is the cleverest thing I've ever heard of.*

As much as he was fascinated by what Special Agent Bishop was telling them, he couldn't miss the emotions of his fellow trainees. To Kim's trained eyes, their feelings were as obvious as the words on advertising billboards.

There was Gaia Moore, the pretty blond girl from New York by way of California—the one who so clearly had some kind of troubled past. Glancing sideways at Gaia, who stood next to him in a well-fitting T-shirt and dark workman's pants, Kim realized that Gaia herself probably didn't realize how troubled she was.

"Serial killers," Bishop said into her microphone. Kim turned his attention back to the podium. "As some of you may know, the pursuit of serial killers is a specific area of study I've pursued for years. I've designed this training course to make maximum use of all the forensic, psychological, and criminal information I've gathered in my study of the subject. So be prepared, ladies and gentlemen: the Hogan's Alley simulation you're about to begin is as close to the living nightmare of serial killer pursuit as you've ever been—as close as you can possibly get without engaging in the real thing. Prepare yourself for many sights and sounds that will shock you, frighten you, disgust you, unnerve you, and push you to your absolute extremes of physical and mental endurance. Prepare for a chess game where the chess pieces are human lives, and those lives will mean less to your prey than real chess pieces mean to you and me."

Someone gave a nervous laugh right then. Looking down the line of trainees, Kim saw that it had been Will Taylor. To Kim, Will was even easier to read. Will was very attractive, Kim had noticed absently, but he wasn't Kim's type. Kim didn't like all-American athletes. Glancing at Will's handsome face, Kim realized that he was much more nervous than he'd let on. Clearly this was a young man who was used to succeeding— and who had developed a personality built around that trait. But Kim wondered how Will would react if he ever *failed* at something. It was an interesting question. There was something in the cast of Will's eyes right then that told Kim that Will was frightened. And his fear was a secret. It was like he didn't want anyone—least of all Gaia, Kim had noticed the day before—to realize that there were cracks in his armor, situations he was afraid of, things he was afraid he couldn't do. But at the same time he looked excited. His eyes shone, and his nervous laugh as he heard the descriptions of serial killers' methods showed how interested he was.

"No doubt some of you are gamers," Bishop was saying. "The Hogan's Alley exercise works very much like a computer or video game—it has the equivalent of a pause button. The town has its own game time—clocks will start moving in just ten minutes, when the bell signals game start. After the first round today another bell will signal that the entire town has essentially 'paused'—and game time will freeze overnight, without the story moving forward at all. It's PlayStation but for real."

Directly next to Kim, on his other side, was Catherine Sanders. Kim had liked her immediately, from the moment he'd knocked on her dorm room door the day before. To Kim's trained eyes, Catherine was clearly possessed of a precise, mathematical mind. She seemed to perk up as Bishop mentioned games, which made sense: it was already clear that machines and computers were second nature to her. Kim had watched her drive her Altima the night before, and he could tell: she knew how to make inanimate objects do what she wanted. Kim figured she was probably good with firearms, too. But there was more to Catherine that he hadn't figured out yet.

"Always remember that investigation is about what you *don't* see. Don't be fooled by distracting foreground details; concentrate on uncovering the hidden truth that lies beneath the world you observe. Remember, too, the lesson you learned yesterday," Bishop warned them, her voice amplified by the loudspeakers. "This game has rules, but just like in real life, the rules are constantly changing. The elements of this manhunt could be anywhere—not just here in Hogan's Alley, but anywhere you go in Quantico, both on and off our campus."

As Bishop referred to the lessons of the previous day, Kim

could see Gaia flinching as if someone was poking her with a sharp stick. Kim couldn't miss it.

"And finally, here's the most important thing I'm going to say this morning. Behavior counts as much as winning, if not more. Those FBI personnel you'll encounter in the game aren't just playing parts; they're also there to watch *you*. Believe me when I tell you that there's nothing you can do or say in these 1.2 acres behind me—or off our campus, for that matter—that won't be seen and reported. So follow the rules at all times. And pay extra attention to the 'FBI Field Behavior Directives' I've handed out. Entire cases have been thrown out of court and killers have gone free because arresting officers didn't do everything 'by the book,' which is why we're very, very serious about ironclad obedience to these rules."

The sun was beating down on the courtyard—already the trainees were casting heavy shadows. It was going to be a long, hot day. Somewhere in the town in front of them were the clues to acts of complete inhumanity. Kim knew it didn't matter one bit that the "killer" they were chasing was fictional any more than it mattered that the nightmare that kept someone awake night after night wasn't real.

Can I do it? Kim thought seriously. *I'm supposed to be so good at reading people. That's what the diplomas say. But can I think like someone who's brilliantly insane—and as dangerous as a wild animal?*

"If you're ready," Bishop called out, "then step forward in an orderly fashion and retrieve your badges and guns. You'll be grouped into five task forces, each with four trainees—the details are included with your badges. Get ready—and good luck."

There was no cheer, no sound at all except the wind moving through the distant trees as the trainees all moved forward. Kim's heart was racing. By his wristwatch, they had two minutes until the bell went off, starting the game. He walked forward with the others.

Can I do this?

Kim sincerely hoped so.

FEDERAL BUREAU OF INVESTIGATION
FIELD REPORT—QUANTICO SPECIAL FORCES TRAINING PROGRAM
DAY: 2
REPORT: Practical Applications ("Hogan's Alley") Exercise, Segment 1
SUPERVISOR: Special Agent Jennifer Bishop, code G44

SUMMARY

[*Note*: Our trainees now number 20, down from 22 this morning; details to follow.]

Trainees assembled in outdoor court A2 as per orders at 0800 EST. They were reminded of the events of the previous day, specifically the emphasis placed on scenario evaluation and situational analysis.

As has been noted elsewhere, I have made several adjustments and enhancements to the Hogan's Alley "serial killer pursuit" game (bringing it to version 3.1); this should address concerns arising from the previous version of the game, which was considered too shocking and unsetting in its details and realization. Agent Malloy and I have stressed the crucial importance of these games being as violently realistic as possible as well as the importance of the games maintaining a level of complexity and subtlety to match real-world criminal investigations.

Several trainees are receiving special observation as has been noted elsewhere; in light of their ongoing rivalry on the training fields during day 1 preliminary exercises (*please see Sgt. Conroy's full day 1 report, filed elsewhere*), I have paired Gaia Moore and Will Taylor on the same team. According to all accounts Moore seemed disillusioned by her failure and by Taylor's contrasting success in the "restaurant robbery" drill the previous day. It remains to be seen whether Gaia has the personal strength to swallow her pride and learn from her mistakes or the intellectual and physical ingenuity to grow to meet the formidable challenges to come. Pairing her with Taylor should exacerbate precisely those competitive/resentful urges that Moore is most troubled by.

Taylor remains an unknown quantity in several respects, as his attention has only turned to law enforcement relatively recently (see accompanying personnel file). For this reason, among others, I have placed Catherine Sanders and Kim Lau on Moore and Taylor's team; the four have already met, and Lau's remarkable psych-op abilities as well as Sanders's digital skills might provide an interesting combination. Whether this combination is a recipe for success or for catastrophic failure remains to be seen, especially after the rather dramatic developments that ensued as day 2 continued.

Full report to come—Bishop, G44.

Gaia

Gaia Moore, FBI.

   Special Agent Gaia Moore.

   Well, today's the day I say those words out loud for the first time. And try to sound like I mean it. I'm finally carrying a badge and a gun. (A fake gun, that is. I've had a long talk with myself, and I think I'm going to be okay around fake guns. They're filled with paint pellets. Paint pellets don't cause senseless murders. Paint pellets don't cut short innocent lives.)

   I think my dad would be proud. Fake gun and all.

   I was thinking about him as I crossed the highway and entered Hogan's Alley. The gun straps under my arm, in a leather cross-draw shoulder holster that attaches to my belt and reaches around my back. You can wear the straps under a jacket and nobody will see them; that's the point. The badge is folded in a leather case in my back pocket. I can feel the equipment's weight as I move around. If Dad saw me right now, he would know—if he were standing right there, with his sad eyes squinting in the sun, he would look at me, and his first thought would be, *Shoulder holster—right-hand cross draw. Government issue—probably a Walther automatic.*

   And would he be proud? Would this be what he wanted?

   Would he understand why I had to do this by myself, without his involvement? I would like to know the answer to that, actually.

   The simple fact is, this is much more confusing than I thought it would be. And it's already much harder. Yesterday I thought, fine—just run faster, jump higher, punch harder, kick more accurately, and think more quickly. But there's more to it than that—a lot more. For instance, I have to deal with people directly—I can't run away from them while pretending to run toward them, the way I've done with so many people in my life.

With my teammates right now, that may not be so easy. I like Kim—he seems very sweet, and I can already tell his mind is like a laser, focusing in on everyone else's personalities. And Catherine's great. I wish they hadn't seen me make a fool of myself yesterday. I thought Will was the big show-off—but it turns out that if anyone's been showing off, it's probably me.

Will. I don't know why we're on the same team, but his superior attitude is a distraction I don't need. I've got to concentrate on solving this crime, not proving anything or competing with anyone.

Except maybe that's the point. *Am* I here to prove something? To myself, to Dad, to Will, to Agent Bishop, to Agent Malloy? Can I win the game? Can I win without proving anything—can I prove anything without winning?

I don't know.

But one thing's for sure—it's absolutely clear in my head as the four of us walk in a line across the road and step between the buildings on the perimeter of this fictional town "Hogan's Alley." I'm not going to make any more mistakes. I'm going to walk into this fake-ass town with my badge and gun, and I'm going to catch a killer.

The bell rang out, as clear and loud as a fire alarm, echoing in the crisp, morning air.

Game start.

They had walked into a wide, treeless town square. Once they were out of view of the official FBI buildings, the illusion was complete. Hogan's Alley wasn't like some strip of fake buildings at Universal Studios. The trainees could have been in any American small town. Catherine saw a barbershop, a bookstore, a small bank. There were newspaper vending machines on the corners, and a band shell in the center of the small civic park at the end of the town square. Cars were parked up and down the main street.

Gaia, Will, Kim, and Catherine stood there, looking around. There were a few passersby strolling down the sidewalks but not that much pedestrian traffic. At the other end of the square Catherine could see one of the other teams of four—the competition.

"So what do we do?" Catherine asked.

Will shrugged. "What do special agents do before anything happens?"

"Stand around looking useless?" Gaia said pleasantly. "But then, you already know that, don't you?"

"Well, since you're clearly watchin' every move I make, you tell me," Will answered.

"Is there something we're supposed to see?" Kim asked Will. He was shading his eyes, gazing up and down the street. "Some detail we're supposed to pick up?"

He's asking Will, Catherine noticed. *Will's established that*

he's the observational wizard—Kim's acknowledging that.
Catherine also noticed that Gaia chose that moment to turn
away, as if she was wincing. Catherine was confused. Was Kim
doing it on purpose? Trying to irritate Gaia?

Or was Kim not thinking about Gaia at all? Was he just
focused on winning the game?

"I can't think of anything," Will said. The wind made his T-
shirt flap against his shoulder muscles. "I think we just wait."

"Did Bishop give any specifics?" Gaia asked. "Did she say
what—?"

Catherine's cell phone rang.

"Hello? Um—Sanders here," Catherine said, answering the
phone. The other three watched her expectantly.

"Agent Sanders, this is Sheriff Landy," a rough male voice
told her over the phone. It was a bad connection. "The regional
FBI headquarters gave me your cell phone number—I hope
that's all right."

"Yes—go on."

"Agent Sanders, we've had a violent homicide," Sheriff
Landy continued. If he was an actor, he was very good; to
Catherine's ears, he sounded completely real. "Circumstances of
the murder are—" *Hiss!* A blast of cell phone static obscured
the sheriff's voice for a moment. "—Take a look."

"I'm sorry, Sheriff; I lost some of that," Catherine said,
squinting impatiently and shielding her other ear with her
hand. "A homicide—"

"Just please come to the police station as quickly as you can,
Agent Sanders. Frankly, we can't make heads or tails of this—it's
pretty gruesome."

Catherine slapped the phone shut. "Police station," she told the others. They all looked around, and then Kim pointed—a low building with long white columns along its facade bore an engraved sign that read Police Station. Without missing a beat, they started walking four abreast in that direction.

"Did they give any details?" Gaia asked. Catherine shook her head.

"A single homicide?" Will asked in his Farm Belt accent, which Catherine had to admit she found charming. "And they've moved the body?"

"He didn't say. Damn phone—I was losing him."

"How did they get the number?" Kim asked as they arrived at the police station entrance. Will held the door for Catherine and Gaia—Gaia clearly didn't like this, but she acquiesced.

"They gave me the phone. It's a private network for the game," Catherine explained.

"Interesting that they gave it to you," Kim noted.

Catherine nodded. "Something tells me communication problems are part of the game."

"Agent Sanders?" the sheriff's voice echoed at them the moment the four of them had arrived in the cool, air-conditioned police station lobby, before their eyes had even adjusted to the darkness. Catherine had never felt more awake, she realized absently, standing up straighter as the sheriff came toward them out of the shadows. With surprise, Catherine recognized one of the "gunmen" from the previous day. He was using a different voice, and he was dressed differently, but it was the same actor. "Thank you so much for coming."

"Sheriff, these are Special Agents Moore, Lau, and Taylor," Catherine said.

"Don't worry, Sheriff," Will said smoothly, stepping forward and smiling. "My colleagues and I will get to the bottom of this."

"Well, I do appreciate it," the sheriff told Will. "I sure am glad to see some FBI agents, I can tell you that, sir."

Kim glanced at Will, and Catherine had the same thought. *Is he playing dominance games? Is he showing off for Gaia? They didn't have time for that. Or is he just giving the sheriff a reassuring "alpha male" presence to deal with?*

"What's the current status of the investigation?" Catherine asked.

"Local police completed their crime scene investigation yesterday." Sheriff Landy was taking them toward a door with a pebbled-glass panel that read Sheriff's Office. "The body was brought here last night. We've not gotten our lab results back yet, but there's a great deal of confusing forensic evidence. By yesterday evening the investigation had yielded not one useful clue, and we began to worry that too much time was slipping away and the trail was becoming cold. At ten this morning Deputy Linden formally recommended that we call in the FBI since it was clear that we weren't getting anywhere at all. I don't mind saying, we're stumped, ma'am. And we've got a grief-stricken family to deal with, too. Such a young boy—what a tragic waste."

They came into the sheriff's office. He gestured them toward a row of four chairs. *Of course,* Catherine thought. *Four-man teams.* She was trying not to think about what they were really doing—to bury herself in this fictional investigation—but she kept noticing details like that.

"Are these the crime scene photos?" Kim asked, reaching

for a thick stack of photographs on the sheriff's desk. "May we see them?"

They began leafing through the photographs, handing them around. Catherine braced herself, taking a deep breath. *It's going to be bloody,* she warned herself. *Get ready.*

She wasn't wrong.

The first picture was of a young boy's bedroom, probably on the second floor of a suburban house. Catherine guessed that the inhabitant was a teenager—in his early teens. Sadly, she was reminded of her college friends, the computer "geeks" with whom she'd spent so much of her time. *This is what their rooms would have looked like,* she thought. *When they were young.*

There was a Christina Aguilera poster on the wall next to a *Star Trek* poster showing Seven of Nine. There was a Gateway personal computer—peering at the picture, Catherine quickly determined that there was nothing unusual about the machine. There was a bookshelf stuffed with paperbacks. The other shelves were untidy, covered with baseball mitts, comic books, colorful T-shirts.

You're stalling, Catherine told herself. *Look in the middle.*

She looked in the middle of the picture. Her breathing stopped, and she felt like a cold wave was passing over her.

"Police logged a 911 call at seven-twenty from the James Hill residence," the sheriff told them. He was reaching for a knob on a reel-to-reel tape deck on his desk. "This is the call."

Beep! "Nine one one; what's the emergency?" A tinny-sounding operator came over the sheriff's speakers.

"My son—!" a woman's voice screamed. The sound went

right through Catherine. She had never in her life heard a scream like that, and if it were up to her, she never would again. The woman was sobbing, choking, and screaming at the same time. "*Oh my GOD—my—s-son—Nathan—*"

"*He's dead; he's d-dead; oh Jesus—*" A man's voice in the background was interrupting. Glancing over, Catherine saw Kim squinting and leaning forward, concentrating on the voices.

"Ma'am, please give us your address."

"*Nathan!!! Nathan!!!*" the woman screamed. There was a fumbling noise as the phone was roughly grabbed away.

"Two twenty-six Emerald Lane," a sobbing male voice interrupted. "*Oh G-God, no, no—*"

"*Jim, he's dead—oh G—*"

Beep! The sound stopped. The reels of the tape machine kept spinning silently until the sheriff reached to turn them off.

Nathan Hill was stretched out faceup across the carpet on the floor of his bedroom. He was fully dressed in jeans, a dark green flannel shirt, and a blue windbreaker. An enormous dark red stain spread out from his torso. His arms were spread left and right, palms upward, hands clenched as if in pain. His mouth was frozen open as if in a scream, and his head was thrown backward.

The boy's chest was ripped open. His ribs had been cracked apart as if with an automotive jack. The blood was everywhere; it had clearly spouted like a fountain, drenching the bedsheets, the wall, the carpet. A spray of drying, darkening crimson had spattered across Christina Aguilera's navel—at first glance, Catherine hadn't even noticed.

"Officers Reardon and McCormack arrived on the scene at eight-o-five and quickly determined that Mr. and Mrs. Hill were unable to participate in the investigation due to their extreme emotional distress," Sheriff Landy went on in his dry, accented voice. "They were moved here to the precinct house as soon as was convenient, but there wasn't much questioning we could do; I understand that both parents had to be sedated."

The next photograph was a close-up of the body.

It's not real. It's not real, Catherine told herself furiously. She felt very sure that she was about to vomit. She was swallowing over and over like one did on an airplane, trying to interrupt her gagging reflex. *That's not really a dead kid. This whole thing is just a game. It's just a—*

And then she firmly stopped herself. That was no way to be thinking. It was technically correct . . . but in the long run it was a mistake. She had to react as if this were real. They all did. Because that was the only way they'd ever be ready to face photographs like this when it *was* real.

"The medical examiner hasn't completed his report," the sheriff was telling them. Will was taking notes, Catherine noticed. "But it seems to be exactly what it looks like: death by disembowelment. There are no poisons, no toxins, no other wounds besides the ones you see."

The wounds Catherine could see were plenty—they would have killed anyone. Poor fourteen-year-old Nathan Hill looked like he'd been attacked with an outboard motor or a lawn mower. It was that bad. His intestines were rolling from his punctured abdomen.

"The parents," Gaia said. "How did they discover the body? Did they wake up and find him?"

Good question, Catherine thought. It had occurred to her, too—wouldn't the kid have screamed? Wouldn't everyone in a block radius have heard his screams?

"We haven't gotten any useful information from the parents," Sheriff Landy drawled. "We won't anytime soon, either, judging from their mental state."

"Hmmm." Kim spoke so quietly that he drew everyone's attention. He was leaning forward, his glossy black hair falling over his eyes as he stared at another one of the photographs. Glare from the window shone on the picture's surface: Catherine couldn't make it out.

"This is interesting," Kim said. "Look."

He held up the photograph. The others looked at it. It showed the opposite bedroom wall—the one that hadn't been visible in the preceding pictures. The wall was unadorned, which was probably why the killer had chosen it for what he'd done.

A word was painted in blood on the wall. It was very neatly done: the letters looked to be about two feet tall, all capitals. There were drips of darkening, brownish blood trailing downward on the wall. The word was

SAVED

Above the word was a cross, also painted in blood.

Catherine, Will, Gaia, and Kim all looked at each other. Catherine couldn't read the others' minds, but she had a pretty good idea what they were thinking because she was thinking it, too. She was completely stumped.

112

We're supposed to figure out who did this? And CATCH them?

She didn't have the slightest idea what to do first. It was very unsettling. Catherine knew she was an exceptional problem solver, but the problems she excelled at solving involved microchips and Ethernet cables and cable modems and CD-ROMs, not blood and strewn intestines and screaming parents driven nearly insane by grief. The gore was much more unsettling than she'd expected—and she was hoping they'd get some kind of break before they had to get close to it again.

Gaia spoke suddenly—and that hope vanished miserably from Catherine's mind as quickly as it had arrived.

"We'd like to see the body," Gaia told the sheriff.

SIGNS OF RESISTANCE

A chest wound, Gaia told herself dully. *It had to be a chest wound.*

She was following the others down a dark, linoleum-floored corridor in the basement of the Hogan's Alley police station. The sheriff was leading them forward, his handcuffs and firearm jingling on his wide belt as he walked. Will, Catherine, and Kim were looking around at their surroundings. Kim was holding the big folder containing the crime scene photographs.

They're all doing the same thing I'm doing, Gaia thought. *They're trying to appear cool, like they're not freaked out.*

At first Gaia had told herself over and over that it wasn't

real. Then she'd stopped. It didn't make it less scary, any more than telling yourself that "it was just a movie" kept you from screaming when the zombies came piling out in *28 Days Later*. All it did was blur your concentration. So Gaia determined to stop; from now on, she would act as if it were utterly real.

But that was harder for her than for the others. *I've seen the real thing,* she told herself again. She even wondered if Bishop had designed the game especially with Gaia in mind.

"Here we are," Sheriff Landy said, reaching for another pebbled-glass-inlaid door, this time with a sign reading Morgue. Gaia glanced over at Will, who, she suddenly realized, looked pale. His eyes were wide open as if in fear or surprise, and Gaia realized that his smirking, I-can-handle-it persona seemed to be gone.

Just then—as the sheriff rattled the doorknob and ushered them in a dark, cool room with a strange, medicinal smell— Will caught Gaia's glance, and suddenly his face was back in its familiar easy smirk, as if he was about to ask a maitre d' to get him a good table.

Is he freaked or isn't he? Gaia wondered, quickly turning her eyes away. *And why do I care, exactly? Concentrate on the case.*

A thin, quiet-looking man in a green doctor's shirt nodded at them. "Agents, welcome. I'm Dr. Pietro, the medical examiner," the man said. He was pulling open what looked like a giant-sized file cabinet drawer. Pietro had to put his back into it—the drawer was heavy. It rolled smoothly out on well-oiled casters.

Pietro pulled back a white sheet, and the trainees got their first look at Nathan Hill.

None of them gasped or winced, which, Gaia thought, was a credit to their self-control. Yes, this was some kind of latex dummy, Gaia realized in the back of her mind, but it didn't matter. It was utterly convincing. Here was the poor young boy, who would never listen to another Eminem song or play another version of "Grand Theft Auto." He was naked, covered only by the sheet. His face still held the wide-open stare of agony. The skin was gray. The blood had been cleared away, and the jagged, torn edges of the wound were clearly visible.

"Passion," Kim muttered quietly, moving closer to the corpse. "Hatred. Look at the violence this took. Whoever did this was very serious about it."

"Speculation," Will argued. "He could just have been in a hurry or afraid of being disturbed."

"It may be speculation, but it's valid," Gaia argued. Will's tone, as usual, was bothering her. And he never argued back—he just smiled that infuriating smile, like he was doing right now.

"Just tryin' to narrow the focus of inquiry, Agent Moore," Will said. Gaia wanted to punch him very hard.

"Doctor," Catherine asked, "based on your preliminary examination, can you draw any conclusions about the crime?"

Well asked, Gaia thought, looking over at her roommate, whose intelligent brown eyes were focused on Pietro's face. *If you don't understand what you're seeing, ask someone who does.*

Unlike the two boys, she thought, who seemed to be competing for who could make the smartest remark.

"Unfortunately, no," Pietro said sadly. "I will say this, however: there are very few signs of resistance. The fingernails are intact; the muscles are unstrained."

"Which means?" Catherine asked.

Pietro shrugged. "Either this happened very quickly, or . . . or the boy was sedated somehow. We won't know until the lab reports are completed."

"You'll be sure to get all your data to these FBI agents as fast as you can, Doctor?" the sheriff said.

"Sure."

There was a pause.

Something's going on, Gaia thought suddenly. It was like the sheriff and the ME were waiting for something. It was a very strange perception—Gaia knew that she could be imagining it.

We're missing something.

Gaia racked her brains. What could they be missing? They had the photographs, they had seen the naked body—

Oh.

"Can we see the boy's clothes?" Gaia asked.

The ME looked at her. Was it her imagination, or were his eyes twinkling, as if the actor was suppressing a smile? She couldn't be sure.

"Right this way," Dr. Pietro told them. "I've got them set up for you."

Okay, I admit it—this is much harder than it looks.

The strange thing about that is, in my experience *nothing* is as hard as it looks. The first time I saw a man hit a home run, when I was just ten and Uncle Casper took me to a ball game, I thought, *That's absolutely awesome. There's no way I could ever do that.* But I turned out to be wrong.

In college it happened all the time—I benefited from the same simple lesson I'd learned when I was a kid. The world is full of people who tell you what you can't do. But there aren't that many people telling you what you *can* do. So you just have to tell yourself.

I've made it pretty far on that principle. "You've made your best time," the track coach would tell me. "You can't get any faster." And I'd think, *How do you know? I'll bet I can.*

Or my knack for seeing things. Growing up, the joke about me was that you could never throw me a surprise party—I'd always pick up on what was going on. No matter how subtle everyone tried to be, how they tried to fake me out, they never could. I'd notice the balloon-store bag in the trash or my aunt's car parked way down the street and the jig was up. Eventually people would challenge me—"Hey, Will, I'll bet you five bucks you didn't see where I put my car keys"—but they'd always lose.

"You'll never make it into the FBI," Casper told me when I was home this past Christmas. He was sitting on the porch drinking a Jack Daniels, which he still does exactly twice a year. The farm smells were rolling in across the fields, like they always do whenever I'm home. And Casper was holding forth on the subject of government agencies.

"It's all a big club," Casper lectured, sipping his drink. I like to think my dad would lecture me the way Uncle Casper does if he was around. "All Yankees, all Ivy Leaguers from the big northeastern cities. I remember Kennedy's war: all the Harvard and Yale boys at the CIA running things. Today's no different." My uncle turned in his chair to look at me. "When they see you, they'll see a southern good ol' boy, and that's it. You may have learned some slick manners and some big words, but that won't make any difference. They'll see you for what you are."

That's fine, I thought, looking out at the beautiful hills of South Carolina. *Bring it on. I love you, Casper, but you've got it all wrong.*

Now, standing here in this freezing cold morgue, there's no reason for me to be thinking about that evening. Except maybe I'm having my doubts. Everyone reaches their best time, right? What's the Clint Eastwood line—"A man's got to know his limitations"? I'm watching Gaia and Kim sort through this pile of bloody clothes, with the blood smearing onto the latex gloves they're wearing, and I have to wonder if I can play in the same league as them.

When Gaia looks at me, I feel like I have a wisp of hay coming out of the corner of my mouth and I'm dressed in manure-covered overalls. Or even worse—I feel like one of those hucksters, a good ol' boy in a shiny suit and a bolo tie, trying to work some angle out of a briefcase—trying to pass for high class, but nobody's buying it. She gives me one look with those wide eyes of hers, and it's like all my pretension melts away.

Because she's what my daddy was talking about—she's as sophisticated as they get. Manhattan to Stanford. I can see it in the way she dresses, the way she talks, the way she carries herself—even the way she uses her upper arm to brush her hair from her eyes right now while she's looking through the dead boy's pockets.

It's possible that Gaia (and the others) feel as over their heads as I do. It really is. But it doesn't seem like it. I won't tell them what I'm really thinking, which is that if I were doing this on my own, I would have no *idea* what to do next. It's a wonder that serial killers are *ever* caught.

But maybe as a team we can do it. I don't know—crazier things have happened. Anyway, I'm determined to think positively. It's my best characteristic, or so they've always told me. It's corny, I know, but it works. And it might make me look like a hick to someone like Gaia Moore, but that's just too bad. It's gotten me this far.

Watching the girls work—the *women,* I mean—I'm impressed with them, too. They've found a bunch of stuff in Nathan Hill's pockets. Not exactly a treasure trove, but a few items that might shed some light on who this kid was. In the windbreaker's pockets they've found the following items:

1) a combination lock, Master brand, with the steel hasp closed

2) a bottle of prescription pills

3) a GameBoy cartridge, slightly scuffed ("Wario Land 4")

4) three quarters and two dimes

5) a Coca-Cola bottle cap with an inset game piece good for a free song download

And that's it. While Gaia and the others dutifully "bag and tag" all the evidence, carefully sealing everything into those Mylar envelopes, I can't help but feel some resignation. I'm *trying* to think positively, like I said. I'm really trying.

But in the movies when the cops do stuff like this, it's exciting. All you have to do is sit back, eat your popcorn, and just wait for the clues to reveal their secrets.

Here it's different. If we don't put the puzzle pieces together, nobody will. Or more accurately, one of the other teams will, and we'll lose the game. And I don't even want to think about that.

Why did nobody hear anything?

Why was Nathan torn open like that?

Does it matter that he was carrying a combination lock?

"SAVED" . . . ? What does that mean?

Like I said, this is much harder than it looks.

just let me be incognito

IT'S A PSYCH-OUT

They were all squinting in the sun, standing in a rough circle on the Hogan's Alley sidewalk. The police station was behind them. The light had changed, Kim noticed, looking at the shadows on the low buildings across the street.

"Now what?" Catherine asked.

"I'm not sure," Kim answered. "Let's see." He ticked the items off on his fingers as he spoke. "We've seen the photographs. We've seen the body. We've seen the contents of his pockets."

"We can't talk to the parents," Gaia said. Her hair was whipping over her face as she spoke; she impatiently brushed it away. "The crime scene is no longer available. We can't see the lab results because they're not ready yet."

"Look," Catherine said, pointing.

Behind them three young women and one young man were emerging from the police station. They all had badges and guns and were carrying a stack of photographs that looked like the ones that Catherine had under her arm. As Kim watched, the four other trainees spared them a haughty glance before moving purposefully off down the sidewalk.

"The competition," Will said. He was staring after them

121

the way a panther stares at his prey across the African savanna.

"Where the hell are *they* going?" Catherine complained.

"They look like they've got something," said Gaia. "Something we missed."

"No," Kim said firmly. "It's a psych-out. They want us to think they've got some sweet clue." He couldn't explain why, but he was absolutely sure of it. It was clear from the way the short, redheaded woman had glanced at them and then purposely moved in front of her teammates as if pulling them along.

"The question remains," Catherine said, squinting up at the blue sky. "What do we do now?"

"I'd say, let's talk to people," Kim suggested. "Let's find someone who knew the kid. Maybe we can learn something about him."

"That's a waste of time," Will argued. "There's no reason to think that anything about the kid's behavior enters into this, Kim."

"There's no reason to think it *doesn't*," Gaia shot back.

She'll take the opposite position to whatever Will says, Kim marveled. He'd been noticing it since the previous day. *It's completely consistent.* "Anyway, how *should* we be spending our time?"

"Starting pointless arguments," Will said, smiling. "But you knew—"

"*Quiet,*" Catherine said urgently, waving at them impatiently. "Shhh!"

Kim heard it suddenly. Catherine's cell phone was ringing.

"Sanders," Catherine said. Again she seemed to have to

strain to hear. "What? Yes, Sheriff, I understand. What? I'm sorry, could you repeat—"

The others were moving closer to Catherine, trying to hear the voice on the other end of her cell phone.

"Yes." Catherine's eyes widened. She reached in her pocket for a pen and scribbled something along the edge of the folder she carried. "I understand. Yes—right away. Thank you."

Catherine hung up the phone. She seemed very excited.

"What is it?" Will asked. "Is it the lab results?"

"Catherine, Jesus. What's wrong?" Gaia had reached to touch Catherine's bare arm.

"It's not the lab results," Catherine said in a strange, quiet voice. "That was the sheriff. There's been a second murder."

Kim felt something like an electric thrill passing through him. He felt cold, even though the warm Virginia sun was beating down on his shoulders and reflecting from the mica in the bright sidewalk.

"Where? *When?*" Gaia asked.

"Called in minutes ago," Catherine said. "The homicide detectives are on their way now. I've got the address."

"Then let's move," Will said purposefully. "We haven't got a moment to sp—"

And right then the bell rang out, as clear and loud as a fire alarm, making them all jump. *Game time,* Kim thought. "Round one" was over. Around them on the sidewalks the pedestrians all stopped what they were doing and began walking toward the road that led back to real life.

In Hogan's Alley time had stopped. It wouldn't start again until the game resumed the next morning. Kim took a deep breath as the others stretched and tried to relax.

"Wow," Catherine said after a moment. It was clear that she was trying to "wake up" to reality—he could hear the stress in her voice as she tried to drain the adrenaline out of her system.

"So how are we doing?" Gaia asked worriedly.

"Great," Will said confidently. He had begun leading them across the big town square, which now resembled nothing more than a movie set. Kim could see other teams in the distance walking in the same direction. "We're doing great. Come on—who's hungry?"

He's faking it, Kim thought. *We have no idea how we're doing.*

But Will faked it well, and Kim was impressed. It was the sign of a leader—the willingness to sacrifice candor for morale. It showed a sensitivity to the team's feelings, and Kim approved.

"I'm going to take a stroll," Gaia told them. "I just need to think for a little while. I'll see you at dinner."

Kim frowned. It was easy to see that something about "the Nathan Hill Murder" had gotten to Gaia. But he had no idea what it was or why it had hit her as hard as it clearly had.

GRAB THE INTRUDER

From the wooded path Gaia could see the fading sky. As she walked over the twigs and dirt, she could hear the sounds of Quantico drifting through the trees: the ever-present echoes of gunfire (*paint pellets,* she'd remind herself, *they're only firing paint pellets*), the shouts from the physical-training fields, the occasional drone of an automobile. But right now all that was out of view.

Gaia wasn't homesick necessarily. She'd gotten over that at Stanford. It was just so *different.* She didn't know if she'd ever get completely used to it. Closing her eyes, she could imagine the sights and sounds of New York as if it were just yesterday that she'd left. The taxicabs, the roar of traffic, the loud cell phone conversations, the honking car horns, the beeping of early-morning garbage trucks.

Now, walking through the Virginia woods, Gaia relished the quiet. She was alone with her own thoughts, and for once that seemed to be a tranquil or even a pleasant thing. She thought about her teammates, who might be turning into her friends. Somehow she'd avoided having friends in college. Now she wasn't sure why. It had seemed logical at the time: no distractions, no lures away from the crystalline purity of her thoughts, no threat that they'd have their lives taken prematurely and without mercy. And inevitably if she tried to make friends—as she was tempted to do a few times, once with a shy girl in her math class named Akeisha, who impressed Gaia with her own conspicuous "loner" routine, hiding her eyes constantly behind Armani sunglasses, and once with a quiet sophomore musician and actor who struck her as being one of the most truly original thinkers she'd met, and finally, of course, fatefully, with Kevin Bender—but she always pulled back because in the end she was afraid of the questions. Where are you from? What do your parents do?

What was high school like? What's the worst thing that ever happened to you?

And Gaia just wasn't ready to answer these questions. *Just let me be incognito,* she wanted to say. *Can we be friends without you knowing me? Because I can't deal with the questions or the reactions the answers will produce.* At least her friends here would be well equipped to defend themselves physically.

Gaia was nearly back to the campus—she could see the dark masses of the FBI buildings looming through the trees. She passed a pair of trainees in running shoes sprinting in the other direction, and they smiled and waved. Gaia waved back.

Here it might be different, she was thinking. These people were the same way. They could trade information like poker players putting cards down—it would be an even, fair game. *My mother was killed when I was a girl,* she would say. *Your turn.* And then Kim or Catherine would tell her something, and it would be clear that it was as hard for them as it was for Gaia. Because they were unusual, too—Gaia could tell. Agent Bishop must have made sure of that.

And Will. Don't forget Will.

But Gaia wasn't sure if she could fit Will into that same category. Yes, she grudgingly reminded herself, he'd done that amazing move in the restaurant the previous day. And he'd come closer to beating her in the physical competitions than anyone ever had—even Jake. But beyond that, was he so exceptional? Was he *really?* Gaia wasn't sure.

A few moments later, exiting the stairwell onto the girls' floor, Gaia stopped walking, staring at the half-open door to her room.

What the hell?

Security was very tight on the Quantico base. Gaia had to show her plastic trainee badge to a guard every time she entered the dorm building—and the campus's edge was rimmed with a high fence and surveillance cameras. No one unauthorized could possibly get in here.

So there was no way she could be seeing what she was seeing—but there it was. A dark-clothed, stooping figure rummaging through Gaia's dresser.

Gaia stood there a moment, getting her bearings, making sure she had the right floor and the correct room. But she did. There was the nameplate that read Moore, G./Sanders, C. Stepping soundlessly forward, catlike, Gaia could see the figure stooped over her drawer—and she could hear clattering noises as her belongings were pushed around.

Gaia barreled forward and swung the door open, ready to grab the intruder.

"Jesus Christ!" Catherine yelled, jumping nearly a foot in the air and then turning around. "Gaia," she gasped, hand on her chest. "Wow—you scared the hell out of me."

"What are you doing?" Gaia looked down at her open drawer. "Can I help you with something?"

"No—I'm sorry," Catherine said, stepping back from Gaia's dresser. She sounded frustrated. "Damn, this looks really bad. Look, have you seen my bracelet? I can't find this bracelet of mine."

Gaia went over to sit on her bed. "No," Gaia said, thinking back. "No, I don't think so. What's it look like? And why would it be in my dresser drawer?"

"I don't *know*," Catherine admitted, collapsing on her bed. "Damn it, I'm just at my wits' end. I'm sorry, Gaia."

"That's okay," Gaia said hesitantly. "Is it really valuable?"

"To me," Catherine told her. She had her hand shoved up into her short Peter Pan haircut. "It's not actually that valuable—it's actually kind of tacky. It's just a silver band, you know, with a turquoise inlay. It was—it was my mother's."

"Oh," Gaia said, leaning back against the wall.

Do I believe that?

Gaia wasn't sure. How well did she know Catherine, anyway? Why would she *really* be looking through her drawer?

Oh, come off it, Gaia thought disgustedly. *She told you why. Drop it—there are actually people who tell the truth, if you can get your head around that one.*

Gaia sensed pain coming from Catherine when she said the word *mom*. She knew this was her cue to ask.

"And your mom . . ." Gaia began, but then trailed off. She has no idea how to complete the question.

"She died," Catherine said quietly.

That's what Gaia had figured.

"Abdominal cancer, two years ago."

"Oh—I'm sorry," Gaia said. A strange feeling had come over her—a feeling of sadness, or loneliness, or some combination of the two.

Do it, Gaia told herself. *Say the words.*

"My mother died, too," she said. "Years ago."

Catherine stopped tapping her foot. She raised her brown eyes slowly to look back at Gaia.

"Really?" Catherine was sitting up. "Wow. I'm sorry, I had no—were you close?"

"Well—yeah." Gaia wasn't sure how to answer that question. She thought about her mother . . . about the smell of her perfume and the sound of her voice when she hummed to the second movement of the Sibelius violin concerto. "Yes, we were close."

"What was her name?"

"Katia."

"What did she look like?" Catherine's questions had an almost avid tone. "I'm sorry; I've just never met someone my own age who lost her mother."

"She looked—" *And how do I answer* that *question?* Gaia wondered. The complexity of her mother's face, the way she'd looked at her—how could she get that into the English language, especially when talking to a girl she'd known for less than forty-eight hours?

"She looked like me," Gaia answered finally. *And I'm sorry I brought this up.* "But much, much prettier."

"Anybody home?" came a sudden voice from outside the room. Whoever it was out there, he was rapping loudly on the door. "Catherine? Gaia?"

"Come in," Gaia called out. *Please,* she thought, *whoever you are, interrupt this conversation. I've made a mistake.*

Kim Lau opened the door. He had changed clothes—again; he seemed to have an enormous wardrobe, and all his clothes were nice. Now he wore a bright red print shirt over loose-fitting khaki trousers and elaborate Puma running shoes.

"Ladies," Kim said. "How goes it?"

"Hey, buddy," Catherine said warmly. "Just decompressing. Come in."

"Thanks," Kim said. He strolled into the room, hands in pockets, his sneakers squeaking on the buffed linoleum. "Nice place you got here."

"Are you kidding?" Catherine was laughing. The room was almost bare. Neither of them had even unpacked all the way.

"Yes." Kim stared at her, beaming. Catherine laughed again. "Garrett and I already put up all our posters. Garrett's my roommate—he's from Los Angeles and thinks he's a gangsta."

"What posters does he have?" Gaia asked.

"Usher, Redman, and Jada Pinkett Smith," Kim ticked off. He had collapsed into Catherine's desk chair. "Hey, did you hear we lost two more trainees today?"

"What? No," Catherine said. "What happened?"

"On two different teams. They couldn't deal—they saw the photos and the corpse, and they freaked. Throwing up, tears, the works. So they're out. Bishop handled it personally."

"Wow," Gaia said.

There's no room for error, she thought. *None at all.*

"Listen, are you guys doing anything tonight?" Kim went on. Gaia and Catherine looked at each other.

"Beyond taking showers and falling into fatigue-induced comas? No," Catherine said. "Why—what have you got?"

"Well, I thought we could, you know, unwind together. Go into town, have a drink . . . and talk about the case."

"Oh, *good* idea," Catherine said fervently. "I'd love to. Roomie?"

"Well, I'm not—" *Much of a drinker,* Gaia was about to say. But for some reason, she didn't. She stalled instead. "Did you have something specific in mind, Kim?"

"Indeed I do." Kim was pointing at her, smiling. He seemed very pleased with himself. "Someone at the shooting range told me about this place called Johnny Ray's. It's not hard to get to—closer than that steak place yesterday. And"—he grinned—"they have gay nights. Like, for example, tonight."

"Gay—Wait, will *everyone* be gay?" Catherine wrinkled her nose as she sifted through the clothes in her closet. "That's no fun."

"No, I imagine only the small percentage you'd find in a backwater burg like this one." Kim was swinging his arms. "Probably like ten percent, but that ten percent gets half-price pitchers and cheap mixed drinks. So I'll be happy, and *you'll* have some beautiful men to look at and never be able to touch. Come on, Gaia—let's go. Get a sweater or something."

"Well—"

The thing was, Gaia thought, she could *use* a drink. Her mind was filled with violent imagery: Nathan Hill's exploded chest and, lurking behind it, the searing images of Jake Montone's final moments on earth. And there was more on her mind: that burning shame she'd felt the day before, standing up from the cheaply carpeted floor of the steak house, releasing the "gunman's" hands while the whole room applauded Will Taylor's "Sherlock Holmes" moment. Yeah, she could use a drink. One of those rare occasions where Gaia Moore would actually imbibe alcohol.

"*Here's* my bracelet!" Catherine was pawing through her

own dresser drawer, apparently looking for her purse. She triumphantly held a silver bracelet aloft. As she'd said, it had a turquoise inlay—it was really quite pretty. "Oh, thank God. Gaia, I'm sorry about before—I just don't know what I'd do if I lost this."

"Don't worry about it," Gaia said, pulling a sweater out of her own dresser. "Lead on, Kim. Are we taking Catherine's car?"

"That's the plan," Kim said as Catherine locked the dorm room door behind them. "Will's meeting us out front."

Gaia's heart sank. *Will's meeting us?*

Great. Gaia kept her face immobile and cursed herself for not finding this information out beforehand—before she'd agreed to come along. Now it was too late—she couldn't back out. It wasn't that Will was so bad, necessarily. It was just that she was in no mood for the verbal sparring that Will seemed to find so indispensable.

"Something wrong?" Kim asked her quietly as they galloped down the cinder block stairwell.

"No," Gaia told him quickly. "Just preoccupied."

"You don't mind that I invited Will, do you?" Kim went on. He seemed concerned. "It just seemed like a—"

"No, that's fine," Gaia interrupted. She gave Kim a bright smile as they came through the glass doors and out into the cool evening air. "I'm glad he's coming."

And you don't miss much.

Gaia was beginning to realize how difficult, if not impossible, it was to hide your thoughts from Kim. *Advanced shrink degrees before he turned twenty,* Gaia remembered.

"Well, hi there," Will said, smiling. He was leaning casually on Catherine's Altima. He had changed into an untucked white dress shirt, jeans, and black loafers. *He almost looks like a guy you'd see in Greenwich Village,* Gaia thought in surprise. *Until he opens his mouth and that southern boy routine starts.* "Are we all ready to saddle up?"

"I'm sitting in front," Gaia told Catherine, quickly moving around the car.

"Hey, buddy," Catherine greeted Will. "Did you hear it's gay night where we're going?"

"No prospects at all—I'll have to dance with *you,* Catherine," Will said, with a wide southern gentleman grin. "That won't upset the clientele, will it, Kim?"

"The 'clientele'?" Kim said, smiling as he opened the back car door. "No."

The sky had darkened; the wind was blowing through the tops of the surrounding trees as Catherine started the engine. Gaia stared straight ahead, hearing Will climb into the backseat right behind her, his aftershave seeming to fill the car immediately. Will's knees bumped into her seat, knocking her forward.

"Watch the knees," Gaia said impatiently. But as she spoke, she could feel her face heating up and, no doubt, turning bright red—and she was glad that nobody could see her in the darkened car interior.

no reason newcomers should put up with this nonsense

YOU'RE BEING SCOPED

Slamming the back door of Catherine's Altima, walking across the gravel parking area in front of Johnny Ray's, Kim knew that the Quantico area wouldn't exactly be a hotbed of activity for the gay community. There was no question that this was a "straight" bar. From the outside, it looked like a roadhouse. A buzzing neon sign advertised Coors Light in one window. A bored-looking young man wearing a sleeveless black T-shirt and a cowboy hat stood by the door. The circumference of his upper arms and his lack of neck suggested he was a bouncer, but God help the poor soul who actually got into a fight—the guy was practically asleep. It was fully dark now: looking up, Kim could barely make out the stars between the heavy electrical cables that stretched across the parking lot. Loud country-and-western music played from within the bar; through the bright yellow windows, Kim could see a blurred, shadowy view of a crowd moving around. In the background, behind the music, Kim could hear the wind rustling in the nearby trees and crickets conducting their nocturnal symphony.

As soon as Kim pushed open the heavy, leather-covered door, he was struck by a wall of sound. The smell of beer was overpowering. A jukebox was playing "Stand by Your Man"—

with a smile, Kim recognized the Dixie Chicks cover. The western theme was continued in the clothes. Beyond the wide floor, dotted with round wooden tables, a dance floor with a glittering witch's ball overhead was filled with a dozen or so pretty boys in cowboy hats dancing to the song, the capped sleeves of their sequined shirts showing off their thick upper arms. All the boys were smiling, clearly having a great time.

"Definitely gay night." Kim leaned to tell Catherine. He had to speak loudly to be heard over the deafening music.

"*All* those boys are gay?" Catherine pouted comically. "What a tragedy."

"Ladies and gentlemen, the first round's on me," Will said grandly, gesturing them toward the bar.

Two couples were just vacating their bar stools. Catherine and Will dashed over and claimed them. Will pulled out a bar stool for Gaia, as if it were the most natural thing in the world.

"That's really not necessary," Gaia told him, speaking loudly over the music.

"Then I'll take it. Thank you, sir," Catherine said, sliding between them and taking the stool Will had pulled out.

"Evening," a young woman called out to them as a surge in the crowd pressed her against them. She was shorter than Catherine but slender, with rough, tanned skin, wearing a blue denim shirt and a waitress's apron. Her honey brown hair was pulled back from her pretty face. "Sorry—I can't move. You new in town?"

"Yes, ma'am—we just got two days ago," Will said. Kim noticed that Will actually made a token gesture toward his forehead, as if tipping a cowboy hat. "Nice place you have here."

"Well, thank you!" The waitress stuck out her hand. "Name's Kelly—welcome to Johnny Ray's."

"Thanks," Kim said. He had to lean toward Kelly's ear to be heard. "This is great—I had no idea there were so many gay men in this town."

Kelly squinted. "Are you kidding? Buddy, they ship in from *all* the neighboring towns, all over Prince William County, every Tuesday night like clockwork. We make more money on these nights than the rest of the week combined—and the pretty boys know how to tip."

They all laughed loudly to be heard over the crowd. The music had changed to "Achy Breaky Heart" as the glitzy cowboys broke into a line dance. Kim was discovering a newfound affinity for Wrangler jeans.

"Whoops! There's my order," Kelly yelped, darting away. "Nice to meet you all!"

They waved as Kelly rushed off. The room had gotten even louder, Kim noticed, and more crowded as they all sat there. "I'm counting on you ladies to defend my honor," he joked.

Kim turned to Catherine. "Hey, you're being scoped." The crowd was pressing against their backs, and glancing that way, Kim saw that many of the men in the bar—the ones at the enormous, wheel-like wooden tables—were staring at Gaia and Catherine. He also noted that a couple of the men were giving him openly hostile looks.

Divided, Kim realized. *The room's divided. The gay guys are dancing, and the straight couples aren't.*

"Evening." A rough male voice came from behind the bar. "Get you something?"

136

Kim and the others looked over. A fortyish-looking man with close-cropped black hair and a dull, sullen expression was leaning on the bar right in front of them. He wore a leather vest over a T-shirt and was unshaven. His eyes were bloodshot, Kim noticed, and there was a trace of scotch on his breath.

"First round's on me," Will said, leaning forward. "As advertised. Should we just get a pitcher? Gaia? Catherine?"

"Sure," Catherine said. After a moment Gaia nodded.

"And how about you?" The bartender had fixed his eyes on Kim. He was chewing a toothpick methodically. "Something a bit more ladylike? Or maybe just a saki?"

Here we go, Kim thought resignedly. After more than ten years of such remarks, he wasn't even surprised. "Saki's Japanese," he told the bartender, meeting his eyes. "My family's from Jiangsu."

"Well, *pardon me,*" the bartender said, smiling in mock deference.

"I'll just take a glass, thanks," Kim said, smiling calmly. There was a pause while the two men looked at each other.

"Hey, friend—did you not get that order?" Will said, leaning forward and squinting. "A pitcher of draft and four glasses."

The bartender swiveled his gaze over at Will and then rolled his eyes. "Coming right up, *friend,*" he said, moving away.

"Do you get that a lot?" Catherine asked. She was munching a handful of peanuts from a dish on the bar.

"Less than you think," Kim said easily. He really didn't want to dwell on it.

"Here you go, ladies," the bartender told Kim, loudly clank-ing a full pitcher of beer on the bar in front of them. He gazed dully at Will as he dropped a stack of four glasses on the bar. "Anything else?"

"Hey!" A female voice came from behind them. Looking over, Kim saw that it was Kelly, the waitress. "What's the trouble here?"

"No trouble at all, Kelly," the bartender said. He was still chewing the toothpick. There was something very unsettling about his dull gray eyes. "Just serving drinks."

"That *better* be all, Jack." Kelly glared across the bar. "I've had just about enough of your nonsense for one night."

"Listen, let me ask you something," Kim said, leaning for-ward. His tone was completely pleasant. "If you don't like Asians, that's your business; I understand. But if you don't like gay guys, why the hell do you have a weekly *gay night* at your own bar?"

Gaia and the others were looking at Kim, wide-eyed.

"Because it's not his bar," Kelly said, her eyes flashing. "It's mine."

Kim and the others stared at her, surprised.

"I'm Kelly Ray," the pretty waitress went on, "and Johnny Ray was my dad. Passed the place on to me fair and square when he died. And *I* started gay night 'cause like I told you, I make more money with this routine than the rest of the week put together. And if you don't like it, Jack"—Kelly gazed at the bartender with eyes as hard as flints—"you can *quit* anytime you like. There are plenty of bartenders in Quantico last time I checked."

A few nearby patrons had glanced over, sensing that some-thing was happening. Most of the people in the room hadn't noticed a thing—the roar of laughter and conversation went on uninterrupted.

"And if you stuck to waitressing like the other girls," Jack said quietly, not meeting Kelly's eyes, "and left the business affairs to the boys, we'd all be in better shape."

Kelly was holding her thumb and forefinger an inch apart. "*This* close, Jack," she said levelly. "You're *this* close. Don't try me 'cause you'll lose."

Jack looked back at Kelly and then turned quickly away, busying himself at the back bar.

"Let me get you a table," Kelly told them, her hands on Kim and Catherine's shoulders. "I'll make sure your drinks get sent over. No reason newcomers should put up with this nonsense. *Grace!*" she yelled out across the bar at someone they couldn't see. "Clear that four top right now! Come with me, folks."

"Thank you, ma'am," Will said as they stood up, doing his quaint hat-tip gesture again. And glancing back at the bar, Kim noticed Jack staring at him.

Kim stared right back. "Enjoyed meeting you," he said without a trace of humor.

TWO YOUNG HOTTIES

"Okay," Catherine yelled across the table. She was getting used to the loudness of the bar—it wasn't a bad place to have a conversation if you didn't mind having to raise your voice. They were on their second pitcher; the first one stood there with just a trace of suds along its bottom and sides. "Let's go through the pockets again."

"*Padlock*," Kim announced with a flourish, pouring more drinks for the others. He was obviously having a good time.

"Not a padlock, my friend," Will said, taking his drink as Kim finished pouring it. He took a sip and wiped the foam from his upper lip. "*Combination* lock."

Kim waved a hand impatiently. "Fine, combination lock—but it was *closed.* So what's it mean?"

"School locker," Catherine said.

"No," Gaia said, sipping beer. "Then it would be *on* the locker, not in his pocket."

"Fine. So what's your theory?"

Gaia smiled. "Bicycle chain."

The others looked at each other, nodding. "Okay," Catherine said. "Score one for you. *If* there's a bicycle; we can check." Catherine had a very nice buzz on from the beer—she felt pleasantly light-headed and very comfortable in her surroundings. "Next: *pill bottle.*"

"Ampicillin," Will said. "It's a low-grade antibiotic, by prescription only."

"How do you know that?" Kim demanded.

"I looked it up on the Web when we got back," Will said. "While you were busy changing into your fancy threads. What we don't know is *why* he was taking it. It could be anything: an infected wisdom tooth, strep throat."

"We'll need to get his medical records," Kim pointed out.

"Next: Wario Land 4," Gaia said, in bewilderment. "Anyone know games?"

"I do," Catherine said, raising her hand. "I'm the geek; you all need to remember that."

"And?" Will raised his eyebrows pleasantly.

The place hadn't quieted down at all—their ears would be ringing in the morning, Catherine realized. She happened to look over at the door right then and saw a small crowd of men arrive all together. They were all in their thirties, and they all had severe brush cuts. As she watched, they made their way over to the bar and loudly greeted and cheered Jack the bartender, yelling and grunting as they clasped his hands and reached over the bar to slap him on the back.

"Nothing I can think of," Catherine admitted, returning her attention to Will's question. "It's a garden variety GameBoy cartridge. I've played it: it's a simple nine-level shooter game. Nothing special. I honestly can't think of any connection."

"Is the word *saved* in the game?" Gaia asked, sipping her beer.

"No," Catherine said, after thinking about it a moment. "There's *save game,* but every GameBoy cartridge has that."

"Well, Ms. Moore?" Will said, filling Gaia's glass. "We need your remarkable intellect. Can't you help us out with some Stanford University insights?"

Gaia affected a classic southern belle accent. "Why, I rightly don't know, Mr. Taylor. Can't you grace us with some simple southern wisdom?"

Will raised his eyebrows. He was crossing his arms, Catherine saw, in a way that he probably knew showed off his heavy forearm muscles. "I just might *do* that, Ms.—"

"Well, what do you think of that," a male voice called out from the bar. "Two young hotties wasting their time drinking with faggots."

Catherine looked over. It was one of bartender Jack's friends—a man in a leather vest with a mustache and a shaved head. He had a U.S. Marines pin on his vest. The crowd in the bar seemed intent on not paying attention. A few people glanced over, but when Jack or his other friends returned their stares, the patrons turned quickly away, apparently intent on minding their own business.

"I see it, too," another of Jack's friends agreed sadly. He was tall and red faced, wearing a denim jacket over a flannel shirt and a wide-brimmed cowboy hat. He was staring at Gaia, his eyes roving up and down her body. "Shame is what it is—here's a girl looks prettier than Britney Spears, and she's wasting time with a boy wouldn't know what to do with her if his life depended on it."

Gaia didn't move or turn. She didn't seem to react at all, Catherine saw—she just slowly put her glass down.

"And that other one ain't nothing to sneeze at," the first man said, and now Catherine had that ants-crawling-on-me feeling that she always got when a man was blatantly eyeing her body. "Like the song says, 'brown-eyed girl'."

Brilliant observation, Catherine thought, keeping her mouth shut.

"Ignore them," Will said quietly. "We don't want to make a scene."

"Right," Catherine agreed, nodding. "No scenes."

"I guess the faggots can't hear me," the first man said—the

one in the leather vest. He began walking toward their table. It was obvious from his gait that he was drunk. "Or the girls neither. Hey, I'm talking to you, Britney! You want to dance with a man who knows he's supposed to kiss girls, not boys?"

Now more people were watching what was going on. Heads were turning around the bar.

"Hey, Walter," Kelly Ray said, stepping out of the crowd. She was more than a head shorter than the ex-marine in the leather vest, but she strode right up to him. "Walter, come on, pal. Let me buy you a drink."

"Oh, I ain't your pal, Kelly," Walter sneered. He was weaving in place. Catherine could see Gaia's eyes narrowing as she sat there, but she figured it was just the beer her roommate was reacting to—or maybe she didn't like being compared to Britney Spears. "I ain't your pal at all. Now, your old man, *there* was a pal—someone worthy of putting his name on the door of this place. But not you."

"Fine, but what do you say you let the customers be," Kelly said more firmly, reaching for Walter's muscular arm. "Come on, Walter—let me get you a Coke or something."

"You get your hands off me, you little whore," Walter said, shoving Kelly away. The young woman stumbled backward, nearly falling over as she collided with the edge of a table. "Don't *ever* touch me again."

Gaia stood up.

All eyes were on her as she slowly turned around and faced Walter. On the side, Kelly was still getting her balance, leaning on the table as she righted herself. Gaia stood absolutely straight, Catherine saw, balanced on both her feet. It was particularly impressive since Catherine *knew* how many beers Gaia had had.

"Well, now," Walter said, grinning broadly at Gaia. "You change your mind, missy? You want to dance with me?"

"Yeah," Gaia said quietly, stepping forward. "Let's dance."

What happened next was so rapid, so blindingly quick that Catherine barely registered what she'd seen until moments after it was over. The noise hit her first: like Will, Kim, and the rest of the customers in Johnny Ray's. She recoiled instinctively. But the funny thing was, she *did* see it—maybe her tipsiness had something to do with it, but through the blur of beer and surprise she found that she could play it back in her mind, move for move, and recall everything that had happened.

Walter stepped toward Gaia with his hand moving toward her waist as if to make good on his promise to dance with her, and Gaia just reached out like it was the simplest thing in the world and took his hand and flipped him on his back. There was a tremendous cracking noise as Walter landed on the floorboards, his eyes wide, and then he *howled* like a dog—the pain made his face turn scarlet like a baby's. The whole room gasped right then—Catherine realized that she'd heard that sound, too, right before she heard the squeak of Kim and Will's chairs on the floor as the two men stood up, lightning quick. Walter's friends were moving in on Gaia, and Jack was hoisting himself over the bar, and Catherine had a moment of fear as the man in the cowboy hat swung his fist, and then Gaia did something so amazing that Catherine thought at first she'd imagined it—she somehow ducked her head under the roundhouse blow, blond hair flying in the amber bar lights, and then threw herself up into the air so that her leg was spinning like a helicopter blade, smashing into the side of the cowboy-hat-wearing man's head. There was another loud, wet smacking sound and then he, too, dropped to the ground with a dull thump.

She kicked him in the head, Catherine thought dazedly, rising to her feet and realizing in that moment just how tipsy she was. *She kicked him in the head and landed in a perfect fighting stance.*

That was exactly what Gaia had done. Kim and Will were arriving behind her, but they needn't have bothered: Gaia launched herself back into the air gracefully, kicking with her other leg and knocking down both Jack and the third of Jack's friends, a sunglasses-wearing obese man whom Catherine hadn't even noticed. The lights were swimming in Catherine's eyes. *I'm drunk,* she thought. *I'm drunk, so Gaia must be, too—how is she* doing *this?*

Sirens were blaring outside the bar—at least Catherine thought so. She wasn't sure. Gaia had dropped back to the floor and was reaching down and grabbing the lapels of Walter's leather vest. Walter's head lolled, blood running freely from his nose and mouth. The entire population of the bar was on their feet, watching in disbelief—it had all happened so *fast.*

"Don't you *ever* touch her again!" Gaia yelled in Walter's face, shaking his weakened frame. "Do you hear me?"

"Uhhh—" Walter moaned.

There was suddenly a loud bang as the leather-covered front door opened and a blast of cool night air as three police officers strode into the room. "All right, stop! Stop this *right now!*" the lead cop yelled. He wore a beige short-sleeve police shirt and a wide-brimmed hat. "Young lady, let go of that man!"

Gaia lowered Walter to the floor. The music had stopped. Someone turned the overhead fluorescent lights on—everyone stood blinking in the glare. The entire crowd watched silently. The only sound was Walter and the other men whimpering, Gaia panting for breath, and the squawks of the police radios.

"Now, what's this all about?" the lead cop yelled out. "I'm waiting."

"They started it!" Jack yelled from where he lay sprawled on the floor. He was holding his hand to his bloody nose and pointing murderously at Gaia, Will, Kim, and Catherine. "Goddamned government trainees or whatever they are, coming into our town and causing trouble. *Look* at them, Gus," he yelled at the cop insistently. One of the other men in the bar was helping him to his feet. "Damn uppity feds; they started it."

"That's a lie," Kelly said. "Gus, you know better than to listen to Jack," she told the cop, striding right up to him with her hands on her hips. "His damn goon squad came in here plastered and looking for trouble. They harassed these four for no reason at all."

Gus, the cop, looked back and forth between Kelly and Jack. Everyone waited. The cop radio on Gus's belt squawked again.

"Jack," Gus said finally, "now, you go on home and cool yourself down."

"Gus—"

146

"Get on out of here before I change my mind and take you all down to the station house," Gus insisted tersely. "I mean it."

"One more false move," Kelly told Jack as his friends helped him toward the door, "and you're out on your ear. I don't care what promises my father made."

Jack was still nursing his bleeding nose. He raised a finger toward Kelly and opened his mouth.

"Don't," Kelly said quickly.

Jack turned away. He and Walter and the others limped toward the door—the crowd shuffled apart, letting them go by. The witch's ball in the ceiling kept glittering, as if the dancing was still going on. Gaia had moved gingerly back to their table and was carefully sitting down.

"All right, folks, the show's over," Gus the cop said loudly. The cool night air was still blowing in through the open door. They all heard a squeal of brakes as Jack's red pickup truck sped away. "Kelly, I think you'd better close down for the night, don't you? It's late enough."

Kelly sighed heavily. She shook her head. "You're killing me, Gus. But you're probably right."

"You know I am."

"All right, people," Kelly said, turning to face the bar's patrons. "You heard the man. Let's move it on out—you don't have to go home, but you can't stay here."

The crowd started shuffling toward the door—and suddenly everyone was talking at once.

"Gaia?" Catherine said, looking over at where Gaia was sitting. "Are you all right?"

"Blacking out," Gaia murmured distractedly. Her eyes looked dull and unfocused. "I'm blacking out—"

And Gaia slid forward out of her chair and onto the floor, unconscious—they all heard the thump as her head smacked against the hard wooden floor.

Will

That was a first. I've never seen *anyone* fight like that, let alone a girl.

Let alone a *pretty* girl.

Okay, I'm admitting it—she's extremely cute.

Dealing with girls isn't so hard. Particularly pretty girls, because they're so predictable. They pretend otherwise, but the main thing on their mind at any given moment is how they look. Take it from me—I've been out on enough dates with them. And the prettier a girl is, the more "natural" and "carefree" she's acting, the more it's all a fraud. The reflections are what give it away. Most people hate mirrors, but pretty girls are *addicted* to them. They're always admiring how they look in whatever cute outfit they've put together.

I learned that one long ago, before I even went away to college. After enough time with southern debutantes, the lesson sticks. I can still see all those shiny dresses and corsages and purses and pearl necklaces. It's like some kind of lesson in reflexes: compliment their looks and they go all giggly and stop thinking. No, thanks.

What I'm dealing with here, on the other hand, is clearly an alien life-form. From the first time I really saw her, moving over those ropes, my eyes were bugging out of their sockets. Gaia moves like a gazelle—like a cheetah. I've never seen anything like it in my life, and I've spent a lot of time among track stars.

Female athletes—the real thing, like Olympic athletes—are much more technically proficient. It was very hard for me to face the fact that I'd never reach that level of physical mastery, no matter how devoted to athletics I've been. That's the equivalent of being a violin prodigy who's playing Chopin concertos in Carnegie Hall at the age of eight.

No, Gaia's not like that, and neither am I. But what Gaia has—and I really don't think she realizes it—is poetry. Gaia's not like a virtuoso violinist. She's more like the best jazz trumpet player you ever heard, the one who never learned to read music but can make you weep with joy when you hear them play a solo.

I still can't get over that *kick*. I don't think Gaia even realized what she did, how technically difficult it would be to reproduce that flying roundhouse kick. But she did it without thinking. She's that rare thing—a true natural athlete.

I keep thinking about watching her fight. And it *was* amazing . . . but I'm shying away from the real point.

The real point is that I'm confused. I'm not saying I like her or anything. There's no reason to think she's a girl I'd want to pursue romantically or anything like that. For one thing, it wouldn't be professional . . . and for another . . .

I don't remember what the other thing is.

I'm *not* interested. That's not my point. I'm just confused. Because like I said, here's an alien life-form—like a perfect fighting machine. Except that she's trapped in the body of a debutante.

It's an interesting phenomenon. I wonder what her life's been like? What was she like as a little girl or in high school? Did the other kids hate her? Were they scared of her? I'd love to find out what it was like. I'm sure her life has been anything but boring.

But I can't let that any of this distract me. We're FBI trainees, and we have to push as hard as we can to succeed. It's driving me nuts, the way she keeps *winning*—the way she keeps coming out on top. And then she just tosses off a casual, bratty remark and keeps going. It's really maddening. I sincerely wish she wasn't here at Quantico, on my trainee team. It's just a headache I don't need.

She really was something to behold, though. I could watch her do that all day—although I'll never admit that to anyone.

But I'm not here to watch anyone else. I'm here to make my mark on the bureau, and I'm not about to let some girl get in the way.

"Gaia?" a soft male voice said. "Gaia? Can you hear me?" The voice was right there—less than two feet away. And she thought she recognized it.

Hello—?

It was someone she could trust—she felt that, without really knowing who it was. But something about the voice finally jogged her memory.

Quantico, I'm in Quantico, Virginia.

The FBI. I'm training with the FBI. This isn't a dream at all.

Gaia experimentally began to open her eyes—just the narrowest of slits so she could barely peer out from between her eyelashes—and wanted to scream at the harshness of the light that shone above her. It was as if the sun itself was right there, suspended above her. She quickly shut them again. Her head was singing with pain. And it was spinning.

"Gaia?" the soft voice repeated. Gaia could feel cool hands on her forehead, brushing her hair back from her warm skin. "Relax—just relax. Shhh. Everything's fine."

"Light," Gaia croaked. "Too bright."

"What? Oh, the *light*. Hang on—"

There was a clicking sound, and then the most incredible, wonderful thing happened: the light was gone. Now there was just soothing darkness and the distant wind and the sound of crickets.

"How do you feel now?" the voice went on. The hands kept stroking her forehead.

"Head hurts," she murmured.

"Hang on," the male voice said, and now there was something soft and cool sliding beneath her head. It felt good. And she was sure she could figure out who the voice was—if she could just concentrate. She felt so weird, so dizzy and weak.

Gaia finally got her eyes open. She could dimly make out a cracked, painted ceiling overhead. She was in a small room, and a dark male silhouette was looming over her. There was a trace of an aroma that she recognized . . . some kind of aftershave.

"Hey," the man said, with just a trace of a southern accent. "Still with us?"

". . . Will?"

"Yeah."

Gaia moved to sit up. It was a mistake to move so fast—her head began spinning, and for a second she thought she would black out again.

"Take it easy," Will warned. "You've got a huge lump on your head."

"I'm fine," Gaia said. She was trying to sit up, but Will was in the way. She couldn't move her feet onto the floor. "Watch out," she told him impatiently.

"All right," Will said agreeably. His shadow moved farther away, which was what she wanted. "Just take it easy. You've had a few too many."

That's not it, Gaia thought hopelessly. It was all coming back to her. *I've been fighting. And I did my thing—I fainted.*

It was a real setback. Had she really believed she was over this? That was a laugh. Recovering after gymnastics was different. Fighting, apparently, was another story altogether. It had been so *long* . . . when was her last fight, anyway? Her last *real* fight? Years ago?

It's the adrenaline, she thought. *Fighting is different from anything else. And I'd better remember that, too.*

The room was coming into focus. It was small, with wooden floorboards that creaked as Will moved around and ghostly, gray shapes on either side that had to be windows.

"Where are we?" Gaia asked.

"Kelly's house," Will told her. He was still nearly whispering. "You remember Kelly Ray? From the bar where you—"

"Yeah." Gaia remembered. She was sitting up, gingerly rubbing her head. She still felt dizzy, and the room was spinning still as if she hadn't completely sobered up.

How many beers did I have? she wondered. *Was it really two pitchers for four of us? Jesus.*

"Where is everybody?"

"They're here." Will's shadow gestured toward the glowing edge of a door, which was the only source of light in the room.

"Okay." Gaia stood up gingerly. She was wobbly, but she could walk. Will immediately vaulted over to take her arm. She quickly pulled away. "I'm fine," she said. "I'm not some fragile southern belle, Will."

"I noticed."

Gaia had made it over to the door—she was squinting, wincing in advance as she pulled it open, but the blinding light still made her eyes water. Through the glare she could make out a small kitchen. There was a ticking Westclox wall clock hanging over the sink. Kelly was standing at the stove, where a silver kettle was billowing steam.

"Good morning, star shine," Kelly said pleasantly. She spoke in a hushed tone. Her smile seemed genuine. "Sit down, sit down. We need to whisper. My Jasmine's asleep upstairs."

"Okay." Gaia sat down at one of the wooden kitchen chairs, leaning her elbows on the oilcloth that covered the table. "Thanks for bringing me here," she said.

Kelly frowned. "That's the least I can do after what you did," she said appreciatively. "You knocked down *all* of Jack's goons. I still can't believe it."

"He shoved you," Gaia said, wincing at the pain in her head. "It was nothing personal."

The kettle was whistling. Kelly turned off the burner and poured water into a mug. An unfamiliar, spicy fragrance filled the kitchen.

"This is my patented hangover remedy," Kelly explained. "Anytime I have a blackout in my place, I whip up one of these. Does the trick."

"But I didn't—" Gaia stopped. She *had* blacked out, but how could she explain? She couldn't explain. *Fine,* she thought, accepting the steaming mug that Kelly put down in front of her. "Thanks," she said. "Really, thank you. You're being very nice."

"No nicer than Sir Lancelot here," Kelly said, smiling as she pulled her honey brown hair back behind her head, snapping a rubber band around it. Her face was damp from the steam, Gaia saw. "How long have you been seeing each other?"

"What—" Gaia nearly dropped the mug. "We're not—"

"We're just friends," Will said quickly. "I mean, not friends. *Colleagues.* We work together—we're training together at the base. You know."

155

"Colleagues," Gaia repeated. The steam was making her flush, she realized. "We all are, the four of us."

"Okay," Kelly said hesitantly. She was looking back and forth between them.

"Kim and Cathy are out on the porch," Will told Gaia, quickly moving toward the kitchen's narrow door. "I'll be right back—I want to tell them you're awake."

They could hear Will's footsteps moving through the house and then a screen door creaking open and closed. Kelly moved behind Gaia, who jumped when she felt a cold ice pack touching the bump on the back of her head.

"Kelly, you don't have to—"

"Shhh. I don't mind," Kelly said. "Relax. You're a jumpy one, Gaia."

That's true—I am. She forced herself to relax. Surprisingly, it wasn't hard. It was nice having Kelly "mothering" her—even though, Gaia realized, she could only be a few years older chronologically. "That feels nice."

"Good."

"There's something I don't understand, Kelly," Gaia said, sipping the "blackout remedy." It tasted like herbal tea, but it seemed to have some kind of broth in it, too. Whatever it was, it was doing the trick. She felt better already.

"What's that?"

"Well—I mean, forgive the question, but . . . what's the deal with that guy Jack, anyway? Why do you keep him around?"

"Because of Dad," Kelly explained. Her hands kept moving the ice pack against Gaia's head. "See, they were good

156

friends. Dad knew Jack couldn't make it on his own—he's got problems. He's angry, and he drinks. But they were close, so at the end, when Dad was sick, he made me promise to keep him on."

"Oh." Gaia thought about it. "But he must hate it. I mean, he's a homophobe to begin with—how can he stand being at that place every Tuesday night?"

"Don't even tell me," Kelly agreed. "It's awful. He's also a . . . what do you call it when you hate women?"

"A misogynist."

"Yeah. One of those. It just gets worse and worse—and I *hate* those damn army buddies of his. I wish I could just fire him."

"But you could," Gaia said.

"Maybe *you* could," Kelly replied. She was looking away through the torn screen in the kitchen window. "I don't know. Maybe it's possible—maybe I could be strong, like you were tonight. Honestly, that's what I was thinking, watching you kick their butts like that. I'm so glad someone finally stood up to them. Maybe I *could* do it."

"You probably could," Gaia agreed. "But be careful. He's dangerous. I'll bet all those men are."

"I'd have to talk to Gus," Kelly said. "Gus is the constable. I'd have to tell him to keep an eye on things—make sure I'm all right. Just in case Jack got angry."

The kitchen was cooling off as the night wind moved through the house. "You're sure that man's not your boyfriend? The good-looking one?" Kelly said, smiling. "Because you sure do fight like a couple. I was watching you at the bar."

"We're just friends. I mean, um—"

"Colleagues."

"Right." Gaia could hear the floorboards creaking again. "Colleagues."

"Hey," Kim whispered, poking his head through the kitchen doorway. "You all right?"

"Yeah." Gaia smiled at him. "Yeah, I'm fine, Kim. Thanks."

"We should go," Kim said. "Catherine's anxious to get moving. We've got to make curfew."

"Okay." Gaia stood up. She felt much stronger now. "Thanks, Kelly," she said.

"Anytime, Gaia," Kelly said, squeezing Gaia's arm.

"Best 'gay night' I've ever seen," Kim said, waving at Kelly. They both laughed.

Then Kim and Gaia were moving through the dark corridor toward the screen door that led to the porch. Gaia could hear a car engine starting, and she saw the headlights of Catherine's Altima flare up, shining in through the screen door and casting its crazy graph-paper shadows on the wall.

"Tomorrow morning," Kim said quietly, "when the game starts, we've got to move fast."

"Right."

"Remember, Cathy *just* got that phone call when the game froze. So the *instant* that bell rings, we want to be moving—we want to be on our way to the scene of the second murder."

"Right," Gaia whispered. "Right."

they just see the blood and they come unglued

ALL BEING WATCHED

"Now hear this—now hear this."

Sergeant Conroy's voice. Catherine recognized it instantly from two days before. It was unmistakable; he must have learned that commanding tone for addressing subordinates somewhere in the armed forces. Its effect was immediate: she was wide awake.

"Please report to Administration Wing A and await instructions," the sergeant barked out. Catherine's eyes were still shut, but she could feel the searing morning sunlight coming in through the dorm room window. She had a headache: nothing spectacular, but it was definitely going to slow her down.

"Now hear this," Conroy continued over the loudspeaker. There had to be speakers in every corridor all through the FBI trainee dorm floors. With her eyes still shut, Catherine could hear the sergeant's rough voice echoing down the cement corridors. *"Now hear this. The following trainees will report to Administration Wing A immediately and await instructions."*

What are they throwing at us now? Catherine thought, forcing her eyes open and sitting up. The room was spinning just a bit. In the opposite bed Gaia was sitting up, too, her hair twisted crazily around her squinting face like a wild blond tumbleweed.

"Roll call?" Gaia groaned. "That's a new one."

Catherine looked at her watch. Six ten A.M. *Give me a break,* she thought resignedly. The game wasn't supposed to restart for three hours. *Can't we get some rest?*

"Lau, Kim," Sergeant Conroy recited.

"Are they going to make us listen to every name?" Catherine complained. She stood up, leaning on the bed's white steel frame. "That's no fair. You want the first shower?"

"Moore, Gaia. Sanders, Catherine. Taylor, Will."

"They must be going by team," Gaia said. She had stood up, too, stretching and brushing her wild hair back from her face. "I don't think we've got time to shower."

"Repeat, repeat," the relentless drill sergeant continued. *"Trainees Lau, Moore, Sanders, Taylor report immediately to Administration Wing A and await further instructions."*

Oh my God, Catherine thought. Suddenly she was wide awake—a bolt of fear shot through her. It was like someone had thrown a glass of ice water in her face. She and Gaia looked at each other.

"It's just us," Catherine said. "Uh-oh."

"Come on." Gaia had snapped into action, yanking open her bottom dresser drawer with a screech of wood and pulling out a folded pair of jeans. "Let's go—we have to get over there." She quickly dressed and tied her shoes. "Ready?"

No, Catherine thought. *Not even slightly.*

"Yeah, I guess," she told Gaia. She only hoped she looked better than her roommate—Gaia's eyes were rimmed with red, her hair was still tangled, and her face was pale. There was a red band across her face from the wrinkled bedsheets.

"You look awful, girl."

"I'm not the only one." Gaia smiled weakly as she scooped her keys off the dresser. "Let's go."

The Quantico campus was still shrouded in morning mist. At 6 A.M., the sun had barely crept over the horizon, and the sky was a weak, pale color. Groundsmen were out, mowing the grass between the buildings, and in the far distance a clump of male and female trainees were jogging along the dirt path. The air was filled with birdsong.

"Where's Admin A?" Catherine asked Gaia. They were shivering in the morning air as they walked out of the dorm building. It was amazing the way that pure fear worked as a hangover cure.

"I don't know," Gaia said. A glass door opened behind them with its unmistakable *kerchunk* sound, and Will and Kim came out to join them. They looked as bad as Catherine felt. Nobody said anything.

"Admin A's over there," Kim said, pointing. The others followed mutely. Up in the dorm building's windows, faces looked out at them.

Enjoy the show, Catherine thought despairingly. Their third day of training, and they were being hauled in for a reprimand in front of all their fellow trainees. A great way to start a career in the FBI.

"Lau, Moore, Sanders, and Taylor reporting as ordered," Will told the guard in the Admin A lobby. He was a severe-looking young man with a brush cut in a marine uniform; he nodded and gestured them toward a nearby elevator.

"Top floor," the marine told them. "Turn left and follow the signs until you get to Special Agent Malloy's office."

Catherine's heart sank. *Malloy—the man himself.* It didn't seem like this could get any more awful, but the day was young.

The elevator door closed and the four of them stood in its harsh fluorescent light. Waiting. "Anyone know what this is about?" Will asked quietly.

"You mean, are we in trouble?" Gaia stared straight ahead. "No. We have to assume we're all being watched—whatever we did wrong, they saw it."

Ding! The elevator doors opened. They were in a wide, featureless, carpeted corridor. Catherine felt like she'd been sent to the principal's office—which had happened to her at least once during her stormy high school career—but the feeling was ten times as bad.

Malloy, Brian, A71, the nameplate on the door read. Will took a deep breath and then rapped his knuckles on the black metal surface.

"Come," Malloy's voice barked out. Will opened the door, gesturing to the others ahead. *Always the gentleman,* Catherine thought bitterly, remembering Will cheerfully refilling their beer glasses over and over again the night before. *Good for you.*

The office wasn't as big as Catherine expected. It seemed very utilitarian. There was a fairly advanced-looking Dell workstation, she saw, with its screen displaying some kind of proprietary windowing system. There were diplomas and badges on the wall and a few pictures of Malloy standing stiffly with several public figures: Robert Mueller, John Ashcroft, Rudolph Giuliani.

The man himself sat behind a bare oak desk, his hands clasped in front of him, reading from a thick sheaf of papers, dressed in his regulation charcoal gray suit. Catherine couldn't have felt more intimidated. She had *imagined* this office—fantasized about being called in here to meet with the boss, perhaps even with her team. But not like this. Now she wished she could be anywhere else.

With a pang of despair, Catherine could just make out a Quantico Police Department shield imprinted on the pages Malloy was reading. The four of them glanced nervously at each other and then lined up, facing the desk.

Malloy finally looked up. He stared fixedly at each of them in turn. The distaste on his face was impossible to miss. Up close, he looked even more weather hardened and severe, like a man who had returned from a polar expedition or an Everest climb. He looked *tough*—there was no other way to put it.

"I have here a police report," Malloy began, "from Sheriff Gus Parker at Quantico Central Precinct. It's a required formality—he has to submit a report to me personally in the case of an incident like this. Needless to say, it hasn't happened very often. We try to keep our relations with the town and the local police as stress-free as possible."

This is bad, Catherine thought desperately. For the first time it occurred to her that they might be expelled from the program. She stared straight ahead and tried to return Malloy's steel-hard stare whenever it rested on her.

"I also have eyewitness reports from agents Reno and Segretti, who were in this 'Johnny Ray's' last night. Dancing, in case any of you were wondering where we'd put them. I won't insult your intelligence by reminding you of what you know very well, which is the fact that the FBI is observing your conduct at all times. It's a fact that you've been explicitly reminded of on more than one occasion."

Malloy leaned back in his chair. He looked extraordinarily angry, as if it was only by force of will that he was maintaining a civil tone.

"As I'm sure you can understand, this is precisely the sort of incident that we take the greatest pains to avoid. The conduct of FBI personnel and trainees, both on and off the campus, is a matter of grave importance—not just for the legal and physical safety of all concerned, but also because of the trust our society will soon be placing in you to act as unswerving upholders and defenders of the law. It's a responsibility that I carry all the way to Washington. Do you understand?"

"Yes, sir," they all said in unison.

"The Field Behavior Directives lay out specific rules governing precisely this sort of incident, in which agents or trainees feel that civilians' safety is in jeopardy—rules that you saw fit to utterly disregard last night," Malloy continued in his harsh voice. "Ordinarily an incident like this is grounds for immediate dismissal."

Ordinarily, Catherine thought. A ray of hope had burst into view. She furiously tried to keep her expression from changing. *He said "ordinarily." That means not every time. It means not this time—you're getting a break.*

"However, there are mitigating circumstances I've got to consider. First, the establishment in question"—Malloy was flipping pages, and from her vantage point Catherine could see that he even had photographs of Johnny Ray's—"has become increasingly problematic for several reasons. According to Gus Parker, who is a very competent police officer, the place is something of a powder keg, especially on Tuesday nights." He was looking right at Kim now. "Issues of prejudice and intolerance can be deeply entrenched in small rural communities, as I'm sure you're aware, and any kind of 'pride' event can have the unintended effect of polarizing a community. So emotions can easily become overheated, and provocative situations are correspondingly difficult to avoid."

"Yes, sir," Kim said. Catherine didn't look, but Kim sounded almost surprised—as if he hadn't expected that kind of perception or sensitivity on Malloy's part.

"The other mitigating circumstance," Malloy said, and now he was glaring straight at Gaia, "is Sheriff Parker's report, which makes quite clear that responsibility for what happened is not evenly borne. For that reason I've decided to dispense with standard procedures and forgo any punishment for trainees Lau, Sanders, and Taylor. There will be no notation in your permanent records and no official reprimand."

Thank you, Catherine thought in a rush. *Oh my God, thank you—I'll never do anything wrong again, I promise.*

But then in the next second she thought, *What's he going to do to Gaia?*

Catherine's thoughts moved so quickly that she was immediately picturing another roommate moving in and another trainee joining their team. And she realized, with a kind of surprise, how much she didn't want that to happen.

"But I want the three of you to remember what I've told you," Malloy rasped. The morning sunlight out his window had grown stronger; it shone in his graying hair. "You've done a good job with our fictional sheriff; let's hope you don't have any more problems with the real one. Dismissed."

"Yes, sir. Thank you, sir."

Will, Kim, and Catherine turned away, moving toward the office door. Malloy didn't move—he was clearly waiting for them to leave. Catherine had one glimpse of Gaia, in her rumpled jeans and the T-shirt she'd slept in, standing at attention before Malloy's desk, before Kim pulled the door shut.

The three of them looked at each other. None of them were smiling. Kim pointed down the corridor, and they got the idea—*Let's get out of earshot.*

"Will he do it?" Will said. He sounded worried, more worried than Catherine would have expected. All traces of his southern brashness were gone. "Will he throw her out?"

"I don't think so," Kim said. "I wasn't getting that feeling."

Catherine and Will nodded. Kim's "feelings" were amazingly accurate—they had learned that much already.

"You could be wrong, though," Catherine said, turning and facing him. "I mean, you don't know for sure."

"Something's going on between them," Kim said quietly. He rubbed his eyes, exhaling with obvious fatigue and stress. "Malloy and Gaia. Some kind of battle or test. I don't understand it."

Will and Catherine looked at each other.

"Would you weigh the odds in Gaia's favor?" Will asked.

But Kim just turned his eyes down to the floor.

If Gaia were capable of being frightened, this would have been an appropriate moment.

Neither she nor Special Agent Malloy had moved since the others had filed out. Gaia had stayed staring straight ahead as she heard the door close and the receding footsteps of her partners. She strained to hear if they were saying anything, but of course she couldn't—those three would wait until they were out of earshot.

The office was quiet except for the hum of the air-conditioning. The sky was gray out the window—it was the beginning of an overcast day. Gaia wanted to move—she wanted to adjust her pants where they were itching her; she wanted to rub her eyes; she wanted to nurse the bump on the back of her head, which was no longer aching but was now itching relentlessly.

Malloy pinched the bridge of his nose. He looked back at her, drumming his fingers on the table.

Go ahead, Gaia wanted to say. *If you're going to throw me out, then* do *it. Put me on a plane back to California or somewhere else.* She could go to Ohio and get her brother off that farm and then find a place of her own somewhere. She could even imagine her own small house, her own kitchen, her own hangover remedy.

"Once again my day is long," Malloy began. He was gazing sadly at Gaia. "I don't want to waste a lot of time on back-and-forth with you. I'm sure you know what I'm thinking."

"Yes."

Malloy squinted at her quizzically. "Since you know what I'm thinking, let me ask you this. What would you do if you were in my shoes? If you were the one seated behind this desk"—he tapped the thick police file in front of him—"and you'd just received this?"

Gaia stared back at him.

"I would expel the trainee."

Malloy raised his eyebrows. "Why?"

Gaia had given what she thought was a truthful answer. There was no room for games here. As soon as she'd spoken, she knew she believed it. There was no escaping the logic. And if Malloy did something else, it wouldn't be due to any argument she could win or point she could make. She had to face reality.

"You've expelled three trainees since we started. One for not being fast enough on the obstacle course. Two yesterday because they couldn't handle the game. They were nauseated by the pictures, so you kicked them out."

"Go on."

"So you have to expel me, if only to be fair. Those trainees didn't get a second chance, so why should I?"

Malloy was nodding, looking down at his desk. "That's reasonable. But it shows how little you understand, Gaia. See, frankly, that's why someone like you is *not* in my shoes. Because this job demands a certain kind of thinking."

Gaia stared back at him. She had no idea where he was going with this.

"Mark Perkins came in last on the obstacle course, so I threw him out," Malloy went on. "But you understand, Gaia—

he was trying as hard as he could. He's just not very strong. His muscles are slack; he's an ex-smoker; he's not very coordinated. I took a chance on him because he's a mathematical prodigy. He can compute crime statistics in his head faster than you or I could type them into a calculator. He'd be an incredible asset to any task force if he learned how to move. If he trains his body hard for two years or more he's welcome to return.

"Squeamishness, on the other hand—that's something you can't change. Did you know that 40 percent of medical students quit in the first year? It's the surgery training. They simply can't deal with it. It doesn't matter how much they want to be doctors. They just see the blood and come unglued. There's nothing to be done about it—it can be quite heartbreaking. Chen and Vasquez discovered this yesterday about themselves in the Hogan's Alley morgue.

"But *you*"—Malloy leaned forward and gazed directly at Gaia—"are a different situation entirely. We both know that there's nothing in this program you can't do. You're strong enough; you're smart enough; you're obviously brave and disciplined enough. You've already had experiences that most agents don't go through until they've been in the field for years. All this I know because Agent Bishop made it quite clear to me when we met in California three weeks ago.

"With you, I'm dealing with a failure of nerve, a failure of willpower."

Gaia stared back at him. The wound on her head was forgotten. She was listening to every word the man said. She had never imagined that Special Agent Brian Malloy would or could talk like this.

"See, those three others are trapped; they can't change. Maybe I'll see Perkins in two years if he remakes himself completely, but right now there's nothing he can do. Those other two are goners. They'll have to find other lines of work; they have no choice. But you—Gaia, you're a different story entirely. Because for you Quantico isn't a physical test or a mental test at all. It's a test of *character*.

"And that's why you don't get thrown out this time," Malloy concluded. He was closing the dossiers in front of him on the desk and putting them away. "That's why you get another chance. *One* more chance." He raised an index finger. "And if you had my job, you'd see the logic. Because you *can* change. Maybe you didn't understand this before, but you have a chance to understand it now. Either Jenny Bishop is right about you or she's wrong. Do you understand?"

"I think so."

"Either you're going to grow up," Malloy said, "or you're not. I don't know. But let's get one thing straight: you've disappointed me severely, and you let me and Agent Bishop down. And I'm holding you responsible, unlike Perkins and the others, because you had the *choice*—you didn't *have* to do what you did. So, if you make one more mistake, just one, you are out the door for good. You will have proven that you don't understand, that you don't care, and that you won't grow up. Then Perkins will have more of a chance than you. Do you understand?"

"Yes." Gaia straightened her posture, looking back at Malloy. His eyes, for the first time, reminded her of some of the CIA personnel she'd met through her father.

"Dismissed," Malloy said.

"Yes, sir," Gaia said clearly. And then, deliberately, she added, "Thank you, sir."

Malloy understood. He seemed to pick up that she was saying more than just the routine *thank-you* that FBI subordinates said without thinking.

Malloy nodded.

Gaia turned and left the office. It took her a few steps to get to the door, and the whole time it was like her head was spinning. Nobody had ever spoken to her the way Malloy just had. She found herself thinking through every word of what he'd said over and over as she pushed her way through the glass doors and out into the humid, overcast sunlight in the courtyard.

Catherine, Kim, and Will were waiting just outside the administration building doors, leaning on the building's granite wall. The moment they saw her, they sprang forward, hurrying over, all talking at once.

"What happened?" Catherine asked.

"What did he do?" Will wanted to know. "What was the verdict?"

Gaia looked back and forth at them, as if she were seeing them for the first time.

They care about me, she realized suddenly. It was the simplest thought in the world—one that, she imagined, people thought every day without even noticing. But for Gaia it was a revelation. *They're not just co-trainees or partners. They're friends. This isn't about the game. They genuinely care what happens to me.*

"Come on, you're killing us," Catherine said impatiently,

tugging on Gaia's T-shirt. "Are you out or in?"

"I'm in," Gaia told them. "I'm still in."

Will grinned at her. Catherine leaped to hug her spontaneously—it was awkward, neither of them knowing how to handle it, and she pulled back quickly.

"So what did he say?" Will wanted to know. "Did he tan your hide but good?"

Gaia shook her head. She was looking at her watch. "We don't have time to talk about this. The game unfreezes in ninety minutes; we have to get ready."

"Right," Kim said.

"We'll take showers and regroup in fifteen; we can go over our notes and refresh our memories of the facts we know. At o-nine hundred we want to be across the road, ready to *run* to that crime scene the moment the bell goes off. Right?"

"Right," Catherine said. Will was nodding.

"Good." Gaia nodded back at her teammates. "Then let's win this game."

CLEVER ANSWER

Five minutes later Gaia and Catherine were re-entering their dorm room and Gaia was looking at the unmade bed that she'd been sleeping in, seemingly, just a few moments before. *It's probably still warm,* she thought dismally. *God, I'd love to climb back in there. . . .*

"You want to take the first shower?" Catherine said. "You look like you need it."

"Sure—thanks," Gaia said gratefully. When she glanced over, she saw something funny in her roommate's face. "What?"

"Nothing," Catherine said, embarrassed. "It's just the way you looked before. When you were psyching us all up."

"What do you mean?"

Catherine looked at the floor. "You have this great 'take charge' thing you do—it's never condescending or anything. It reminds me of my mother."

"Really?" Gaia was taken aback. "It does?"

Nobody's ever said that *before,* Gaia thought. She remembered how Catherine had hugged her spontaneously just now. *Did I really distrust Catherine? Did I* really? *Or am I just not used to making friends?*

"Yeah, my mom had this 'rally the troops' voice she would use," Catherine said shyly. She had grabbed Gaia's bath towel, and she tossed it at her face. Gaia caught it. "Come on, hurry up. I thought New Yorkers did things fast."

"Okay," Gaia said, picking up her toiletry bag. She couldn't think of a clever answer fast enough, so she just hurried out of the room.

Teammates and colleagues, Gaia thought. *I still can't get used to it.*

Kim

When Agent Bishop recruited me, she told me the FBI would be a chance to study behavior.

And Jennifer Bishop is clearly no fool. She was clearly playing to what she thought my priorities are.

It was obvious what she really meant. Not just *criminal* behavior—that's where my academic interests are the same as the FBI's—but *team* behavior.

I think of it as music. As a little kid, when Dad was still forcing me to study classical music, I learned about harmony—about how notes sound good together. Melody happens over time, but harmony happens all at once—the instruments and voices all sing different notes at the *same moment,* creating something magical.

And the same magic exists between people. It's a different kind of music, and most people can't hear it. But I can. It's in the faces and voices, the way people interrupt each other, all talking at once. Every person's reacting to every other person, and if you can hear that music, it's almost like you can read minds.

The FBI knows what I'm good at. They want me working for them for that reason—they always need good profilers, and I could be one of the best.

But they knew enough to realize that they had to make it *enticing* to me—to give me a good reason to turn away from what would probably have been a lucrative, plush career as a high-priced shrink of some kind.

But an empty one. I mean, I didn't give up the guitar in order to sit in some office all day.

If you join us, Bishop told me, sipping coffee in a Colorado Starbucks, *you'll quickly become an expert in team behavior. You'll see how small crime-fighting forces work. You'll have an opportunity to study authority structures from the inside. After a few weeks you'll know enough to give a dozen lectures on the subject.*

The idea did fascinate me. And I have to admit, so far she's been right.

The case—the serial killer hunt in the game we're playing—is absolutely first rate. I've studied things like this in the readings I've done: examinations of criminal behavior or pathology, of crime patterns. And you couldn't ask for a more perfectly drawn presentation of the craft. As far as I can tell, Agent Bishop has created a flawless simulation of the real thing.

SAVED, the blood on the wall said. I keep coming back to that. What could it possibly mean? How are people "saved"? The cross suggests a straight Christian reading, in which salvation is the opposite of damnation.

I'll have to think about that. I suspect that might be the key to this case.

And in the meantime I'm getting another opportunity altogether. I'm observing my teammates. Team behavior is a new field of study, and I'm getting more interested in it with each passing hour.

Catherine's waiting for her chance to shine. That's clear. She's a very confident young woman—so confident that she doesn't ever brag or show off at all. I'll bet there's something she's *really* good at—and we're going to find out very soon.

Will Taylor is an interesting case study. I get the sense that everything's come easy to him. He's probably spent his whole life in an environment that provided him with almost no com-petition. So he had to make his *own* competition—set higher and higher goals for himself and then knock them down.

And now he's met his match. It's clearly confusing him since he's obviously attracted to Gaia and challenged by her at the same time. It's probably the first time in his life that's happened.

And Gaia—with Gaia, I draw a blank. The girl's a mystery to me.

There's something deeply unusual about her psychological makeup. And it makes it nearly impossible to read her. Clearly she's got a complex, tragic past. It's probably a grand story, like a long, passionate opera—the kind of experience that's more satisfying to study or read about than to actually live through.

Gaia Moore's *wounded* somehow. I have no doubt at all about that. She's torn, and she's trying to make herself com-plete. She's been doing it all alone, too—all by herself. And that's probably the hardest thing in life. But people who can do it, who can make themselves whole by force of will, become very strong indeed.

I'm pulling for Gaia. Whatever mysteries are in her past, I hope she can overcome them. Not just for her, but for all of us. And if we ever make it through Quantico—if we become "real" FBI—I imagine that Gaia will really shine.

But first things first. Now we've got to solve this puzzle Agent Bishop's created for us.

Which means that I have to figure out what SAVED means. They're counting on me to solve that. No, we're *all* counting on *each other* to solve all of it.

I hope we can do it.

a catastrophe had been created

STABBING CUTS

The four of them stood in a line on the asphalt road that bordered Hogan's Alley, wearing their guns and badges. They had showered and cleaned up and were dressed in the simple, quasi-business attire that befitted FBI trainees. They all had sunglasses on; the overcast sky was brightening, and through its haze the hot Virginia sky was shining down above the canopy of trees.

Will glanced at the others, looking at his watch. Just a few more seconds until game time. He checked again that Catherine had her note from the day before, when "Sheriff Landy" had called with the location of the second murder.

"Everybody ready?" Gaia asked.

She was talking like a leader now, Will noticed. It was a subtle change, but it had started when she'd had that private conversation with Malloy two hours ago. Will was dying to know what the boss had said to her. Not out of any personal curiosity, he quickly told himself, but out of professional interest in the workings of the FBI.

So who's in charge here, anyway? Will wondered. Was it Gaia? Was it himself? He didn't know. His behavior—acting like he was running the show—was really just routine, he was realizing. He took over situations because it was easier, and generally people *wanted* him to—they need a clear, direct voice to tell them what to do.

And now Gaia was talking like a leader. Will wasn't sure what he thought about that. *Does there have to be a leader?* he asked himself. It was a genuinely new thought. He wasn't sure what the answer was.

Fifty yards away, down the asphalt road, Will could see another group of four trainees. Another team. He couldn't see their faces—they were too far away. It was three women and one man. They cast long, sharp shadows on the asphalt as they stood there, waiting, just like Will and his team. *More competition,* he thought.

The bell went off.

It was very loud, just like the day before. Will and the others jumped, even though they were ready for it.

"Let's go," Catherine said, launching ahead. She had her notebook open; she was leading them between the Hogan's Alley flanking buildings toward the town square.

"Where are we headed?" Kim asked, hurrying to catch up. His leather cross-draw shoulder holster flapped against his shirt as he ran.

"Hogan's Alley Retirement Home," Catherine said. She pointed. "This way. Can you hear the sirens?"

They could. As they rounded the corner of the town's red-brick bank, they could see something that looked like flashes of lightning—the strobelike rhythm of police car flashers.

The Hogan's Alley Retirement Home was a drab, modern, three-story building with a horseshoe-shaped driveway in front of it. The entire area was roped off with yellow police line tape. Three police cruisers were parked inside the tape in a crescent around the driveway. Five or six uniformed police-men were positioned around the building entrance. Will could see several elderly men and women gathered to one side, where a uniformed cop was detaining them, keeping them from entering the building. Catherine led Will and the others in that direction.

It's only been "five minutes," Will remembered. *Just five minutes since we got the call.*

It was a strange sensation, dealing with the game's "frozen time." It was almost like everything that had happened the night before—the trip to Johnny Ray's, the fight Gaia had got-ten into, the detour to Kelly's house, and the early-morning reprimand from Special Agent Malloy—had never happened. They were back in Hogan's Alley, where just minutes before they had been going through the pockets of a murdered four-teen-year-old named Nathan Hill.

"FBI," Gaia told the uniformed cop. She flashed her badge. "Where's the officer in charge?"

The cop pointed at a plainclothes detective, closer to the building's front door. Will thought he recognized the cop as one of the busboys from the steak house exercise two nights before—clearly the same actors played multiple roles. He firmly put the thought out of his mind. *It's real,* he told himself. *Not playacting—real. If you don't believe it's real, you can't win it.*

"I'm so glad you're here, ma'am," the investigating detective told Gaia. He was a small, dark-haired man in a baggy brown suit and a beige shirt, his gold detective shield clipped to his belt. "I'm Detective Okuda. The lab boys just got here—they're upstairs—but nobody's touched anything yet."

"Could we have the particulars, please?" Gaia asked. Beside her, Kim closed his eyes, getting ready to listen.

"Yes, ma'am." Okuda flipped open his spiral notebook. "Uh, at ten-twenty this morning, fifteen minutes ago, residents of the home"—Okuda gestured behind himself—"called 911. They explained that Mr. Abe Kaufman, a resident here, uh, seventy-eight years old, grandfather of six—had not come down for breakfast. The callers—they explained that they'd gone upstairs to room 231, Mr. Kaufman's door, where, uh—"

"Slow down, Officer," Will said, in what he hoped was a soothing tone. "Take it easy. You're doing fine."

Okuda nodded. "They knocked on the door, and there was no answer. So they called 911. Unit 631 responded; uniformed officers Kagan and Duff went upstairs and couldn't get an answer at the door, so they forced it open. Once they got a look inside—" Okuda swallowed, clearly shaken. "Well, they called in for backup. This was now twenty minutes ago. I got here, and Detective Goldblatt, who's upstairs; we knew there was a federal investigation in progress, so Sheriff Landy called you."

Okuda spread his hands, indicating that his narrative was over.

"Thank you, Detective," Gaia said, giving Okuda what Will noticed was a dazzling smile. Seeing her smile that way, Will forgot all about the case. He was imagining Gaia in a dinner dress, smiling at the arriving guests, the South Carolina sun flashing in her blond hair. He had to deliberately, firmly shake the image out of his head.

The four trainees were vaulting up the stairs to the second floor. Will and Catherine were looking around, inspecting the stairwell for any obvious clues. Gaia had a package of white latex gloves and was handing them out.

"That wasn't much from the cop," Catherine said. She was snapping the rubber gloves onto her slim hands.

"He's freaked," said Kim. "Cathy, any significance to the room number? 231?"

"What?" Catherine said derisively. "No. These aren't numerological crimes."

"Why are you so sure?" Will wanted to know. They were moving down a drab, badly lit corridor, looking at the room numbers. He could already smell an unpleasant, metallic aroma—the smell of blood.

"SAVED," Catherine explained simply. "Look, if I see what I think is a significant number, I'll let you know."

The door to 231 was wide open. As they got there, Will had a strange feeling—he felt his legs wanting to slow down. *I don't want to go in there,* he thought plaintively. It was like some part of his mind was six years old again. *Daddy, don't make me go in there.*

"Come on." Gaia was poking him in the back, propelling him forward. "Get moving."

"Yes, ma'am," Will said absently, but his heart wasn't in it. Now he could see into the room, and the first thing he saw was bright red blood—that particular, rich, dark red that was unmistakable. It was *wet*—whatever had happened had happened not that long ago.

The room was fairly large and well lit. Its single, plateglass window faced the street, where the white, overcast sky was shining brightly. The walls were covered in cream-colored wallpaper. The wallpaper was spattered with blood wherever Will looked.

All four trainees stopped walking instantly. They were alone in the room except for two criminologists crouching down, swabbing the floor, a young man in a beige jacket with a mop of curly, sandy hair who had to be Detective Goldblatt, and the body of Abe Kaufman.

This is worse than looking at pictures, Will thought, swallowing weakly. *Way worse.*

The old man had been skewered repeatedly. He lay on his back, his arms curled defensively by his sides. There were bloody slice wounds in his gnarled, arthritic hands. It made Will want to cry. You could *picture* old Mr. Kaufman flinching on the floor, trying to ward off the stabs that he knew were killing him.

The coffee table had been upset, pulled to one side so that a stack of *Retirement Life* magazines had spilled onto the floor. A side table had fallen over, spilling an ashtray full of brown cigarette butts. There was a great deal of clutter in the room, standing on various antique-looking side tables, including what had to be pictures of grandchildren.

They'll all grieve, Will thought sadly. *Every one of them. They probably came over here to watch TV with Grandpa, or they saw him for the holidays.*

It didn't matter that this was a staged setting. Will knew that Agent Bishop had drawn from real crime files when she had put together this masterful simulation. Maybe this scene wasn't real, but it was probably based on something that had really happened.

"Detective Goldblatt?" Gaia said, walking up to him. "Gaia Moore, FBI."

"Hi," Goldblatt said roughly. He seemed choked up. "I'm sorry. It's just—I knew him. Abe—he came in on my poker game sometimes. I'm—" The mop-headed detective's jaw clenched.

"Detective, this is Special Agent Sanders," Gaia said. "She's taking complete control of the crime scene as of right now. Your people are to follow her orders down to the last detail."

Catherine's eyes widened as she looked at Gaia.

"Detective," Gaia said more quietly, "given your personal relationship with the victim, maybe it would be best if you left the crime scene to us. It will give you a chance to compose yourself and adjust to the shock, and our team is going to need all the room we can get in this small apartment."

"Well, yeah," Goldblatt said, nodding. He seemed embarrassed. "Okay. I'm sorry—I'd like to stay and help."

"You've already done all you can," Gaia said soothingly. "It's not your fault, Detective. When it's someone you know"— Gaia seemed hesitant, swallowing before going on—"it's different."

Will realized he was gazing at Gaia in frank admiration.

You'll get points for that one, he thought. *Very well done, Ms. Moore.*

"Okay, um—you two," Catherine said to the criminologists. They both stopped their work and looked up at her expectantly. "I want you to give fiber analysis a high priority. The wallpaper's going to need a complete fingerprint scan, along with—we'll have to get people to come with ultraviolet equipment. In the meantime do everything you can to retrieve the most fragile and perishable materials from this rug."

"Yes, ma'am," one of the criminologists said.

"And the ashtray," Catherine continued, pointing. "I want distinct samples of the ash, and I want the butts individually bagged and tagged, with vacuum seals. Be particularly careful with the butts; they could have tooth marks on the filters."

"Gaia," Will said quietly. He was crouching by Abe Kaufman's body. Gaia came over and after a moment crouched beside him. She seemed hesitant about getting too close to the body. Will pointed. "See the way the chest cavity was cut open? You can't see it on Nathan Hill since the ME cleaned it up. But here—"

"What?" Gaia leaned closer. From her face, Will guessed that it was the last thing in the world she wanted to do, but she was making herself do it.

"These aren't stabbing cuts," Will explained, pointing at the lacerations. "See how the fabric of his shirt is separated? These are *lateral* cuts. Like, I don't know, slicing a steak."

"You're right," Gaia said. She leaned on Will's shoulder in order to stand back up, and for a moment the feel of her hand pressing on his shoulder was all he could think about. "Hey, Catherine?" Gaia called out. Catherine was on the phone, giving instructions to someone. She covered the phone with her hand and looked at Gaia inquiringy. "Make

184

sure a photographer is coming—we need much better pictures than they got with the previous victim."

"Gaia," Kim said, stepping over.

"Yes?"

Kim didn't answer. Instead he pointed off to one side, at the darker corner of the room. On the wall, in the shadows, behind a standing, shaded lamp, a word was painted on the wall.

SAVED

The word had a cross painted above it.

Will felt a chill crawl over his body. It was such an acute feeling that he actually reached to pull his jacket collar closer to his neck.

Identical MO, he thought. *It's official—we're looking at a serial killer.*

"Gaia," Will said. "Something just occurred to me."

Gaia raised her eyebrows.

"Nathan Hill was killed in his bedroom," Will said. "With his mom and dad a room away. The killer couldn't go anywhere else; he had to be careful not to awaken the parents."

"Right."

"But this is a private apartment. So we've got to pay real close attention to the other rooms." Will was pointing at the three doors they could see: bathroom, bedroom, and kitchen. "The killer had free run of the place probably before, during, and after the murder."

With Gaia following, he walked into the bathroom, reaching with his latex-gloved hand to snap on the light.

It was an ordinary bathroom. Will's nostrils caught the geriatric scent of soap, medicine, and that nameless "elderly person" scent that wasn't unpleasant, but that he couldn't really identify.

He and Gaia looked around. There was a white porcelain sink, a toilet, a bathtub with rubber daisies stuck to its bottom so that you wouldn't slip in the soapy water. There were more pictures of grandchildren—just snapshots—in small frames on the wall. The medicine cabinet was open—its white shelves were bare except for a hairbrush with a silver handle.

"Guys!" Catherine called out. She was slapping her phone shut. "We should get over to the crime lab. Data's coming in from the other crime scene—from the Nathan Hill murder."

Gaia nodded. Will wasn't sure if she was listening—she was staring through the bathroom doorway at the corpse and at Abe Kaufman's bloody torso. The old man had a thick head of white hair—he was probably very proud of it. Will's uncle Casper wasn't much younger and was totally bald.

Will looked over at Gaia, who was chewing on her thumbnail, staring at the corpse—and, more specifically, at the wound in Abe Kaufman's chest.

Something about that really gets to her, Will thought. *But why?*

He couldn't begin to think of an answer.

"You're right," Gaia said to Will. It was like she had suddenly come out of a trance. "We've got to inspect all the other rooms. Catherine, why don't you and Will head over to the lab and we'll join you?"

Catherine nodded, all business. Will raised his eyebrows.

"You don't want me to stay?"

"I want *Kim* to stay," Gaia explained. "He needs to see this

186

place close-up, not on a computer monitor. Meanwhile you can make some of your brilliant deductions at the lab."

Will was listening for traces of sarcasm—and he couldn't detect any. He was surprised. Gaia wasn't even thinking about him anymore, he realized—she was moving toward the bedroom door, walking carefully to avoid disturbing the spilled magazines.

She's not messing around, Will thought. *No jokes, no distractions.*

Will didn't know what Agent Malloy had said to her, but whatever it was, it had certainly had a potent effect.

She's trying to overcome something. She wants to win—to prove something.

But Will didn't understand it any more than that.

I WAS BLIND

The crime lab was outside Hogan's Alley, in one of the drab FBI campus buildings. It was early afternoon, still muggy and overcast—about an hour after they'd begun their inspection of the new crime scene. Rain was coming.

Gaia and Kim strode across the concrete court, where they'd all first been debriefed by Special Agent Bishop about the Hogan's Alley game. Gaia's handgun was bouncing against her side under her left arm as she walked. It was a strange feeling but one that she imagined she'd have to get used to.

"What are you thinking?" Gaia asked Kim.

It seemed to her like a reasonable question. Kim's mind

was very interesting to Gaia, not just because he was so insightful, but because he was so *disciplined*. Gaia had trouble imagining being as directed as Kim was. She admired it—it was a capacity she was realizing that she'd never really developed in herself.

"I'm thinking," Kim said, "about what we have to do to win this game."

"And?"

"I'm wondering whether we'd be thinking the same way if this were a real case," Kim went on. They had gotten to the base of the looming criminology building, and a blast of air-conditioning came out of the glass door that he courteously held open for Gaia. "See, in a *real* case, right now, having recognized that we're dealing with a serial killer—someone killing a *series* of victims—we'd be desperate to prevent the next death."

"Uh-huh."

"But this is a game," Kim went on. They were headed toward a bank of elevators, and they got their ID badges out. "So nobody's really getting hurt. Which means if we *wait* for the next murder, we get more clues, and our investigation gets further along."

Gaia thought about what he was saying. "But we lose serious points for each death."

"Exactly," Kim said. "I think the *wrong* way to play this game is to wait for more clues."

The elevator was chiming softly as it passed each floor. "You think we've already got the clues we need."

"Yes," Kim said as the elevator slowed and stopped. "What we have to do is *connect* the murders. We need to figure out what the victims have in common."

Nathan Hill and Abe Kaufman, Gaia thought. *An old man and a young boy. What do they have in common?*

Nothing.

The corridor was bustling with people: lab technicians and business-suited agents passing back and forth. They followed the signs that pointed to Criminology Laboratory 18—below that were handwritten signs that added, Closed for Trainee Operations.

"Then we can maybe find the *next* victim," Kim went on. "And try to catch the killer before he strikes again. *That's* the way to win this game."

Gaia could find nothing wrong with Kim's logic. She nodded, more to herself than to him. *Catch the killer.* Maybe before he struck again—and maybe in the act.

She realized she was shuddering. The air in the corridor was cold, but as they passed through a big metal door, it got colder still.

The door read Crime Lab 18.

Inside was a large, cool, dark, windowless room. Computers were lined up along all four walls, and in the middle of the room were stainless steel tables holding microscopes and other technical equipment. Lab technicians in white coats and with cloth masks over their noses and mouths were working intently around the room. The main wall was lit up like a movie screen; several enormous bright images were enlarged there by digital projectors hanging from the ceiling. The left image showed a color photograph of the Nathan Hill murder scene. The right image showed a large statistical chart—Gaia wasn't sure what it was, but she could recognize chemical formulas.

Will and Catherine, also in lab coats, were walking around the room, talking to the technicians. Catherine seemed to be in charge. Will was holding a large plastic bag with an evidence tag that held the combination padlock from Nathan Hill's pocket. They both looked up as their teammates entered the room.

"Find anything else?" Will asked quietly.

Kim shook his head.

The four trainees looked at each other. None of them bothered to hide their disappointment. *We don't know how to do this,* Gaia thought plaintively. It was a little girl's thought, the whining of a young kid who wanted her daddy to fix everything. She shoved the idea firmly out of her head.

"Catherine," Gaia began. "Any progress?"

Catherine nodded. In the dim light the computer screens around the room reflected in her large brown eyes.

"I've got all the lab results from the Hill murder in the computer and all the victim data," Catherine said. "We're working to feed in the material from the Kaufman murder, but it's taking some time."

"And?"

"There are fifty-six separate blood deposits around Nathan Hill's bedroom and *none* elsewhere in the house. The problem is that *all* the blood is the boy's."

Kim had quietly moved off to talk to one of the technicians.

"Fingerprints?" Gaia asked.

Catherine nodded at Gaia's question. "Plenty. Again, all the boy's. We had a few minutes when we got excited because Will found a partial that was from a different hand."

"It's the father." Will shook his head. "Back to the drawing board."

"Anything *else?*" Gaia was in the grip of a sinking feeling.

"Not really," Will told them. "No footprints. No identifying marks anywhere. Plenty of fibers and chemical samples everywhere, but that's taking a long time to process."

"Guys," Kim called out, pointing at the big projection screen on the wall. "Look at this."

Gaia and the others looked up at the screen.

On the left a negative image of Nathan Hill's wall came into focus. They could see now in white against black the jagged, dripping letters that spelled SAVED—and the cross painted above it.

"Go ahead," Kim told the technician he'd been talking to. She tapped her fingers on her computer keyboard.

On the right-hand screen another negative image appeared. It was much smaller, and the contrast was more washed out. But it showed a very similar image: the word SAVED and a jagged cross. *That's the new one,* Gaia realized. *From the old man's apartment.*

"Can you bring them together?" Kim asked.

The technician did what he'd asked. The two images moved together, their sizes adjusting until they overlapped in the center of the screen. By now most of the technicians were watching.

"Well?" Will asked.

"The same," Kim said firmly. "The same handwriting. The same person."

"You're sure?" Gaia asked.

"What? Oh, absolutely," Kim said quickly, pointing at the screen with a pen. "Look at the downstrokes. Look at how the drips go—the cross stroke of the *A* smears the blood on the left side. One person did both."

But we knew that, Gaia thought impatiently. She admired what Kim had done, and she saw the logic behind it. But it didn't get them any closer to solving anything.

"Agent Sanders," another technician said suddenly. He was a tall man with a close-cropped afro and gold-rimmed glasses. "I've found something."

Gaia and the others gathered around. The man was carefully holding up a microscope slide.

"Well?" Kim asked.

"Some kind of red powder," the man said excitedly. "We thought it was dried blood, but it's not. It's got impurities, but it's basically a consistent compound. It's *not* organic—not food or bodily material."

"Which crime scene?" Gaia asked.

"Both," the technician said triumphantly. He was holding up another slide. "We just got this from the Kaufman murder. It's the same stuff. Personally, I'd say it was clay. Some kind of red clay."

Red clay? Gaia thought in confusion. *Red clay? What does that mean?*

"Any ideas?" she asked the others. They shook their heads.

Suddenly they heard a rapping sound from the direction of the door.

"May I come in?"

Gaia looked over and saw Special Agent Jennifer Bishop.

"I'm sorry to interrupt," Bishop said. She was wearing an impeccable business suit with her FBI identification badge clipped to her lapel. Her dark red hair was combed flat as usual. "I just wanted to drop by and see how you're all doing."

"Hello, ma'am," Catherine said in a forced-sounding cheerful voice. Kim, Will, and Gaia all said hello.

"Making any progress?" Bishop asked casually, gazing around at the technicians and their machines. "You all look so busy."

"We're not sure, ma'am," Will said, in his patented aw-shucks southern manner.

"You've certainly got all the data under control," Bishop was saying to Catherine. "I'm impressed."

"Thanks, ma'am," Catherine said sullenly. She was rubbing the bridge of her nose, as if the traces of her hangover were refusing to go away. "It's not like it's doing a lot of good."

"Oh, I don't know," Agent Bishop said teasingly, casting her eyes down the rows of computer screens, the stacks of crime scene photographs, the microscope slides. "Actually, I'd say you've got everything you need. You could solve the case right now just from the information in this room."

Kim and Catherine were staring at Agent Bishop. "But we can't *find* anything," Catherine burst out in frustration. "I'm sorry, but I can't see any patterns, any information, anything."

Agent Bishop smiled peacefully.

"'I once was lost,'" she recited quietly, "'but now I'm found. I was blind, but now I see.'"

"Is that a clue, ma'am?" Kim asked.

"No," Agent Bishop said. She was looking at her watch.

"Just some advice. The bell's going to ring in two minutes. Make sure all your data's safe in the computers."

And then, with a parting glance at Gaia, Agent Bishop turned and walked out of the room. When the door was shut, Catherine slammed her fist against the lab table.

"Easy," Kim said. "Take it easy."

"I *can't*," Catherine said. "I'm *frustrated*. We're not *getting* anywhere."

Will had come over to Gaia. He was standing close to her, a look of concern in his eyes.

"Hey," Will said. "You all right?"

Gaia shook her head. "I don't know. Maybe. What's it to you?"

"I'm your colleague," Will said quietly. "Remember?"

The bell went off. It was as loud as usual. With a loud clicking noise every computer screen in the room went off all at once. Fluorescent lights in the ceiling began buzzing to life. The technicians put down what they were doing and began filing from the room.

"Gaia," Will said. She looked at him.

"Yeah?"

"Let's go for a drive."

It wasn't what she was expecting him to say. Catherine and Kim were putting their notes into file folders across the now-empty room. Gaia looked up at Will's ice blue eyes, and suddenly she felt enormously *tired*—tired of clues and orders and ticking clocks and computers and the whole ordeal. *And he realized that,* Gaia thought. *He knows I need to get away. He's actually being the "gentleman" that I thought he only played on TV.*

"What do you say?" Will went on. "Just a drive into town. To relax and get away."

"All right," Gaia said, sighing. She was reaching to take off her shoulder holster, which was rubbing painfully against the back of her neck. "Yeah, good idea. Let's get the hell out of this place."

OLDEST, LAMEST TRICK

The sky was darker and still overcast, and rain seemed likely. Gaia stared at the gray clouds through the blue-green strip of glass along the top of the windshield of Catherine's car.

Will was driving. They weren't talking much. He seemed to understand that she just wanted to think.

And I don't need to be alone, she thought. *Not necessarily.*

Usually when Gaia felt like this, she went off to spend time by herself. She had done it just yesterday after round 1 of the game, when "the body of Nathan Hill"—just a latex dummy, she knew, but what difference did it make?—had reminded her of Jake. Years ago, in that other life, she had spent time in Central Park, looking for low-grade criminals to attack.

Agent Malloy was right, Gaia thought, watching the houses and trees pass by the car. *I thought I was "doing good" back then, but I wasn't, not really.*

Gaia was slumped in the car seat, her knees against the dashboard. She and Will had changed out of their trainee outfits and back into regular, comfortable clothes. Glancing over, she watched his hands on the steering wheel, strong fingers gripping its rubber surface.

This time, in daylight, as they passed the mowed field near the edge of town, Gaia had a clear view of the World War II memorial statue. In the bleak, fading, overcast light, she could clearly see the bronze soldier's tired, brave face, his eyes shaded by his wide, round helmet. The sculptor had managed to convey the strain in the infantryman's limbs, the unimaginable weight of battle on his wide shoulders, the burden that pressed his heavy combat boots into the soft mud of Normandy or Italy or Iwo Jima or wherever this nameless soldier had fought and, maybe, died.

The soldier's rifle barrel held a bouquet of white roses. Gaia remembered that from last time. The wide, blooming white petals opened to the sky, as simple and beautiful as notes of music.

Now, after another half hour of aimless driving, Gaia felt a little better. Will still hadn't said a word. They both looked over as they passed Johnny Ray's, not yet open for business, and Montano's steak house, where a chipped plastic sign advertised Special Bar B Q and Surf & Turf Shrimp Special.

That's where Will proved how good he is, Gaia thought, remembering two days before. Had she really been that consumed with being "better" than him? Was their competition really so meaningful? Gaia wasn't sure now. They continued through the town, and Gaia looked at the cars and newspaper machines and pickup trucks and papers blowing in the breeze beneath the overcast sky.

This is a real town, she thought with some satisfaction. *Not like Hogan's Alley. This place makes Hogan's Alley look like Disneyland.*

That was a bit of an exaggeration, but it was essentially correct. The stage set where they played their game was a thin, pale imitation—a drive through a genuine American town made that clear.

"A little dose of reality," Will said, letting out a long breath.

Gaia looked over at him with her head leaning on the car's window.

That's not the first time he's done that, she thought. *Read my mind somehow.*

Will glanced over, saw Gaia looking at him, and quickly turned his attention back to the road. Gaia did the same thing, self-consciously sitting up, turning her attention to the buildings outside the car's windshield. They were passing a small apartment complex with a row of cars parked in front. The building was low and wide, the kind of place Gaia could only imagine living in if she couldn't find a stand-alone house. The apartment complex had a row of fenced-in tennis courts, their red clay surfaces framed by white painted lines, behind the—

Wait.

"Stop the car," Gaia told Will.

"What?"

"Stop. Look over there."

Gaia pointed. Will followed the direction of her arm and then stepped on the brakes. The Altima lurched to a stop, and a driver behind them honked angrily. Will waved and quickly pulled out of the street's traffic lane and over to the curb.

The building had tennis courts, and they were surfaced in red clay.

Red clay.

"Well, don't that beat all," Will said quietly.

"This is it," Gaia whispered. "This is the next clue. This is part of the game."

Will frowned at her. "Gaia—come on. That doesn't make sense."

"Why not?"

"Look where we are," Will said patiently. "We're on the far side of Quantico. We're nowhere *near* Hogan's Alley."

"So?"

"So how could this be a clue? We're not even on FBI property."

"We weren't on FBI property," Gaia said slowly, "when they pulled that stunt with the restaurant gunman. You remember: you were the big hero of the hour. It was your moment of—"

"Okay, smart-ass, I get your point. Continue." Will smirked.

"And we weren't on FBI property at Johnny Ray's when two agents were watching us either."

Will was clearly thinking. He stared out the car window at the clay tennis courts. Then he slowly reached to shut the engine off and pulled the parking brake.

"So . . . *assuming* you're right, what do we do?" Will asked skeptically.

Gaia thought about it. She wasn't sure what the answer was.

"We wait," she said quietly. "We sit here and we watch the building. And we see who comes in or out."

Will squinted. "Are you sure?"

"Not really. I'm waiting for your brilliant idea that will make me look dumb."

Will closed his eyes in mock resignation. "All right, all right, Ms. Moore—I concede the point. Just trying to make you laugh," he said. "You've got these little dimples that appear when you laugh—I've seen it before."

"I don't have any *dimples*." Gaia could feel her face reddening, heating up. "Honestly, Will, I don't know where you get this stuff."

"Come on, you must like me a *little*," Will said, smiling. His arm was still along the edge of the car seat—Gaia was suddenly aware of his thick upper arm muscles just inches from her T-shirted shoulder. "I can't be all bad. And you were looking at me before, ma'am—I caught you at it fair and square and you might as well admit it."

"What?" Gaia was almost sputtering her objections. "That's the most—"

"Remind me never to move to New York," Will said, squinting and grinning as he turned his face away. "If all the girls are like you, the boys must have prematurely gray hair, and I like my hair the way it is."

"Okay," Gaia said. "Okay, I admit it. I think you're all right. I think you're very smart, for one."

"And I'm a handsome devil," Will said, smiling maddeningly. "You might as well admit that part, too. Look how close to me you're sitting right now."

"*Conceited* is what you are," Gaia said. "It's amazing. We're in a car—there's nowhere to go."

"Fine, but I'm not conceited. I'm truthful," Will argued.

"I mean, should I act like you? The way you go around pretending you're not beautiful?"

"What?" Gaia had no idea what to say to that. Somehow she was having trouble thinking clearly or breathing regularly—and it made her even more frustrated with Farm Boy. "Don't change the subject. Anyway, *you're* the one with the arm on the car seat. Didn't anyone tell you that's the oldest, lamest trick in the book?"

"I'd heard that," Will said.

Gaia was looking into Will's blue eyes from just inches away. Somehow she had moved her fingers up to brush against his chest. He was staring right back, and as he did, his hand moved, and his fingers gently grazed across her shoulder, through the smooth cotton of her T-shirt. Distantly, Gaia expected herself to flinch. But she didn't.

Will brushed the hair from her neck and ran his fingers across her cheek. Then his face moved closer, and before Gaia even allowed herself to think, she let hers move closer to his.

"Stop that," Gaia murmured.

"You first."

Their mouths came together smoothly, gently at first, slowly, and then more firmly. Will's left hand came up onto Gaia's shoulder, his strong arms pulling her forward as the kiss grew deeper and deeper. Gaia's eyes were closed, and with Will pressed against her, a trace of his aftershave in her nostrils, and his strong chest pushed against her, she felt like her entire body was softening, going more and more limp in his arms. Now Will's hands were delicately framing her face, gently brushing her hair back as he kissed her again more powerfully and then pulled back. Her eyes were open now; their faces were pressed together, forehead to forehead, her hands on his wide shoulders, his forearms resting on either side of her long neck.

"Well," Will murmured. His eyes were very close; she could feel his eyelashes brushing against hers. "Interesting development."

Gaia didn't know what to say.

"Does this mean we're not 'colleagues' anymore?" Will asked.

"I'm not sure I'd— *Oh my God.*"

"What?" Will seemed startled. "It was just one kiss; it's not—"

"*Look,*" Gaia whispered urgently. She was squeezing Will's shoulder, pointing past him out the car window at the apartment building.

Will turned and looked. Crouching her head down, Gaia could see into one of the second-floor windows. The window was partially shaded, but the room behind the shade was brightly lit.

Shadows were moving on the blinds. Gaia and Will could clearly make them out.

A hulking male figure. Holding something menacing—the shadow was blurred, but it could have been a knife or a gun.

Cowering before the huge male shadow, a smaller figure. Pretty clearly female—Gaia could make out the shadow of a ponytail.

It's happening, Gaia thought. *This is it—the killer is in there.*

"Come on," she snapped at Will, pulling on his sleeve. "Come on, let's go. This is it—this is the third murder."

"What?" Will was squinting incredulously at her. "Gaia,

wait—that doesn't make sense. *Now?* While we're watching?"

"We *staked the place out,*" Gaia argued. "It makes perfect sense—it's exactly what Bishop would do. What did she say? I'm blind, but now I can see? I can *see* it, Will. It's *happening.*"

"I don't know." Will seemed agitated. He was rubbing his neck, squinting up at the building. In the window the menacing male figure was moving again—drawing closer to the female silhouette. "I know how badly you want to win, Gaia. But this is just—Look, can we at least call the others?"

"Come on," Gaia snapped impatiently. "We don't have time and you know it. Look, he's hurting her."

"What?" Will was looking at her quizzically. "Gaia, it's just a *game.* Even if you're right, what can a few minutes—?"

"No. We've got to *stop* the crime," Gaia explained impatiently. She was practically hopping up and down in her seat. "Kim explained it to me. Look, are you coming?"

"Gaia, think about what you're doing," Will said patiently. "The red clay doesn't prove—"

"Fine," Gaia said. Turning away, she got the car door open and vaulted out into the street.

Come on—time to move fast, Gaia told herself, propelling her body up onto the sidewalk and over to the Truro Apartments door. She tried to open it; it was locked. After shaking it back and forth she slammed her fist against the glass. The glass broke loudly and Gaia reached through the opening and twisted the knob, getting the door open.

Then she was racing through the dusty, badly lit entryway and up a narrow flight of linoleum-covered stairs toward a wooden apartment door that had to led to the room she'd been watching. She banged on the door.

"Open up," Gaia yelled.

No answer.

With a surge of effort Gaia took a running leap and banged her body laterally against the door. There was a crunching, smashing sound and the door collapsed inward, its hinges giving way. Gaia regained her balance and rushed forward into the room. She could hear Will on the stairs behind her calling her name.

She was standing in a small, one-room apartment. Wind was blowing through it, thanks to the door she'd smashed open. The room's two inhabitants were looking at her, their eyes wide with surprise and fear.

Kelly Ray was sitting on a footstool by the window. Her honey brown hair was pulled back into a characteristic ponytail.

Jack, the bartender, was standing over her. He was twisted in place, staring at Gaia as if she were mad. The object in his hand was a cordless telephone.

"Leave her alone," Gaia yelled, running forward, grabbing Jack by the shirtfront and throwing him against the wall. "Leave her alone, asshole."

"Gaia?" Kelly yelled in confusion, leaping to her feet. "Gaia, honey, what are you doing?"

"You son of a bitch," Gaia told Jack, slamming him back against the wall. "You remember me, right? I beat the crap out of your friends and I'll do the same thing to you."

"Yeah, I remember you," Jack said, squinting down at her.

"Lady, you got this all wrong. Let go of me, will you? Or you'll get hurt."

"*You're* the one who's getting hurt," Gaia insisted. She could hear Will coming into the room behind her. The light from the window was illuminating all the sawdust in the air from the smashed door. "How dare you threaten Kelly?"

"He *wasn't threatening me,*" Kelly insisted, trying to get ahold of Gaia's shoulder. "Please, Gaia—let him go!"

"I'm not letting anyone go," Gaia insisted. She knew about battered women, how they walked around disguising their bruises behind sunglasses, always insisting that nothing had happened, that it was *their* fault—and how some of them kept insisting the same thing all their short lives, all the way into an early grave.

"You let go of me right now," Jack said quietly, his scotch-scented breath in Gaia's face, "or I'm pressing charges. I'll call that damn base of yours and have you all subpoenaed and worse. You'll be buying me a new apartment door, and that's just for starters."

Gaia's head was spinning. It was the adrenaline—suddenly she felt like she might faint again, as she had the night before. *No,* she thought weakly. *Not now. Not until I figure this out.*

"Gaia, we were just having an argument," Kelly said angrily. "Jack wanted his two-week bonus early; that's all."

"*Gaia,*" Will said urgently. His hands were clamped powerfully on her shoulders from behind, and he was gently but firmly pulling her away from Jack. "Gaia, we *have* to go right now."

"You got that right," Jack muttered as Gaia's hands finally slipped off him.

"Sir, ma'am," Will said, as smoothly as he could, "clearly this has been a terrible mistake. Let me apologize right now for my friend here. I'm sure we can straighten all this out amicably."

What's going on? Gaia thought miserably. She still felt light-headed, but she was riding it out—the moment when she was afraid she'd black out had passed. *Oh, Jesus, what kind of mistake did I make now?*

Jack was leaning on the wall, getting his breath back. He pointed furiously at his own broken apartment door. "Get out," he said. "Get out as fast as you can, or you'll be in even more trouble than you already are."

Gaia couldn't think of a thing to say. She darted her eyes back and forth between Kelly and Jack and then turned wordlessly and let Will lead her through the cloud of sawdust and out of the room.

My God, this is bad, Gaia thought weakly. It was just beginning to sink in what a catastrophe had been created. *This is just so bad.*

What have I done?

FEDERAL BUREAU OF INVESTIGATION
TRAINEE EXPULSION FORM

Note: **This document is an official registry of trainee expulsion.** In accordance with FBI regulation #34RB-6 this form must be submitted by registered courier to FBI National Personnel Office, J. Edgar Hoover Building, Washington, DC.

The FBI trainee named below is hereby **DISMISSED** from all training exercises. All existing arrangements and agreements with the below-named trainee are hereby suspended. In addition, the below-named trainee is hereby **REMOVED** from all low-level security clearance lists and is required to sign an oath stating his or her willing compliance with the terms of trainee dismissal.

NAME OF TRAINEE: Moore, Gaia
SUPERVISOR: Special Agent Jennifer Bishop, code G44
OVERSEEING SUPERVISOR: Special Agent Brian Malloy, code A71
REASON FOR DISMISSAL: Violation of regulations #21EE-5, #54EE-5
The above-named individual is hereby judged unfit for participation in the Federal Bureau of Investigation's Special Forces Training Program (Quantico Facility).

Signatures (please press firmly):

Jennifer Bishop, G44

Brian Malloy, A71

controlled artificial reality

A FREAKING MESS

It's not signed, Gaia thought. *They haven't signed it yet.*

She was standing at attention, facing Special Agent Malloy, who sat behind his big, bare oak desk. Jennifer Bishop was beside him at the edge of the desk, her legs crossed. Between them was a single sheet of paper. From where she stood, Gaia could see what it was, even reading upside down.

Trainee Expulsion Form, it said in bold type, below an FBI seal. There were open spaces at the bottom of the page, where Malloy's secretary had typed the agents' names.

Agent Bishop had a thick fountain pen in her right hand—she was fiddling with it as she looked over the form and then returned her gaze to the carpeted floor. She had avoided Gaia's eyes completely.

She doesn't want to look at me.

Out the window, behind Agent Malloy, the sky was thickly clouded and menacing. A rainstorm was on its way. In the far distance, beyond the gravel and concrete courts that bounded the back edge of Administration Wing A, the dark trees were tossing in the wind. The only sound in the room was the drone of the air-conditioning. Since she'd entered the room, nobody had spoken.

I've got to talk them out of this, Gaia thought insistently.

She was having a hard time keeping herself still as the two agents sat there, maddeningly silent, looking at the expulsion form. *I've got to make some kind of argument before they sign that form.*

"Agent Bishop," Gaia said.

Bishop slowly raised her eyes from the form and looked back at Gaia. She looked very upset. It was as if the woman's most pessimistic view of human nature had been proven correct; that the innocent hopes she'd nurtured had been dashed to the ground.

"Agent Bishop—ma'am, I'd like a chance to explain this."

Neither agent spoke. Finally Bishop put down her pen. It clicked against the desk.

"Go ahead."

Bishop didn't sound very enthusiastic. Gaia forced herself to return the woman's ice-cold gaze. "Ma'am, I'm not—I'm not sure you understand the circumstances of what happened. See, we were—Will and I—"

Start over. Make sense. Talk like an agent—in straight lines.

Gaia took a breath. "Ma'am, Mr. Taylor and I believed we were following a clue in the game. We had good reason to believe that part of the game took place off the Quantico base. The test at Montano's steak house, the speech you made about how the rules changed all the time—all of this led us to believe that the clay we saw—the red clay outside that building—was a clue in the Hogan's Alley game."

"Go on," Bishop said.

"Ma'am, after staking out the building, I saw what I believed was the game's next crime in progress. We saw what looked like an assault of some kind through the window. So then we—"

"A crime that didn't in any way fit the profile of the killer you and your teammates were pursuing," Bishop interrupted impatiently. "A crime that happened to be taking place right in front of you, involving a 'weapon' you couldn't see and a tenuous line of evidentiary reasoning at best."

"But—"

"No, go on," Bishop snapped. Gaia began to realize just how angry she was. "I want to hear about what you did next. I want to hear about the 'procedure' you followed. How you *didn't* call for backup, how you *didn't* identify yourself, how you *didn't* discuss your mode of entry with your partner or in any way coordinate your efforts to stop the 'crime' in progress." Bishop pointed at the wall. "Back in my office, I've got Will Taylor's report. He does his noble best to deflect blame away from you, but it's quite clear what happened. Do you want to *read* his report, or would we be wasting our time?"

"Ma'am, I was convinced that every second counted," Gaia insisted. She was looking at Bishop, but she could feel Malloy's eyes boring into her like drills. "I thought that a woman was being attacked, and I didn't like—"

"For an FBI agent that's *routine,*" Bishop said angrily. "Moving fast is part of the job. But it *never* means you get to break the rules. You broke into a private residence, unarmed, with no badge or shield, with no *warrant,* without *identifying* yourself, without *questioning* the suspects, without following FBI procedure in *any way.* And all this after a specific, direct warning about your behavior. All because you *didn't like* what you thought an innocent man was doing to an innocent woman."

All true, Gaia thought hopelessly.

Bishop sighed. Out the window behind her, as Gaia watched, the first few drops of rain hit the window. The air-conditioning was very cold.

"The game," Bishop finished quietly, unscrewing the cap from her fountain pen, "is a controlled artificial reality—a simplified environment. If you can't behave like an FBI agent in my game, how can you be expected to do it in the real world? In the real world your actions have real *consequences*—and with this unprovoked assault you've created a bureaucratic and legal mess that I and other members of the FBI will have to go to great pains to straighten out. The bureau could even be sued."

There was nothing Gaia could say—nothing she could do except stand there and watch Jennifer Bishop sign her name on the expulsion form. The scratching of the fountain pen was very loud.

Please don't, Gaia thought plaintively. *Please don't do this to me.*

She remembered that day in Palo Alto—the crowd along the edge of the roof, applauding. Before she'd met any of these people, before Catherine and Will and Agent Malloy and Hogan's Alley and Quantico. It seemed like so long ago.

Bishop finished signing her name. The second line—where Malloy would add his own signature—remained blank. Without looking at Gaia, Bishop slid the sheet of paper and the pen across the desk to Special Agent Malloy.

"Jenny," Malloy said, looking down at the page, "this means continuing with only nineteen trainees. Would you want to keep the teams as they are?"

"I don't see an alternative," Bishop said quietly, looking at the floor. Once again she seemed unwilling to make eye contact with Gaia. "Lau, Sanders, and Taylor can continue as a team. I'd recommend staying with the current configuration until the game ends."

Malloy nodded. Gaia was struck by his attitude. All the time she'd been waiting outside his office after the summons had come, she had expected Agent Malloy to be angry. But this was worse. He was quiet, resigned—almost sad.

"Thank you, Agent Bishop," Malloy said. "That will be all."

It took Gaia a moment to realize what Malloy meant—that he was asking Bishop to leave. Bishop didn't seem to get it either: there was a pause while Malloy's words sank in, and then she quickly rose to her feet. She looked at Gaia sharply and then looked away, as if she couldn't bring herself to say anything. Malloy waited while Bishop crossed the room, and they both heard her open the office door, walk out, and pull the door loudly shut. He was staring down at the expulsion form. Finally he looked up.

"I want to show you something," Malloy said quietly.

In the window's dim light the lines around his face seemed sharply drawn, as if carved in stone. As Gaia watched, he opened a desk drawer and pulled out a thick, heavy folder the size of a telephone book. He dropped it on the desk, where it thumped loudly. A red paper ribbon around the file said Quantico Code X—Director Only. On the folder's front panel was a seal that Gaia recognized instantly, even upside down—an ornate shield with three letters across it.

CIA.

"Agent Bishop doesn't know about this," Malloy told Gaia, tapping the massive folder. "This is the result of extensive inter-bureau communication and cooperation—of two separate trips I took to Langley, Virginia, to visit CIA headquarters . . . of meetings with Martin Rodriguez and with a well-respected ex-agent named Thomas Moore."

Dad, Gaia thought.

"You were never just another trainee," Malloy went on. He had folded his hands on the desk. "Even on that rooftop in Palo Alto, we knew exactly who you were. The FBI can't put together an operation like the Kevin Bender arrest without finding out everything about the suspect in question. When we fed your name into our computers, we got a *lot* of information back. Once you were on our list of potential trainees, we realized that we had a very special situation—with a very special trainee."

Gaia was struggling to absorb what Malloy was telling her. Out the window the rain was spattering against the building, louder and louder as the storm began. *Does that mean he knows all about me?* she thought. Everything *about me?*

"The CIA and the FBI have agreed," Malloy went on, "that a person with your capabilities and skills could be placed on what we call a 'fast track'—an accelerated program that would lead to rapid deployment as a full agent. All you had to do"—Malloy sighed heavily, rubbing his eyes—"was finish the training program."

"*Fast track to agent*"—Gaia could barely believe what she was hearing. A special arrangement just for her, and as suddenly as she'd learned about it, it was gone.

"I didn't—" Gaia took a deep breath. She was imagining her father and Agent Malloy talking about her. It had happened more than once. There had been *meetings* about her. "I didn't know."

"Of *course* you didn't know," Malloy snapped. "You weren't *supposed* to know. All you needed to know was that you were one of my trainees. I warned you—I told you exactly what the rules were. Now you've done *exactly* what you promised me in this office that you would never do. And now I have to get on the phone to Virginia and tell them that I played our hunch as far as it would go, and it was a bum steer."

My God, Gaia thought weakly. *I've made such a freaking mess.* She stared back at Malloy, and she couldn't stop a tear from running from her eye onto her cheek. *I've got to say something,* she thought. *I've got to stop him from doing this.*

But there was nothing to say.

"Crying won't help," Malloy said harshly. "Weakness isn't the answer or appealing to others to save you. Nobody else can solve your problems—only you. I thought you knew that. I'm sorry to see that I'm wrong."

As Gaia watched, Malloy unscrewed the cap of the fountain pen and wrote out his name on the blank line below Bishop's signature. Gaia watched him write every letter.

I'm fine, Gaia tried to convince herself. *I've handled worse than this. This is nothing. This is just a moment in my life. I'm fine.*

But Gaia had no idea where she would go now. She would never go back to New York. She didn't want to go back to California, not really. What she wanted, more than anything else, was just to stay in Quantico.

"You're dismissed, Ms. Moore," Malloy said formally. Gaia could hear thunder in the distance. He turned back to her, the lines in his face seeming more pronounced. "I'll expect you off the Quantico campus by the end of the day."

HER OLD LIFE

At four-thirty, an hour after her final meeting with Agents Bishop and Malloy, Gaia was sitting outside. She was down on the cement ground, crouched against the outer wall of the dorm building around the corner from the building's main door. The rain was coming down all around, splashing in the gravel and making shallow pools across the concrete pavement, pools that reflected the threatening sky. Where she was sitting, her back against the rough, damp concrete wall of the building, she was sheltered from the rain by an overhanging metal eave—but just barely. Her hair was wet and tangled, and dark rainwater stains were spreading through the gray sweatpants she had on. She was also wearing her running shoes, although she didn't quite remember when she'd put them on.

I came outside to go running, Gaia remembered dully. *It didn't make sense, but I couldn't just sit in the dorm and let Catherine find me.*

As it was, Catherine would find her bags. Gaia had packed

very quickly, shoving everything into her suitcases and duffel bags. She had considered leaving a note for Catherine but hadn't done it. What would she say? *Good luck with the game? Hope you have a nice life in the FBI?* She had no idea.

Lightning flickered in the sky, and Gaia found herself automatically counting the seconds until the rumble of thunder. It was something she'd always done since she was a little girl. It was soothing somehow—a memory of earlier in her life. Maybe that was why she'd pulled on sweatpants and sneakers; she realized that in her misery, she was reliving old habits from her old life, years ago, in New York.

Gaia had looked at the train schedules, but she didn't know where she wanted to go. The best thing was to head toward Ohio, at least initially. She'd gone ahead and made the reservation, putting it on her credit card, but she wasn't sure where she'd end up.

"Here you are." A familiar voice came through the rain. Male, with a southern accent.

Gaia looked up and saw Will moving across the courtyard toward her. He was wearing a Nautica windbreaker, which he had pulled up over his head to shield himself from the pouring rain. It wasn't working—the rain had darkened his buzzed blond hair.

"None of us could find you," Will said.

Go away, Gaia thought.

This time he wasn't able to read her mind the way he had before. Will dropped down onto the ground beside her.

"Will," Gaia began, "I don't want to—"

"What the hell is the matter with you?" Will said angrily. "Are you crazy?"

"Yeah," Gaia said dully. "I'm crazy. You nailed it."

"I saw you doing it and I couldn't believe it. Why would you throw all this away? Why, Gaia?"

Because I'm not whole, she thought helplessly. *Because I'm incomplete—I always was. Because I'm not as strong as any of you. I thought I was, but I'm not.*

"I don't know," she said finally.

The rain came down, harder than before.

"Look on the bright side, Will," she told him. His face was dripping with rainwater, and she wanted to brush it away, but she didn't move. "Now *you're* the best. Nobody to compete with anymore."

"You said it," Will agreed. "I thought we'd have months to piss each other off."

Will moved, and Gaia thought he might touch her, but he didn't—he just changed his position on the wet ground. They looked at each other.

"We were just getting started," Will said.

Gaia nodded.

"Look, I've got a train," she said in a voice that came out hoarse, like a whisper. "I have to get ready."

"Right," Will said as they both stood up. "We've all got some kind of drill at the shooting gallery in an hour. But winning won't be any fun without you there."

"With me there, you'd lose."

Will chuckled. "Good-bye, Gaia," he said. Then he quickly turned and walked away into the rain.

216

Gaia wasn't sure how long she stood there, but the next thing she knew, she was running. She had some time before the train left, and she figured she could get a cab to take her to the station. In the meantime she didn't want to sit still—she wanted to run.

Now she was on the road, the long two-lane blacktop that led into town. The road was soaked, its yellow meridian line shining in the rain. Gaia splashed through the wide puddles, soaking herself to the bone, diverting into the sand-packed road's edge as cars roared by, their headlights shimmering through the rain.

It doesn't matter if I miss my train, she told herself. *I don't really have anywhere to go.*

It didn't take long for Gaia to get up to a respectable speed. Soon her legs were pumping in their old rhythm, her breathing was labored, and she didn't have to think anymore. Wet telephone poles passed and rusted green metal signs for Virginia's numbered state roads.

Looking up, Gaia realized that she was almost in town. On her left she could see the mowed field with the World War II memorial approaching. The bronze statue of the infantryman was shining with rainwater, protruding above the wet trees that surrounded the field.

A figure stood next to the statue. Gaia couldn't see the person clearly. Only the bright yellow rain slicker the person wore. Running closer, Gaia peered over, wondering what the person was doing. As she watched, the figure reached up and placed white roses in the barrel of the infantryman's gun.

Gaia left the road, slowing to a walk as she crossed the muddy, sodden field, moving toward the statue. Lightning flickered as she got closer, seeing the gray granite pedestal that the statue rested on. Her lower legs were soaking wet now as she walked through the grass. The thunder rumbled across the sky and the figure turned. Gaia realized it was a young woman—a woman with long blond hair. Up close, Gaia saw that she wasn't as young as she'd looked from a distance; there were lines of care in her plain face.

"Oh my Lord, you're soaked," the woman said. Her voice was fairly high but sweet and pleasant. Gaia saw that she wore small silver earrings. Her eyes were green. "Haven't you got a raincoat?"

"I don't mind," Gaia said, walking closer. "I like running in the rain."

The woman made a face, as if to say, *It takes all kinds.*

"The roses are pretty," Gaia said, pointing. "I've seen them before, driving by. I wondered who put them there."

"Guilty," the young woman said, raising her hand. She held it out to Gaia. "I'm Ann Knight."

"I'm Gaia Moore," Gaia said, shaking hands.

"What a pretty name," Ann said. "Glad to know you, Gaia. You don't mind if I finish this, do you?" She held up the roses she still had in her hand. In the dim, rainy light the white petals seemed to shine.

"Go ahead," Gaia said. "Do you do this every day?"

"Every day," Ann said, standing on tiptoe to carefully put the last of the flowers into the bronze soldier's gun barrel. "I've been doing it for years now. My husband was a United States

Marine—he was killed in Kuwait after Operation Desert Storm."

She lost the man she loved, Gaia thought heavily. *And she never got past it.*

"So every morning and every afternoon, rain or shine, I put flowers in the soldier's gun," Ann went on. "I live right there—I grow the roses myself."

Ann pointed, and Gaia turned and looked across the road, where a small, shingled frame house stood near the highway. There was a bed of white roses in front of the house. On the porch, shielded from the rain, a young boy was swinging on a porch swing. As she watched, the boy waved—and beside her Ann waved back.

"Isn't he great?" Ann said. "That's my son. He never knew his father. When he's a little older, I'll tell him the whole story."

The little blond boy waved again. Gaia waved back.

"Your boy's beautiful," Gaia told Ann. "I'm sure your husband would be proud."

"Thank you," Ann said.

Is this what's going to happen to me? Gaia wondered. *Just stuck in a state of permanent mourning? My mother, Mary, Jake . . . Is that why I'm doing this? Why I'm wrecking this? Destroying it and running away?*

Gaia's cell phone rang.

"I'm sorry," she told Ann. "Just a second. Hello?"

"Where the hell are you?" It was Catherine's voice, broken up by dropouts and static. "I've got your bags in the car—I'm ready to take you into town to the train station. I've been driving around looking for you."

"I'm *in* town," Gaia said. "I went running. I'm at the memorial park at the end of the road—you remember?"

"I don't know what you're talking about," Catherine said impatiently. "End of the road, huh? Wait there—I'll see you in five minutes."

"You want to come in and have a cup of coffee, Gaia?" Ann asked when Gaia had put her phone away. "You're welcome. I've got some cookies, too."

"No, thanks," Gaia said. "I've got to go. I'm leaving town."

"Oh, that's too bad," Ann said. She reached to shake hands again. "I'm glad we met."

"Me too," Gaia said. "What's your son's name?"

"Sam."

"That's—" Gaia had to clear her throat. Her first boyfriend was named Sam. "That's a good name."

"Bye now," Ann said. Gaia stood by the bronze statue and watched as Ann crossed the field, her yellow slicker shining in the rain.

MYSTERIOUS TALK

The headlights on Catherine's Altima shone through the mist, coming closer as Gaia stood in her soaking wet sweatshirt and running shoes by the side of the road. Ann and her son, Sam, had gone inside across the road. The rain was easing up—it might stop soon, Gaia thought.

Catherine pulled over, waiting for Gaia to circle to the passenger seat. The windshield wipers were grinding loudly back and forth. Gaia got into the car and slammed the door.

"You're all wet," Catherine complained.

"Sorry."

Gaia was nearly shivering—Catherine had the air-conditioning on. Behind them, in the backseat, Gaia saw all of her luggage.

"Thanks for getting my bags," Gaia said.

"Don't mention it." Catherine was hunched forward, peering through the wet windshield. "I'm going to have a hell of a time finding the train station. Where are you *going,* anyway?"

"Ohio," Gaia said. "At least to begin with. What's this?" There was something pressing into her back from the seat. She reached behind herself and pulled it out. It was a thick black plastic folder.

"What? Oh—nothing. Just the crime scene photos," Catherine explained. "They just arrived over in the crime lab. From the game. Those are all the pictures of Kaufman's apartment."

Gaia started opening the folder. There was no reason to do it—it didn't make any difference anymore—but she found herself leafing through the photographs.

"This sucks," Catherine said. She looked over at Gaia as she drove. "You realize that, don't you?"

"Yeah."

Everyone's in a bad mood, Gaia thought miserably. *But can I blame them? Look what I've done to them.*

"Oh, and Kim says good-bye."

"Thanks," Gaia said. She didn't want to think about it. "Tell him good luck with the game."

"Yeah—there's just the three of us now," Catherine said

gloomily. "I don't really like our chances. I mean, all Bishop's mysterious talk about 'seeing what isn't there' and everything; I still have no *idea* what to do next. There's nothing at either crime scene except—"

"Wait," Gaia said. "Just a second."

She was looking at one particular photograph—a wide-angle color image of Abe Kaufman's bathroom. She remembered standing there with Will not that long ago, looking at the pictures on the walls, the empty medicine cabinet, the porcelain sink. Closing her eyes, she was standing there again, hearing Will's voice next to her, smelling that nameless medicinal aroma in the air.

Seeing what isn't there.

"Turn the car around," Gaia told Catherine.

"What?" Catherine stared at her in complete confusion. "What are you talking about? We're almost to the train station."

"Catherine, come *on*—turn around. We have to go back to the base."

"Why?"

"Do you have the victim's insurance records?" Gaia asked urgently. "They're part of the case file, right?"

"The insurance records?" Catherine squinted as she drove. "Sure, but—"

"Then *turn the car around,*" Gaia insisted, grabbing Catherine's sleeve. "Take us back as fast as you can."

"Why?" Catherine said. She was slowing down and looking at the traffic, trying to find a place to make a U-turn. "To do *what?*"

"To win the game," Gaia said.

as far as the train takes you

DOOR TO A TOMB

Catherine was completely confused, and she didn't mind admitting it.

Here they were, early in the evening—at almost exactly the time that they were supposed to be at the train station, saying good-bye. And instead they were storming across the Quantico base's courtyard toward the administration building.

The rain had stopped, and the courtyard was brightly lit by a row of floodlights on metal poles, like a parking lot. She and Gaia cast multiple yellow shadows on the wet concrete as they walked.

This is so crazy, Catherine told herself again. Catherine had gotten the bad news about Gaia from Will and Kim, who had come upstairs to tell her hours ago.

"Come on," Gaia said. She was carrying the black folder of photographs and a thick sheaf of papers she'd picked out of Catherine's copy of the Hogan's Alley game case file. Catherine didn't understand what was so important about the victims' insurance records, but Gaia had refused to take the time to explain.

"Do you know what you look like?" Catherine asked as they barreled into the admin building's lobby. Gaia was a fright. Her wet, tangled hair hung over her forehead like a janitor's mop. Her sweatpants were soaking wet, their cuffs painted through with green grass stains. Her running shoes were black with caked, drying mud. Only her hands were dry—they carefully cradled the documents she'd gotten from Catherine's file.

"I can't help that," Gaia said absently. "Come *on*—let's go."

"Can I help you?" the guard in the lobby of the administration building asked.

"We have to talk to one of the administrators," Gaia told him. She had handed over her own FBI trainee badge when she was expelled, so Catherine had to show hers.

The guard was shaking his head. "There are no unauthorized—"

"This is a Quantico Code X matter," Gaia told him in a severe tone of voice. "Do you understand? Straight to the top. Call Agent Malloy if you want, but you really don't want to be obstructing this."

Code X? Catherine had no idea what Gaia was talking about, but she tried her best to look official.

The guard looked back and forth between them.

"All right," he said grudgingly, turning a clipboard around and handing over a ballpoint pen. "Sign your name and time of arrival. But if I find out you're abusing a Code X, there'll be hell to pay."

Catherine had barely scribbled her name. Gaia grabbed her hand and pulled her forward, past the guard and into the nearest open elevator. After a maddening pause, the elevator doors rolled shut.

"'Investigation is about what you *don't* see,'" Gaia told Catherine as the elevator rose. Catherine realized she was quoting Special Agent Bishop—somehow Gaia was getting it exactly correct, word for word. "'Don't be fooled by distracting foreground details; concentrate on uncovering the hidden truth that lies beneath the world you observe.'"

Ding! The elevator opened. Gaia stormed out, hurrying down the carpeted corridor, following the wall signs until she got to a wide metal door.

Bishop, Jennifer, G44, the nameplate on the door read.

Gaia didn't bother with knocking—she just twisted the chrome knob and pushed open the door.

The office was smaller than Malloy's but still pretty big. It had a deep brown carpet. The walls were covered floor to ceiling with brown fabric bulletin boards on which dozens and dozens of index cards in all different colors had been tacked. There were stacks of file folders on the floor in neat rows and other folders on the black leather couch that spanned the center of the room. Agent Bishop was sitting behind her own oak desk, a white FBI mug of coffee beside her, typing at her computer. She looked up, startled. Her eyes widened in surprise—and then narrowed as she recognized Gaia and Catherine.

"How did you get in here?" Agent Bishop demanded. "By breaking more rules, I'd imagine."

"Please," Gaia said, stepping forward. "Please, Agent Bishop, if I could just have a few moments of your time—"

Bishop was already shaking her head. *This isn't going to be easy,* Catherine thought, seeing Bishop's face. There wasn't a shred of sympathy or kindness behind those tortoiseshell glasses. "Not a chance," Bishop said severely. "No trainees should be in this building unless summoned, and *you,* Gaia

Moore, shouldn't even be on FBI property."

"'End of the day,'" Gaia argued urgently. She was clutching her folder and papers in both hands. Her wet hair flew haphazardly around her head. "He said 'end of the day'—I'm still allowed here for few more hours. If you could just listen to me . . . I've figured out something important."

Let her talk, Catherine found herself thinking. She could hear something in Gaia's voice—some kind of desperation or finality—and she wasn't sure Bishop was catching it. The sound frightened her. *Just let her talk, Ms. Bishop—that's all I ask. Expel her if you must, but don't humiliate her.*

"It's too late," Agent Bishop said. She stood up, her short red hair swinging against her cheeks as she stepped around her desk. "I'm sorry, Gaia. Really, I am, but we've been through this. The Quantico training program has very clear rules, and they must apply to each trainee equally. Otherwise they have no value. In fact"—Bishop looked at Catherine as she kept moving toward her office's smooth metal door—"I'm surprised that you would let yourself get pulled into this, Catherine. If you're going to ruin things for yourself, Gaia, that's your affair, as sorry as it makes me. But there's no excuse for dragging another trainee down with you."

"She's my friend," Gaia said.

That's right, Catherine thought, with a sudden burst of feeling that surprised her. *That's right, I am.*

"But you don't understand," Gaia persisted. "Please, this is different. It's not about me—it's about being an agent, about solving crimes. I've finally figured out—"

"'Being an agent,'" Bishop said sharply, her hand on the open

226

office door, "is about following orders and obeying regulations. Something you've already demonstrated that you don't understand. And it's something *you* seem to be forgetting, Ms. Sanders. Now get out of my office before I have you taken out—and you won't like the consequences of that one bit, I assure you."

"Don't you remember California?" Gaia asked Bishop. They were both halfway out the door, and Gaia had turned back, making this final plea. To Catherine, she was sounding more and more like a young girl or a high school student and less like an adult. "Agent Bishop, don't you remember what you told me about taking a chance—about changing my life?"

"Good-bye, Gaia," Bishop said. She was tapping her fingers on the edge of the door. "Please, let's part on good terms at least. Let's not have a fight."

Gaia sighed. Catherine saw her shoulders sink under her rain-soaked sweatshirt, and then she turned and walked out of the office. Catherine followed, and the metal door swung shut behind them. To Catherine, it sounded like the door to a tomb.

LIKE SLEEPWALKING

Gaia took a step away from Agent Bishop's door. It felt like sleepwalking. She was still holding the Hogan's Alley papers and folder in her hand, but she had nearly forgotten what they were—she knew they were supposed to be important or have some kind of value on some past life of hers, but in that moment she couldn't really remember why.

She and Catherine were in a wide, gray-walled corridor on the top floor of Quantico Administration Building A. The corridor widened out into a waiting area with padded chairs and a big plate glass window a few yards away. The rain-speckled window showed the same dim gray view they'd gotten used to all day.

What happens now? Gaia thought distantly. It was strange— she was trying to collect her thoughts and focus on what was important, but she couldn't seem to think of anything important. It was kind of soothing, in a way. It was restful. With nothing important to care about, she could give in to a peaceful feeling. *None of this really matters, anyway,* she told herself, taking another step forward. It was like a weight lifting off her. *I'm not really sure what* does *matter.*

What she really wanted to do was go to sleep. Her legs ached after her long run—she suddenly felt the burn in her calves and thighs that she'd been ignoring up to now. And her body was cold and dirty. A hot bath and then sleep. Long, peaceful sleep now that there was nothing to worry or care about.

Except I don't have a bed, she thought dismally. There was a bare mattress and a set of luggage in a dorm room two buildings away, and soon she and that luggage would have to be gone.

Damn. It was inconvenient.

"Gaia."

Catherine's voice from behind her. It was a nice, sweet voice but with a rough edge beneath it—a voice she'd come to know pretty well over the last few days. *And a voice I might as well forget,* she thought. *Since after today I'll never hear it again.*

"Gaia," Catherine said more insistently. Gaia realized she'd walked forward into the waiting area, facing the big window. It really was like sleepwalking. There was nobody around; the neat row of padded chairs were empty. There was a brass inlay of the FBI seal on the wall. "Gaia, can you hear me? Are you okay?"

I'm fine, Gaia thought calmly. She was staring out the window past the beads of rain at the wide grass training field. A group of male trainees were doing calisthenics, lined up like bowling pins along the grass. *I'm fine, Catherine—don't worry about me. Don't let me get you into any more trouble.*

"Hey," Catherine said sharply, stepping in front of Gaia and taking her wet shoulders. "Snap out of it. Come on."

"What?" It was a stall—Gaia had heard her perfectly. She didn't want to talk. She wanted Catherine to move out of the way so that she could stare out the window. And maybe go to sleep right here in one of these chairs, if they would let her. Which they wouldn't.

"Gaia, what's the matter with you?" Catherine said angrily. "This isn't like you at all."

"How do you know?" Gaia said impatiently. "What do *you* know about me, anyway?"

"More than you think," Catherine said. Her dark brown eyes were inches from Gaia's. They stared intently back at her. Gaia wasn't interested in making eye contact—she kept trying to gaze out at the gray sky. "You think I'm blind? You think I'm stupid? You think I haven't learned *anything* about you in the last few days?"

"All right," Gaia said weakly, sinking into one of the chairs. It was every bit as comfortable as she'd predicted. "All right, I'm sorry."

"You didn't answer my question," Catherine persisted. She crouched down in front of Gaia, taking the papers and folder before Gaia let them slip to the carpeted floor.

"What's happened to you?"

"Nothing. You heard," Gaia said weakly. "It's over. I'm kicked out. I haven't got what it takes."

Catherine was shaking her head. "I can't believe I'm hearing this. Don't you realize we've all been learning from *you?*"

Gaia finally let her eyes focus on Catherine. "What?"

"*All* of us," Catherine insisted. She had Gaia's wrists in her hands. "Will, Kim, me. What's your problem, anyway? The *steak house?* That was nonsense—it was a trick and you fell for it. Big deal. The fight? So you started a fight. It's not *important,* Gaia."

"So what is?" Gaia had never heard Catherine talk like this.

"Look." Catherine's arm snaked out, pointing at the wall— at the brass seal mounted there. "Look at that symbol. Think about what it means. Think about what we're all doing here."

Gaia turned her head and followed Catherine's gesture. Federal Bureau of Investigation, she read. He eyes followed the curves and lines of the emblem as if she'd never seen it before.

"Look at them out there," Catherine went on, hooking a thumb to point behind her back out the window, where the trainees were doing jumping jacks. "Look how hard they're working—how proud they are of what they're part of. Just like me. *This is as high as the elevator goes, as far as the train takes you.* These people are a force for good. And they're the best in the world. They solve crimes; they fight for justice. And you could be the best of us all—you know it as well as I do. So why are you letting this"—Catherine pointed back at Bishop's office behind Gaia—"this *BS* stop you?"

Gaia looked at Catherine, who was actually panting from the exertion of everything she'd said. She looked as surprised as Gaia was.

"Wow," Catherine said sheepishly, brushing her hair back from her forehead. "Sorry. I didn't mean to make a speech."

Gaia put her hand on Catherine's shoulder. She pushed down, leaning on Catherine as she pulled herself out of the soft chair and rose to her feet.

"That's okay," Gaia said. She held out her hand. Catherine took it, and Gaia pulled her to her feet.

"We helped each other stand up," Catherine said, smiling.

"Right," Gaia said, squeezing Catherine's hand and then letting go. "What do you say we keep doing it?"

"It's a deal."

Gaia took a deep breath. She looked back over at the FBI seal on the wall. Her mood seemed to have changed: that strange, irrefutable desire to hide somewhere and fall asleep had gone away.

You give a good speech, Catherine, Gaia thought. *A very good speech.*

"You seemed to think these were important," Catherine said, holding out the Hogan's Alley folder and papers.

"Yeah," Gaia said, taking them. "Follow me."

LATERAL THINKING

Catherine watched as Gaia flipped through the photographs in the folder. They were full-page, glossy color prints of the "crime scenes" from the case. Each had an evidence stamp from the lab next to an embossed FBI seal. She still had no idea what Gaia was thinking as she followed her back to Agent Bishop's office.

Finally Gaia had what she wanted. She pulled out a single photograph. It was the same picture she'd studied in the car: the photograph of Abe Kaufman's bathroom, showing the pictures of the old man's relatives, the open, empty medicine cabinet, and the spotless, cracked porcelain sink. Catherine had no idea what the picture meant—if anything—or what it had to do with the insurance records Gaia had asked about.

Gaia slid the photograph under Agent Bishop's door.

What?

Catherine still didn't understand, but she was impressed with the unexpected maneuver. What would Bishop do? How would she respond?

They both stood there, waiting. Through the door Catherine heard the muffled sound of Bishop's phone ringing. She also heard footsteps and then, distinctly, the ruffling sound of the photograph being picked up.

Gaia and Catherine looked at each other.

Open the door, Catherine thought frantically. *I don't know what Gaia's got, but I hope it's good—open the door and we'll both find out.*

With a loud, metallic click the door swung inward. Agent Bishop stood there, one hand on the doorknob, the other holding the photograph. She was squinting quizzically.

"Gaia," Bishop began, "I'm not sure what you—"

"The *medicine cabinet*," Gaia said. "There's nothing in it.

Which doesn't make any sense. Have you ever known an old guy to have an *empty* medicine cabinet? Doesn't almost every person over seventy have at least some prescribed medication?"

Agent Bishop didn't answer. She was listening. It was impossible for Catherine to interpret her facial expression.

"I've *never* seen an old person have an empty medicine cabinet," Gaia went on. "I could even *smell* the medicine in the air. That was your point before, right? That a crime scene can tell you what a killer is thinking."

Gaia had another document ready—it was a folded computer printout that she pulled out of the thick file. Behind Agent Bishop the phone continued to ring.

"The killer emptied the cabinet. He *took the bottles away*—he didn't want us to see them. Look." Gaia held up the printout. "Abe Kaufman's insurance records, routinely submitted for police verification in the case of a violent death. It lists the insurance holder's medical data. And here"—Gaia stabbed her finger down on the document—"it lists all prescribed medications. In particular, heart pills. And it gives the doctor's name. Look: Dr. Byron Eastmann."

Bishop was framed in her office doorway, still holding the chrome knob. She hadn't interrupted—Catherine was glad for that. It seemed that Gaia had somehow managed to get her full attention.

"Nathan Hill's pockets," Gaia went on. She had pulled out another photograph and held it up next to the others. "A bottle of ampicillin, an antibiotic prescribed for any number of minor infectious conditions. Will looked it up on the Web. And here's the bottle."

Catherine looked over at the photograph. She could clearly read the text on the bottle's label. It showed the drug's name and the prescribed dosage. And below that the doctor's name:

Eastman, Byron, MD

Oh my God, Catherine thought. Finally she was following Gaia's logic completely.

"Both victims had the same *doctor,*" Gaia finished, leaning on Agent Bishop's desk. That's the connection—that's the key to finding the killer. All because the medicine cabinet was empty. The killer didn't want to leave clues, so he took away the old man's prescription medicine. But when he killed the boy, he was moving so fast—afraid to wake the parents, probably, that he didn't have time to check Nathan's pockets." Gaia took a breath. "That's what you mean about seeing what's not there. Isn't it?"

"Don't you answer your phone, Bishop?"

Catherine jumped. It was a harsh male voice right behind her. Turning around, she was shocked to see Special Agent Brian Malloy, as big as life, close-cropped hair, severe gray suit and all. There was no way of knowing how long he had been standing there.

"Brian," Bishop said, looking flustered. "I'm sorry. I was just—"

"Who the hell used a Code X clearance without my authorization?" Malloy demanded. "Willis downstairs called to check with me, luckily. What's going on here? Who's responsible?"

"Me," Gaia told him. Looking over, Catherine saw that Gaia was standing straight upright again. Her hair and clothes seemed to be drying; she had lost the drowned-blond-rat look she'd had before. "I did it."

Malloy looked down at her. He seemed more stunned than angry. "Why on earth would you do that? Are you trying to get into even more trouble?"

"No," Gaia said calmly. "I did it because I've cracked the case."

Malloy was nodding. "The prescriptions. That's right, isn't it, Jenny? That's your famous impossible clue?"

"Well—" Agent Bishop was still holding all the photographs and documents that Gaia had handed her. "Yes. Yes, technically she's quite correct. But that doesn't mean—"

"Has anyone ever cracked it that quickly?" Malloy was squinting, his arms crossed. "It seems to me that nobody ever has."

"Well—no," Bishop said tightly. "I suppose not. But Brian, what are you saying? We've had this discussion already. There is more than one reason to expel this trainee, and the rules of the program don't change just because—"

"She wouldn't stop," Malloy said, looking down at Gaia. "It's interesting. She's showing persistence. Wouldn't you agree?"

"Fine," Bishop said, holding up the photographs. "He's right, Gaia—this shows a talent for what's called 'lateral thinking,' and that's very commendable. But there's more to my game than just this clue. You haven't caught the killer yet."

"I'd be interested to see what would happen," Malloy said slowly, "if Gaia rejoined her team and reentered the game."

"Put her *back in?*" Bishop's eyes were wide. "Are you serious? After all the rules she's broken? Just this morning you yourself said—"

"You'd be on probationary status," Malloy told Gaia sternly. "And you're still in a lot of trouble with me—this Code X trick you pulled makes it worse. Do you understand?"

"Yes, sir," Gaia said. "Thank you, sir."

"The expulsion form is on my desk, Jenny," Malloy told Bishop. "It's not going away. It can stay on my desk a little longer. Maybe long enough for someone to win the game, if they're particularly good."

Catherine took the opportunity to reach over and grab Gaia's hand. She squeezed it. Gaia looked back at Catherine. Gaia's eyes gleamed. Neither of them spoke, but it was clear what they were saying to each other.

You did it, Catherine thought. *You did it, Gaia—you cracked the case.*

Gaia nodded soberly. *But it's not over yet.*

cement exploded
in the ground

PULL THE TRIGGER

At just before nine the next morning Kim stood in his FBI agent clothes at the perimeter of Hogan's Alley. The ground was still damp from the previous day's rain, but the sky was clear, a deep, rich blue. Kim was standing with Will and Catherine, listening to Gaia, who was pacing back and forth in front of them with the morning sun glinting off her sunglasses.

"When the bell rings," Gaia said, "we'll go straight to the commercial plaza, on the south edge of Hogan's Alley. It's like a two-minute walk. Then we'll try to talk to Dr. Eastmann."

"You don't want to follow up with Sheriff Landy?" Will asked. Kim could tell, watching his body language, that something had happened between him and Gaia the previous afternoon, when they'd gone for that ill-fated drive into Quantico. He wasn't sure what it had been, exactly, but his theory was that they had kissed. "By now those two detectives will have canvassed the neighborhood and talked to everyone who knew Abe Kaufman."

"That's the obvious move," Gaia agreed. "But I don't like it. The *doctor's* the key. That's the connection between the victims. If he can give us a list of his patients, we might get one step ahead of the killer."

"Fine," said Will agreeably. "Just tell us what to do, and we'll do it."

"Catherine?" Gaia asked, looking at her watch. "Anything to add? We've got twenty seconds."

"Get the doctor's patient data on a disk," Catherine advised. "Then we can match it up to the rest of our database. Beyond that, I'm just awaiting your orders."

"We all are," Kim said.

"All right, then," Gaia said. She smiled a little weakly and then held up her hands with her fingers crossed. "Let's go."

The bell rang.

Is she right? Kim wondered. Gaia's plan was like betting everything on black when you played roulette. If they were wrong, they'd be hopelessly behind the other teams. Right now, as they sprinted across the Hogan's Alley town square, veering left to follow Gaia toward the "town's" small commercial plaza, Kim could see two of the other three teams behind them, sprinting toward the police station.

They could be right, Kim thought. *And Gaia could be wrong. But would Bishop have reinstated her if her gambit didn't make sense?*

Kim didn't know the answer to that question.

The commercial plaza was just two buildings, each two stories tall, facing each other across a small plaza with park benches and a fountain. A balcony ran along the second floor, leading to the upstairs offices. Will had gotten there first and was scanning the framed array of shingles that showed what businesses could be found there. They saw signs for real estate offices, insurance firms, a notary public, a small law firm . . . and a sign that read Byron Eastmann, M.D.—2nd Floor, East Building. Will looked at Gaia, pointing at the sign.

"Let's go," Gaia said. She led them up the cement stairs to the balcony.

They arrived at the door to the doctor's office. Gaia pressed the doorbell, and after a moment the door buzzed open.

The four trainees walked through the door.

They were standing in a small waiting room, with easy-listening music playing from concealed speakers. There were two overstuffed cloth couches facing each other and between them a laminated coffee table with a large glass ashtray and a stack of magazines. A fake painting of a sailing ship was hanging from one wall, casting a shadow on the yellow, floral wallpaper.

An elderly woman with a walker and a bandage on her arm sat in one of the chairs. She looked at the four trainees in confusion as they came into the room.

At the back of the office was a small secretary's desk. A young man in a white lab coat sat behind the desk, thumbing through an old-fashioned card catalog. The man had a slight build and thinning chestnut hair. An engraved nameplate on his desk read Bill Oakley. Oakley flinched at the sound of their entry and then smiled pleasantly at them.

Startled, Kim thought. *He has no idea why we're here—it's unnerving him.*

"Good morning," Oakley said pleasantly. "Can I help you?"

Gaia held up her badge. "Federal Bureau of Investigation,"

she said. "We'd like to speak to Dr. Eastmann if he's available, please."

Oakley frowned. "He's here, but I think he's busy. It's a very busy morning," Oakley told them. He was reaching for a phone. "Just a second—I'll see if he's available."

"Thank you," Gaia said.

"Dr. Eastmann?" Oakley said into the phone. "Federal agents to see you."

There was a brief pause, during which Kim could hear a metallic-sounding voice on the other end of the phone.

"I don't know what it's about, Doctor," Oakley said. "Shall I send them in? Yes. All right."

Oakley hung up the phone and pointed at the door behind him. "You can go right in," he said.

Gaia and the others trooped through another door into a small office with an adjoining examination room. A severe-looking, powerfully built man was seated behind a desk. He had close-cropped black hair and a small goatee. Medical texts filled the bookcases lining the room.

"Yes?" the doctor barked in a strong German accent. "What is this intrusion?"

All the other trainees are across "town," Kim thought nervously. *Talking to the sheriff and his detectives. What are we doing here? Do we trust Gaia that much?*

"Sorry to bother you, Doctor," Gaia said, holding up her badge, "but we're federal agents investigating two homicides."

"Yes?" Dr. Eastmann said brusquely.

"Nathan Hill," Will said, "And Abraham Kaufman. Both have been killed."

240

"Yes—I have heard," the doctor said, nodding stiffly. "A tragic thing to be sure. Very bad for the town. But what do you come to me for?"

"We understand that they were both patients of yours," Catherine said.

Dr. Eastmann raised his eyebrows. "You are insinuating something? Accusing me, perhaps? Do I need to call my attorney?"

"No, no . . . nothing like that," Will said, smiling broadly. "We're just trying to get some more information about the victims. Can you tell us anything about them that the investigating detectives might have missed?"

Dr. Eastmann was already shaking his head. "There is nothing of note," he said. "Kaufman, he had a weak heart valve; he required an anticoagulant. It was part of a recovery program following heart surgery he had last year. And the boy . . ." Dr. Eastmann squinted. "I don't recall. Something about infection—he had a weakened immune system and a wisdom tooth was infected. Yes."

Evasive answers, Kim thought. *Is he hiding something?*

"Can you go into more detail?" Gaia asked. "Can you think of anything, even something trivial, that we could—"

"Nothing, there is nothing," Dr. Eastmann said impatiently, standing up. "Please, now—I have patients to see. Perhaps if you come back later, I can provide you with medical records, but I am very busy right now. I must ask that you go."

"But—" Gaia began.

Will grabbed her arm suddenly.

"Did you hear that?" Will said. "A door slamming."

241

Kim looked back at the door that led to the outer office. Hadn't they left it open? It had just swung shut, as if blown by a sudden breeze.

Gaia and Will looked at each other and then strode over to the door, pulling it open. They all walked out into the waiting room.

It took a moment for Kim to notice what had changed. The elderly woman was still sitting at the coffee table. The fake painting was still hanging on the wall. And then he got it.

The front desk was empty. Bill Oakley had gone.

Walking closer so that he could see behind the desk, Kim felt something like an electric current passing through him. On a shelf below the desk he saw a large black-leather-bound Bible and next to it a book of Old Testament scriptures.

"Gaia," Kim yelled suddenly, pointing.

Below the religious books he had seen a pair of hiking boots. Their soles were encrusted with red clay.

"Ma'am," Catherine said to the elderly lady with the bandaged arm, "did you see what happened to Mr. Oakley?"

"What—?" The woman cupped her ear, frowning.

"Did you see what happened to Mr. Oakley? The desk clerk?"

"Why—" The woman pointed at the front door. "It was the strangest thing. Once you'd gone into the office, he suddenly got up and bolted out of here."

Gaia and Will didn't need to be told twice. They dashed out the door onto the balcony.

Meanwhile, looking out the office's window, Kim suddenly saw a slim figure in a white lab coat running across the parking lot below.

"*Parking lot,*" Kim yelled, vaulting forward. He had to jump over the coffee table to catch up with Catherine, who was dashing out the office's front door, her gun drawn.

Will and Gaia both vaulted over the side of the balcony. They hung from its railing side by side for a moment and then dropped lightly to the ground, rolling as they landed.

Blam! A gunshot rang out, deafeningly loud, echoing like a repeated drumbeat across the narrow plaza. *Blam!* Another gunshot.

Will and Gaia dove behind the fountain just as a bullet smacked into the other side of the fountain's stone base. *That's a nice effect,* the back of Kim's mind thought. He was so adrenalized that he didn't realize he'd drawn his own gun until he looked down and saw the sun glinting off its magazine. Falling back against the wall that ran along the back of the balcony, he worked his way over to the balcony's rail, holding the gun down in both hands. Below, he could see Gaia moving along the edge of the courtyard, her gun drawn.

"APB, APB," Catherine was saying intently into her cell phone behind him on the balcony. "Hello? Hello?" She shook the phone, obviously having lost the connection, and then began redialing.

In the parking lot below, Bill Oakley was crouched behind a car, pointing his gun over its hood back at Gaia and Will. From his aerial vantage point Kim could see that nobody had a good shot.

"Hello? Hello? This is Agent Sanders calling—" Catherine repeated behind him.

Resting his hand on the balcony's railing, Kim carefully

aimed his gun at Bill Oakley's shoulder and pulled the trigger.

Blam! A shot rang out and a bit of cement exploded in the ground in front of Oakley. In that moment Gaia leaped over the fountain's edge and ran forward, gun drawn, her blond hair flying behind her.

"Freeze! FBI!" Gaia shouted, pressing the gun barrel against Bill Oakley's head. "You have the right to remain silent—"

"Sheriff?" Catherine said into the phone behind her. "Sheriff? This is Agent Sanders. We're putting out an all points bulletin for Bill Oakley, a Caucasian male who—what?"

"It's over," Bill Oakley yelled, smiling. He was waving up at Catherine, handing his gun to Gaia. "You got me!"

The game bell rang right then.

"Attention, attention." Special Agent Bishop's voice came over the loudspeaker. *"The Hogan's Alley game is completed. Repeat, the game is over, and we have a winner. Kim Lau, Gaia Moore, Catherine Sanders, and Will Taylor are the winners of the game."*

Will

There are moments I like to call "sublime." Not many of them, but once or twice they come along.

Kissing Gaia in the car was one. But it didn't last. I think I've wanted to kiss that girl since the first moment I saw her, when she came out of her dorm room and ran smack-dab into me. I can't believe that was only a couple of days ago. I remember that I could barely think straight—I babbled some nonsense about her name meaning "Goddess of the earth" and was actually lame enough to bring up, for no reason, the fact that I'm a track star.

But I couldn't help it. The word *Goddess* came into my head because in that moment, I felt like a starstruck, romantic little kid. This stunning blond creature in a dirty T-shirt had just run into me, as if I *hadn't* already been thinking about her nonstop after her performance in the obstacle course.

So I finally kissed Gaia Moore. And it was sublime.

But that moment, that sweet moment when the loudspeaker announced we'd won, was somehow even better. I actually felt light-headed. I laughed like a little boy and looked up at the cloudless blue sky hanging over that wonderful fake town, and I actually hugged the actor playing "Bill Oakley," the "killer," as he was congratulating me.

How about that, Uncle Casper? I thought deliriously. *We won the game! We're at the top of the damn class! How do you like that!*

And then Gaia and I hugged, and she kissed me again, very quickly, very shyly, while Kim and Catherine were on their way down the balcony steps and couldn't see. Like I said, sublime moments.

The rest of that day is a blur. I remember that we all got the rest of the day off, and all the trainees, winners and losers both, ended up at Johnny Ray's, where we got to mingle with all the "Hogan's Alley" actors and talk about the game.

I remember sitting at one of those round wooden tables, on my third or fourth beer, with Kim next to me, grinning as "Dr. Eastmann" and "Detective Okuda" talked about how they'd laid bets on our team.

"I knew you guys had it," the "Okuda" actor said.

"No way," said "Dr. Eastmann," who really has no accent at all. "I had you completely fooled."

Agent Bishop made a surprise appearance at Johnny Ray's and even joined us for a drink. She explained the rest of the game—how Bill Oakley's murder spree was based on an actual case study, in which a fundamentalist born-again Christian turned psychotic and decided that all medical science was mankind interfering with God's plan. Whenever people who were "supposed" to die received medical treatment, the killer believed that he had to "release" them from their "sinfully pro-longed" life—and when he had "saved" them, he wrote what he'd done on the wall in their own blood, "baptizing" their spirits as he rescued them from purgatory.

"Amazing," Kim said, shaking his head as Catherine refilled his beer glass. "And that's just the tip of the iceberg, isn't it? So many different psychoses to study . . ."

"That's just the tip of the iceberg," Agent Bishop confirmed.

"Hey," Gaia said, dropping into a chair beside me. Kim and

Catherine came over, too, and we all looked at each other. I think each of us wanted to say something clever, but nothing was coming to mind.

"We're going to head back," Gaia told us, indicating Catherine and herself.

"You don't want another beer?" I said. But I knew the answer before I'd even finished asking.

"I'm going to be drinking as little as possible for a while," Gaia said, standing up and reaching to squeeze my arm. "I'll see you back there."

"Whatever you say, Ms. Moore," I told her.

"What?"

"Like I said before—we did meet again on the field of battle, and you won fair and square."

"Oh, please," Gaia said. The light of the setting sun silhouetted her as she and Catherine walked out of Johnny Ray's and into the night air. And behind her back this South Carolina boy silently raised a glass in her direction.

The sun was setting, a golden panorama above the canopy of trees to the west, as Gaia walked across the gravel toward Catherine's Altima. The music and laughter from Johnny Ray's continued behind them. Gaia slowed down, dialing a number on her cell phone while Catherine got out her car keys.

1 . . . 212 . . .

How long had it been since she'd dialed a New York phone number? Gaia didn't remember. A very long time. Years, maybe. She pressed send and lifted the phone to her ear. She could hear a phone ringing miles and miles to the north as she looked out at the beginning of the sunset.

What's it like right now in New York? Gaia tried to picture it. The air wasn't this clear, that was certain. There would be traffic noises, the drone of air conditioners, passing planes and traffic helicopters, the constant murmur of more than a million people on a slim island a few miles long.

"You've reached Tom Moore."

Gaia's father had a new answering machine message—or at least, one she'd never heard before. *"I'm not here to take your call, but if you leave a message, I'll get back to you."*

And then the beep, so quickly that Gaia hadn't had time to collect her thoughts. She stood there on the gravel in the sunset, the car in front of her, its taillights already lit as Catherine idled the Altima engine.

"Um—Dad, it's me," Gaia said awkwardly. "I'm calling from Quantico."

And what else did she want to say? Gaia wasn't sure—but

she had to keep talking or the machine would cut her off.

"Um, I just—I just wanted to tell you that everything's fine. I'm working for Special Agent Malloy now. I've had a couple of snags, but I've—I've made some friends, and I guess things are going okay. So I guess I'm with the FBI now."

The wind was blowing through the Virginia trees—Catherine tapped on her car horn impatiently, just once.

"So I just wanted to say," Gaia started, "thank you. For everything. I love you."

Beep! The machine cut her off. Had it picked up that last part?

Gaia hoped so.

"I can't wait to take a shower and get into bed," Catherine said, stifling a yawn as she drove them out of the gravel parking lot and onto the highway. Soon they were cruising toward the FBI base, and the sky was darkening to gold. There were still puddles in the highway left and right as they drove.

"I feel the same way," Gaia said, leaning back against the car seat. "We've got firearms training tomorrow when I get back from my drills."

"Drills?"

"Running and calisthenics," Gaia explained. "Six-thirty in the morning, while you're still fast asleep. It's part of my probation."

Gaia was staring out the window, watching the landscape go by as they drove. She was thinking about New York, and the life she'd run away from, and the new life she'd started here. *I almost ran away from this one,* she thought sleepily. *I'm really glad I didn't.*

"Almost there," Catherine said, pointing. "She lives right around the corner from the bar."

Through the windshield Gaia saw Kelly's small, two-story house coming nearer. It had a red-shingled roof and its siding was painted a restful blue color. Gaia had never seen the outside of the building in daylight—the last time she was here, she'd been carried inside, unconscious.

"Are you sure about this?" Catherine asked, idling the car in the driveway. "We can do this later."

"No, I want to do it now," Gaia said firmly. It was true—she'd made up her mind. No matter how ashamed she was of what she'd done, it was time to make amends.

"Do you want me to come with you?" Catherine asked, killing the engine and dropping the Altima into park. The evening crickets' song filled the car. With the engine off, both women could hear the soft, distant sound of a baby crying.

Gaia shook her head. "I'll just be a minute."

Gaia slammed the car door and crossed the gravel drive to Kelly's porch, which was littered with brightly colored plastic toys and a small tricycle. She hesitated a moment and then knocked on the edge of the screen door.

"Just one second," Kelly's voice sang out. Gaia waited and Kelly appeared behind the screen door, rocking her baby in her arms. She wore a Johnny Ray's T-shirt and a pair of faded jeans. She was barefoot. "Hello, Gaia," she said without expression.

"Hi, Kelly."

Kelly squinted. "You here for more of my hangover remedy? Welcome to it, if you want some."

If she's angry at me, Gaia thought, *I deserve it. I'd better take it and move on. I can't avoid it—not in a small town like this.*

Not if I'm staying here.

"No, thanks," Gaia said. "Listen, I came around to apologize."

Kelly looked back at her and smiled tightly, but Gaia thought it was just politeness. In her arms the baby woke up and began to cry.

"Shhh, Jasmine," Kelly murmured soothingly. The baby had bright blond hair, as wispy as the puffs on a dandelion. Gaia could barely see in the evening light. "Shhh. This is just a friend. Say hi to Gaia."

"Hi, Jasmine," Gaia said through the screen door. "She's pretty."

Kelly smiled. "Thanks."

"I really wanted to apologize," Gaia said awkwardly. "I'm sorry I hurt Jack. I mean, I'll tell him myself," she added quickly. "And I'm supposed to tell him that the agency will pay for all the damage I did to his apartment. But I—but I wanted to talk to you first. I don't know why I did what I did. I guess I'm kind of a confused person."

"You don't seem that confused to me," Kelly said. She kept rocking the baby. "A part of you is very angry."

"That's right."

"But not all of you. It's the same way with Jack. With all of us, really." Jasmine had fallen back asleep, but Kelly kept rocking her. "Are you going to be staying on?"

"I hope so."

Kelly smiled. "Glad to hear it," she said. "Come around again and I'll buy you a drink. But just one."

Gaia laughed and then waved and turned back toward Catherine's Altima, its headlights glowing in the growing dark.

A POOL OF BLOOD

Catherine and Gaia rounded a curve in the road, and now they were passing the mowed memorial field, with the large bronze statue of the infantryman standing in his endless vigil against the oncoming night. Gaia stared up at the dark silhouette of the statue as they passed, thinking about grief—what it could do to people and what it had done to her. It was almost as if—

Wait.

Gaia twisted in her seat, looking back at the statue.

"Catherine," she said quietly, "stop the car."

"What? Jesus, now what? I swear, driving with you is—"

"Look," Gaia said, pointing.

There were no flowers in the bronze gun barrel.

Every morning and every afternoon, rain or shine, I put flowers in the soldier's gun, Ann Knight had said.

I live right there.

Catherine was idling the car. Gaia stared at the empty bronze gun barrel and then slowly pivoted her head and looked over at the small house across the road.

The lights in the house were out.

The front door was ajar.

The windows were open.

"Catherine," Gaia said. "You know how there are always flowers inside the gun?"

"Yeah, so?" Catherine asked, sounding impatient.

"Well, I met the woman who puts them there. She told me she never misses a day, rain or shine."

"That's really touching, Gaia. But do you mind if I drive while we talk about this?"

"I think this is a crime scene, Catherine."

"What?" Catherine asked.

"Like Bishop said, in a crime scene see what's not there," Gaia said. "Here's what I recommend we do. We'll get out of the car. We'll walk over to that house. We won't go in or even step onto the porch—we don't want to do anything to disturb the scene. We're just going to look."

"But the game's over," Catherine said.

"*That* game's over. But remember the steak house. The rules," Gaia recited, "are constantly changing."

"Okay," Catherine said. "Okay."

"You want to kill the engine?"

Catherine killed the engine. The headlights flicked out, and now they were in total country dark. The sky had faded to a dim, pale blue. Gaia and Catherine got out of the car and walked toward the house.

Careful, Gaia told herself. *Careful, now. Do everything by the rules. The rules are there for a reason.*

She got to the porch. The only sound was the crickets around the house.

"Hello?" Gaia called out. "Ann?"

No answer. A twig cracked behind Gaia—it was Catherine, walking closer.

"Ann?" Gaia called. *"Are you there?"*

"Mommy?" a voice called from inside the house. It was the voice of a small child.

"Sam?" Gaia yelled. She was staring at the house's darkened door. It was pitch black—like staring into the entrance to a mine. "Are you okay?"

"My mommy's hurt," Sam's plaintive voice called out. *"I'm scared."*

"Don't be scared, Sam," Gaia said. It was so dark now that she could barely see the outlines of the house against the sky. "You remember me? The blond girl from yesterday? I'm your mommy's friend."

"I'm scared," the boy repeated.

"Sam," Gaia called out, using as calm and friendly a voice as she could muster, "why don't you come out here?"

"Okay . . ."

There was a long pause and then, deep in the darkness of the house, Gaia heard footsteps. The footsteps got closer and stopped.

"Can't see," Sam called out. His voice was much closer.

"Can you turn the light on?" Gaia answered.

"Okay . . ."

After a second there was a click, and inside the house the living room's bright overhead light snapped on.

Catherine screamed.

Ann Knight was lying dead in the center of the room. Her head was twisted at a strange angle and there was a pool of blood spreading out around her body. It was remarkably realistic—maybe even better than the "Nathan Hill" body they'd examined days ago. It was also really strange, Gaia thought. Seeing the "corpse" of someone with whom she'd already established a connection. Another element of the game she'd have to get used to.

Sam, the boy, was standing in the rear doorway, his hand still on the light switch. In his other hand he held a large red lollipop. Catherine was gasping for breath. She had stopped herself from screaming again but just barely.

"Catherine," Gaia said. "Stop it! Snap out of it!"

"Okay—" But Catherine was still staring into the room. Her eyes were as big as saucers. "Okay. Okay. Um— What do we do?"

"Follow procedure," Gaia whispered.

"Still here," Sam called out. "He gave me a lolly!"

Catherine and Gaia looked at each other. Gaia could barely see Catherine's brown eyes shining in the dark.

Catherine pointed wordlessly toward the edge of the house. Gaia nodded. They both understood—because they clearly had both heard the same broken branch at the same time.

The killer's still here.

Catherine leaned her head extremely close to Gaia's "Got to go in there," she whispered, so quietly Gaia could barely hear. "Kid's in danger—"

"No," Gaia whispered back. "Crime scene. Means 'do not disturb.'" She pointed at the flanks of the house. "You go right—I'll go left."

Catherine nodded firmly. She squeezed Gaia's shoulder, and

they moved off in opposite directions as quietly as they could.

Gaia crept step by step along the edge of Ann Knight's house. Her feet sank into the grass and soft mud beside the house's cement foundations. With her right hand she guided herself along the house's rough siding. Her left hand was stiffened, thumb rigid—a karate weapon.

The crickets were nearly deafening. Gaia could barely see; the harsh overhead light from the living room—the crime scene—flowed out a window overhead and behind her. Now she was moving through tall weeds, passing the glass globes of power meters on the side of the house. And she heard it again—a footstep on a twig in front of her.

Squinting, Gaia could barely see a silhouette against the dark woods ahead. A male shape, with some kind of hood or hat pulled over the head. Powerfully built—and moving slowly away from her.

"Freeze—FBI!" Gaia shouted.

The shape of the man darted away toward the woods. Gaia sprinted to catch up, nearly twisting her ankle in the cold, muddy ground. "Hi-*yaaa*," she yelled, launching into a flying tackle.

Her shoulder collided with the man's torso. Even through his thick clothes, Gaia could feel how strong he was. The man lost his balance, grunting as he slammed forward into the mud. Gaia lunged on top of him, trying to grab his wrists and pin him down, but the "murderer" was too fast—he had twisted around, aiming a powerful jab at Gaia's head that she barely managed to dodge before slipping away and regaining her feet. Gaia stretched out her foot to trip the man and he went down again, collapsing with a grunt while Gaia, winded, tried to regain her feet. This time his blow connected, catching Gaia on the side of her forehead. The chop was expertly delivered—a flash of light shone in her left eye as a stinging sensation spread over her face. *Get ready,* she told herself dully—*here comes the pain.*

And a wave of agony bloomed over her face as she stumbled and fell in the soft earth. The man scrambled to his feet, a dark shape like a child's cutout, and bolted away, panting, into the woods.

Damn it, Gaia thought, regaining her breath while lying on the wet forest floor. *Damn it—it's so hard when you can't see.*

"Agent Bishop?"

Catherine's voice behind her, on her cell phone.

"Agent Bishop, it's Catherine Sanders. We've found a murder victim."

I thought the game was over, Gaia thought as she followed the sound of Catherine's voice out of the woods and back toward the dark mass of Ann Knight's house. *What does this mean? What's happening now?*

Now that the man was gone, Gaia recognized a slight aroma—a faint smell in the air. A sugary smell that reminded her of childhood.

Candy, she thought, rising to her feet and delicately probing the tender bruise on her forehead. *Or lollipops.*

WAITING ALL MY LIFE

Gaia looked out across the road, away from the glaring police lights. The stars were out, but the western horizon was still light enough for her to see the silhouette of the bronze infantryman outlined against the sky.

It was fifteen minutes after Catherine called Agent Bishop and left word on Kim's voice mail that he and Will should come to Ann Knight's house. Two of the familiar FBI blue sedans were parked in front of the house, their flashers shining red and white in bright revolving flickers against the dark surrounding forest. Two men in FBI windbreakers were unrolling yellow Crime Scene—Do Not Cross tape across the front of the house's porch. It looked the same as the tape they'd seen across the Hogan's Alley Retirement Home after "Abraham Kaufman's" murder. From a distance Gaia could hear Catherine's voice, issuing calm orders to the forensics squad.

We stood and talked right there, Gaia marveled, looking out at the dark statue where she'd met Ann Knight. *Amazing—so real.* She realized she'd have to rack her brains, trying to find clues in everything the woman had told her. The dead husband, the flowers, the little boy—it was all significant now.

Another car was slowing to a stop in front of the house. As Gaia looked over, its headlights went out and Special Agent Brian Malloy stepped from the driver's seat and slammed the door. He took a moment to appraise the scene in his unreadable, ice-cold way and then came over to Gaia.

"Moore," he said. There was, as usual, no expression in his voice at all.

"Sir."

"Ready to report?"

"Not yet, sir," Gaia told him, turning back to face the

brightly lit house. "Agent Sanders has taken charge of the forensics, but they just started to secure the scene a few minutes ago. She would know more than I would about—"

"You're hurt," Malloy said in a softer voice, looking at Gaia's forehead. "You'd better get that taken care of."

"Yes, sir."

Malloy stood there, looking at Gaia, as if waiting for her to say something else. Gaia was confused. *Am I doing something wrong?* She thought quickly. *Some detail I missed? Something I did or didn't see or hear?*

"You fought with the killer," Malloy said slowly.

"Well, briefly, sir," Gaia said. "He got away almost immediately. I did what I could, but it's difficult to fight under those conditions."

Malloy was waving a hand impatiently, leading her forward toward the well-lit porch. "I know, I know. I just meant that you came in physical contact with the killer. Would you recognize him again? His body type and mobility profile, I mean."

Gaia wasn't sure. "I think so," she said hesitantly.

"You seemed to have learned a thing or two since you got here."

What's he getting at? Why is he talking like this?

"I hope so, sir," Gaia said, following Malloy up the stairs. Catherine was busy examining muddy footprints at one end of the porch—she didn't even look up. Malloy was leading Gaia into the house along the narrow, chalk-marked track of clean floor that had already been fingerprinted and fiber scanned—the only place in the room anyone was walking. The track led toward the "corpse" like a path into a forest.

"Remember when I asked you what you would do in my shoes?" Malloy said.

"Yes, sir." Gaia didn't look at Malloy—she was carefully following him toward the "body."

"I'm going to ask again," Malloy said. He was looking at her seriously, his face flickering red and white in the police flashers from outside. "Would you put two young trainees in charge of investigating this murder? Even if one was coming off a temporary suspension?"

Gaia was confused. "Sir, isn't that the point? This is a new game, isn't it?"

Malloy smiled humorlessly. "I suppose you could put it that way. A whole new game."

They were standing over the figure on the floor—and the room, Gaia noticed, was filled with that sweet, cloying lollipop smell.

"Look, we've got a lot to do," Malloy snapped. "Sheriff Gus Parker is on his way, and his men will want to question you, but I'll help with that. The point is, you saw the killer. In the dark but you were *here*. You and Sanders got that all-important first look at the crime scene while it was still live—before all *this*." He gestured around at the chalk lines and evidence bags, the flickering glare of the cars' flashers outside. "And Sanders seems like a good partner for you—a very smart operative, Bishop tells me. So, let's not waste time. That piece of paper on my desk—the one with the two signatures—do I tear it up?"

What?

Gaia was staring back at Malloy and trying to make sense

of what she was hearing. *Sheriff Parker—? I "saw the killer"?*

More cars were arriving outside. Glancing out there, Gaia saw that they were local police cars.

Slowly she turned her eyes down toward the body. Crouching, looking up close, Gaia could *feel* the realization flowing over her like tide rising unstoppably across the surface of a beach.

Oh my God.

Reaching out, Gaia gently touched the side of "Ann Knight's" face.

Flesh. Not plastic—real skin. Ann Knight, the real Ann Knight, was dead. Brutally murdered, in cold blood.

I saw the killer.

Gaia took her hand away as fast as she could—not out of disgust, but because she didn't want to leave any fingerprints on the corpse. Her heart sank. A vast feeling of sorrow and grief rolled over her right then as she remembered the afternoon in the rain with Ann Knight, who was, finally, a real person, as real as herself, lying here dead on the floor in front of her.

Now nobody will ever put white roses in the statue again, Gaia thought suddenly, wishing that Will and Kim were there for moral support. *Kim probably hasn't had the chance to pick up his messages yet.*

"Well, Moore?" Malloy snapped, standing impatiently above her. "Am I putting you and Sanders in charge of the investigation? What's it going to be?"

Gaia slowly stood up, tearing her eyes away from poor Ann Knight's body and turning back toward Malloy. Her eyes flooded with tears, which she quickly wiped away so that Malloy wouldn't see.

"Let's get some gloves on," she told him.

Malloy allowed himself a very slight smile. His eyes glittered as he gazed at her.

"Gaia!" Catherine called from the front porch. "We need you!"

Have I been waiting all my life to hear that?

"Excuse me, sir," Gaia said to Malloy. She moved past him and went to join the other FBI agents. She had a killer to catch.

Britney is the girl everyone
loves to hate.

She's **popular, blond,** and **fabulous.**
Sure, people are jealous. . . .

But jealous enough to **want her dead?**

killing britney

A thrilling new novel by Sean Olin

from Simon Pulse • published by Simon & Schuster

the party room

by Morgan Burke

The party room is where all the prep school kids drink up and hook up. All you need is a fake ID and your best Juicy Couture to get in.

One night, Samantha Byrne leaves with some guy no one's ever seen before . . . and ends up dead in Central Park. Murdered gruesomely. Found at the scene of the crime: a school tie from Talcott Prep.

New York is suddenly in the grip of a raging media frenzy. And a serial killer walks amidst Manhattan's most privileged—and indulged—teens.

From Simon Pulse
Published by Simon & Schuster

As many as one in three
Americans with HIV...
DO NOT KNOW IT.

More than half of those
who will get HIV this year...
ARE UNDER 25.

HIV is preventable.
You can help fight AIDS.
Get informed. Get the facts.

www.knowhivaids.org
1-866-344-KNOW